THE MEMORY OF A KISS

Back on the main path with its string of gas lamps hanging from trees, Zachary steered Sydney into one of the conveniently situated, dimly lit alcoves. She made no protest as he slipped an arm around her and lifted her chin.

"Are you all right?" he asked.

"I am now."

In her eyes he saw relief and gratitude and an indefinable something else. Longing, maybe. He couldn't help himself; he lowered his mouth to hers. With no hesitation, she responded passionately, her arms around his neck, her need as urgent as his. He hugged her even closer, his hands caressing her back, and she leaned in to him. He buried his face in the curve of her neck.

"I have dreamed of this for so long," he murmured.

"I have too. Nearly three years."

He pulled back to look into her eyes. "Really? Since that day in the park in Bath?"

"Yes. Since then."

He kissed her again, a long, searching exploration of her mouth and was delighted as she responded in kind . . .

Books by Wilma Counts

AN EARL LIKE NO OTHER

THE MEMORY OF YOUR KISS

Published by Kensington Publishing Corporation

The Memory of Your Kiss

WILMA COUNTS

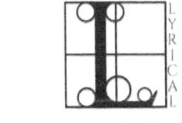

LYRICAL PRESS
Kensington Publishing Corp.
www.kensingtonbooks.com

LYRICAL PRESS BOOKS are published by

Kensington Publishing Corp.
119 West 40th Street
New York, NY 10018

First Electronic Edition: March 2015
eISBN-13: 978-1-60183-316-7
eISBN-10: 1-60183-316-4

First Print Edition: March 2015
ISBN-13: 978-1-60183-317-4
ISBN-10: 1-60183-317-2

Printed in the United States of America

To Marilee Swirczek
for your help and support.

And to Wayne Connaway for the same!

EVERYONE should be so lucky in their friends!

CHAPTER 1

1811

At eighteen, Miss Sydney Isabella Waverly thought of herself as very practical, firmly planted in the world of reality. When she was much younger—at that age when young girls see in themselves the first inklings of the women they will become—Sydney had determined that she could only ever be considered "plain." Not ugly, mind you, or even homely. Just, well, plain. Her hair was unexceptional: light brown, not honey blond or exotic black or saucy red. Just brown—with blond streaks, for she spent an inordinate amount of time in the sun. Her nose was straight—but then noses generally were, were they not? Her mouth? Unexceptional. Maybe a bit wide, and with one of her front teeth very slightly overlapping another. She considered her eyes to be her best feature, but gray-green eyes with dark lashes and brows were hardly up to the task of making a plain young woman into the heroine of one of the Minerva Press's romantic novels. Anyway, eyes were fine so long as one could see with them. Which she could. Such was the decided opinion of Miss Waverly.

She disdained the romantic nonsense exhibited by young women with whom she had once attended Miss Sebastian's Select School for Young Ladies. Even her name proclaimed her down-to-earth, no-nonsense approach to life: Miss Waverly preferred to be called Sydney once she was all grown up. Her late mother had also been called

Sydney and taking her name had helped ease the loss. She persuaded her school friends to adopt that form of address, though her father, her siblings, and neighborhood friends in Devonshire often ignored that preference and still called her *Bella*, a name that suited her well enough when she had been a mere child not allowed to put her hair up.

As well as being eminently practical, she was something of a bluestocking. She showed a most unladylike interest in politics and the machinations of the Corsican monster then rampaging across Europe. Moreover, she immersed herself in the histories and literature of ancient Greece and Rome rather than the modern novels and romantic poetry that fascinated her former classmates. She recalled with contempt how others had swooned over the star-crossed lovers, Romeo and Juliet. A single glance in a crowded room? Ridiculous!

Then it happened to her.

Well, not exactly a single glance in a crowded room, she assured herself. And *lovers* was far too strong a word, but something had, indeed, passed between her and Lieutenant Zachary Quintin when her cousin Herbert introduced them at one of the weekly assemblies held for both citizens and visitors in Bath, England's most popular spa.

And, whatever it was, it came at a most inconvenient—not to say impossible—time in her life.

CHAPTER 2

Sydney had not wanted to come to Bath, but she had finally acquiesced to her father's urging her to do so. It seemed important to him, and, given the circumstances, who knew how many more opportunities she would have to do something that would truly please her beloved papa?

She had known—months before he told her of the doctor's diagnosis of the wasting disease—that her father was seriously ill. He finally called her into the book-lined study of the vicarage to tell her.

"Oh, Papa. I feared it was something like that." She sat dry-eyed in a leather chair in their favorite room; he occupied a matching chair opposite her. She remembered how the afternoon sun of a fine day in mid-August shone in slanting shafts through the window. The soft leather had felt cool and smooth against the skin of her bare arm as the harsh reality of potential change asserted its power over her life. And not just hers. Also her father's, of course, but her thoughts immediately flew to her younger brother and sister.

"H-how long?" she asked quietly, not allowing the choked-back sob.

"A year. Maybe less. Maybe more. We must try to be positive. So far, I do not *feel* so very bad. Tired, but not ill. I would not burden you with it now if I could avoid doing so, but God has given me ample time to provide for you and your brother and sister. I am grateful for that at least."

"What's to become of us? Geoffrey? Marybeth? Me? I suppose *I* could hire out as a governess. But what about Geoff and Marybeth? An eleven-year-old boy and an eight-year-old girl? Would any of the Howard family take them in? Or Aunt Harriet?" She named relatives of her dead mother and her father's sister.

"Agatha Howard might be persuaded—or shamed—into taking them," he answered, "but it would be a miserable life for them. Harriet manages for herself and her two children on her navy widow's pension, but I think it is not easy for her. I have no doubt you *could* be a governess—quite a good one, in fact—but that is a hard life and not many wives would be willing to hire someone as young and pretty as you. No, my daughter. I have given the matter a great deal of thought, and, if you are amenable, I believe your marriage to the Earl of Paxton would offer the best solution for all three of my children. I would not have you unhappy in marriage, but we've known Paxton for many years. He comes with the usual human complement of faults, I'm sure, but I've never seen anything truly untoward in him."

"What if he does not want such a match? I have not even *seen* Henry Laughton since he succeeded to the title over a year ago! And—and before that, I saw him only occasionally on school holidays. Not since we were children . . ."

Her voice trailed off as she fought a rising sense of panic. Yes, she had always known of the arrangement her father and the previous earl had once concocted to blend their families. The two men had practically lived in each other's pockets most of their lives—from the time two lonely, bookish young school boys had met at Harrow until the earl had died, tragically of the same wasting disease that was stealing her beloved papa from her. This same Earl of Paxton, on succeeding to the earldom some twenty-plus years ago, had forcefully insisted that his friend accept the position of vicar in the village of Windham where the earl's principal holding, Paxton Hall, was located. It was he who had initiated the arranged marriage, going so far as to draw up settlement documents, though neither father had been so arrogant or autocratic as to consider the plan binding on adult children should they object.

Over the years, she and Henry had made a light joke of the plan when they happened to see each other—but that was not often. After all, a seven-year age difference did not allow much common ground between children. As adolescents, they had tacitly agreed to deal with the situation "when the time came." Now the time had come. Right on top of her being shattered by facing full-on the reality of losing her father!

Her father broke into her thoughts. "He wants it."

"What? Who—?"

"Henry wants the marriage."

"How do you know that, Papa?"

"I saw him in London last week."

"London? Last week?" This was all going much too fast. "I thought you went for a bishop's conference."

"I did. And I also saw Henry Laughton, Earl of Paxton, eighth of that line." His light tone was intended, she knew, to put her at ease. "He agreed to marry you if you are amenable to the idea. Didn't seem surprised or reluctant at all." He cleared his throat noisily. "I—uh—did not want to bring it up to you if he were now unwilling."

"You and he agreed? Without consulting me?"

"I am consulting you now, Bella," he said gently.

"Do I have a choice?"

"Yes, of course." But she knew, and she was sure her father knew, that, really, there was no choice. Not for a young woman of her station in this day and age. Governess, paid companion to some rich old widow, a convent, barely tolerated dependent relative—or marriage: Those were the alternatives. In Sydney's case, with Geoffrey and Marybeth to be considered, the first three possibilities were out of the question.

Two weeks later the Earl of Paxton made a hurried trip to his primary holding in Devonshire to propose marriage to the vicar's daughter. She received him in her father's study where she silently subjected him to a rather critical examination. He was taller than she by two or three inches; he had dark brown hair; his features were not exactly handsome, but were certainly easy to look at. Clear blue eyes sparkled with amusement.

"Do I pass inspection?"

She felt herself coloring up and gestured at chairs which they took. "I do apologize, Hen—uh—my lord." In truth, he had been subjecting her to the same degree of scrutiny, though perhaps he had been a bit more subtle about it than she. She gave an embarrassed laugh. "Yes, you do. And do I?"

He nodded. "Oh, yes. I daresay you will be the best looking countess England has seen in many a year."

"I do not need fulsome compliments, my lord," she said quietly.

He raised an eyebrow. "Nor do I hand them out willy-nilly. And *Henry* will do as nicely now as it did when we were children, Bella."

She was relieved to find the grown-up Henry Laughton as amiable a person as she remembered. He had then gone through the motions of going down on bended knee and mouthing that "happiest of men" nonsense.

"Do get up, Henry. Of course I will marry you. We both know the circumstances, so do let us always be honest with each other."

If he was surprised by this plain speaking, he did not say so. His response was, "I say, I do believe we will rub on well together."

"I hope so," she said.

Then he kissed her. It was a warm, seal-the-bargain sort of kiss. Not having had many kisses with which to compare it, she tried to respond in kind.

They called her father in—he had been hovering in the hall—and told him the "news," then the three of them set a date some weeks hence, for Paxton had engagements he felt obligated to keep in the meantime. They agreed there was no need to announce the forthcoming nuptials; it would be a very small, private affair in October and they would send newspaper notices after the fact—as was the custom for marriages such as theirs. Meanwhile, they would communicate the happy news privately only to such people as might have interest in knowing.

Henry had spent an extra three days at Paxton Hall during which he devoted much time to his prospective bride and took several meals with her and her father. Since his sisters, nine-year-old twins, were also at the Hall, he brought them one afternoon to spend a few hours with Sydney and her own siblings. Sydney and her family had seen the twins at church from time to time, but they were not well acquainted with Lady Amy and Lady Anne. The four children, ranging in age from eight to eleven, seemed somewhat wary of one another. Sydney thought it fortunate that the three girls were very nearly the same age.

That evening—his last in the area until he returned for the wedding—Henry had said of the afternoon visit, "I think that went tolerably well. I do not foresee a family uproar in our future." Her father having discreetly allowed them this time alone together, Henry sat next to her on a couch in the drawing room and patted her hand, then continued to hold it, twining his fingers with hers.

"Nor do I," she agreed, then added, "I am sorry you must leave so soon. I have enjoyed getting acquainted—reacquainted—with you."

"And I, you," he said, slipping his arm around her and drawing her close. He kissed her, his lips moving sensually over hers, eliciting a physical response from her that rather surprised her. When she felt his tongue stroking the seam of her lips, she was startled and pulled back slightly.

He laughed softly and she was embarrassed. "I-I'm sorry," she stammered.

"Don't be." He rose and pulled her close to murmur, "We'll be all right. I promise." He smiled at seeing her blush, then kissed her again and bade her good night.

Somewhat to her surprise, she found she missed him when he did not appear the next day and those following. Two weeks later her father called her into his study. He sat in his usual leather chair and motioned her to the other one. It was evening and light from a gas lamp on a side table near his chair emphasized lines and strain in his face.

"I want you to have a holiday of sorts before you settle into the life of a married lady," he announced abruptly.

"That is truly not necessary, Papa. I am quite happy to spend the next weeks right here preparing for the wedding, though, truth to tell, aside from some packing—my clothes, a few knickknacks and books—there is simply not much to do. I shall wear Mama's wedding gown. There will be only family and a few others to witness the ceremony. Paxton's staff are planning a breakfast celebration for estate people."

"I wish your mama could see you in her gown."

"I do, too."

There was a long pause during which Sydney thought they were both thinking of the woman who last wore that gown, she who lay in the graveyard only a short distance from where her daughter would be married. Her father reached for his handkerchief to clean his glasses. She recognized this as a familiar ritual he used to help him through painful or difficult conversations. Then he sighed and said, "Your mama should be here to tell you those things a woman needs to know before she gets married, but she isn't, so—"

He sighed again.

Sydney laughed. "Never mind, Papa. I know about the birds and the bees. Dorian Dunlop sneaked an anatomy book into our rooms at school. My biggest worry now is what flowers should I carry in my bouquet?"

Her father's sigh this time was one of relief. "Would you rather have had a grander affair, my dear?"

"No. Not at all. I much prefer it this way. I was immensely pleased when Henry wanted to keep everything very simple."

"Still, I regret that we could never afford either the expense—or, now, the time—for you to have a season in London. The great-grandson of a duke—albeit one whose grandfather was born on the wrong side of the blanket—should be able to do better by his daughter."

She jumped up and moved behind his chair to put her arms around him and touch her cheek to his. "Not to worry, Papa. I am very happy to have my life as it is. As for a holiday—I'd much rather spend time with you."

"We shall have plenty of time together. I am not done in yet! As Paxton's wife, you will be only a mile away. We may visit every day. Meanwhile, I should like you to have at least a taste of the life you might have had as a carefree girl." He patted her hands clasped over his chest and reached toward the side table for a letter lying there. "I wrote your aunt Harriet and she replied immediately to invite you to Bath."

"Papa!"

Sydney was torn. On the one hand, knowing her father's time was limited, she wanted to spend as much of it as possible with him. On the other hand, a part of her wanted to escape duty and responsibility for a tiny while—to dance at a ball, go driving in the park, shop for a frivolous bonnet—all without a thought of what an uncertain future might bring. And her father seemed to want so much for her to do this . . .

So, here she was at Bath, visiting her aunt Harriet.

CHAPTER 3

Harriet Carstairs, a navy captain's widow, lived with her daughter and son, Celia and Herbert, in a modest house on Queen Square in Bath, several blocks south of the more exclusive homes found in the Circus and the Royal Crescent. Celia was the same age as Sydney; Herbert, a year younger. The two girls had attended school together. Sydney arrived one afternoon—along with the maid Maisie whom her father had insisted should accompany her—and found herself immediately thrust into what amounted to the social whirl of Bath. Her aunt and cousins were entertaining callers in the drawing room. Later there would be a small gathering at the home of retired Admiral Crowley for cards and charades, and, tomorrow, a ball in the assembly rooms.

It was at the ball that Sydney met Lieutenant Zachary Quintin, who had come to Bath on convalescent leave from the Iberian Peninsula. There, he served with the inimitable Arthur Wellesley, Lord Wellington, whose troops continued to wage a hard struggle against Napoleon's French and Spanish armies. Quintin, leaning on a cane, stood on the sidelines of the ball with two other uniformed soldiers, the three of them watching the dancers and undoubtedly commenting on the young women present.

When the Carstairs party arrived, Aunt Harriet waved the younger people off to the ballroom as she joined her friends, the Crowleys.

On spotting the soldiers, Herbert immediately steered his sister and their cousin across the room. "Celia. Sydney. You must meet these fellows. Great guns, all."

Sydney suspected Cousin Herbert of a serious case of hero worship, or envy at least. One of the trio, Ensign Trevor Harrelson, had been in a class two years ahead of Herbert's at Winchester. The third man, Ensign Robert Pelham was of an age with Trevor and Herbert, while Lieutenant Quintin was three or four years older than they.

When he had made the introductions and the others bowed or curtsied as custom required, Herbert added, "Did I not assure you that I would arrive with the prettiest girls in all Somerset?"

"That you did," Ensign Harrelson said, looking at the golden-haired, blue-eyed Celia. "Amazing how pesky little girls grow into such phenomena of beauty."

Celia laughed and tapped him on the arm with her fan. "No, Trevor. The amazing thing is that boys finally notice us. I remember very well *begging* you and Herbert to let me go riding or climb trees with you."

"Well, you needn't beg now! And if I'm not too late, may I claim you for the dance just starting?" She agreed and Harrelson cast a look of insincere sympathy at his fellow soldiers. "Sorry, fellows. It falls to me to uphold the army's honor on the dance floor."

Sydney had felt a strange sensation pervade her body as her eyes met those of Lieutenant Quintin and she quickly lowered her lashes, lest he and others standing near perceive her confusion. Despite a still angry-looking scar—a jagged red slash running from his left temple nearly to his chin—and the fact that he had to rely on a cane to walk with ease, the lieutenant was a very striking figure. Seen only from the right, he was breathtakingly handsome with brown eyes so dark as to be almost black. He had black hair, too, and distinct black brows, a straight nose, and a firm jawline. He had a rather wide mouth and white, even teeth that shone against a suntanned complexion.

And he is probably a conceited ass, she told herself, trying to assert control over what was, for her, a most unusual reaction to any man. Good heavens! This was probably what her friend Marianne had meant when she had told the other girls, in a forbidden midnight gab session—and with sigh-bedecked gushes of praise—that she felt "all squashy inside" whenever, William, Viscount Asterly, chanced to touch her hand. Of course Viscount Asterly was now Marianne's husband and there was absolutely no possibility that this, this Lieutenant Whatever, could ever be anything but the merest chance acquaintance to Miss Sydney Waverly.

Herbert's voice abruptly drew her out of this moment of reverie. "I say, cousin, having arrived in Bath only yesterday, you may not know that you stand in the presence of genuine war heroes."

"Oh?" Her tone evincing polite interest, she gestured at a group of empty chairs nearby. With Harrelson's parting comment about the army's honor, she had noticed that Pelham, too, leaned on a cane, so she added, "We surely *are* standing. Let us sit and you may regale me with tales of heroism and derring-do."

"Carstairs exaggerates," Lieutenant Quintin said as the four of them sat down.

"Only when he includes me in that description." Freckle-faced, sandy-haired, and displaying boyish enthusiasm, Pelham reminded Sydney of her young brother. He jerked a thumb at his companion. "Quintin here is the genuine article. He single-handedly held off twelve or fifteen Frenchies on a bridge at Badajoz to allow others to escape. Captured one of Soult's cannons in the process."

Sydney thought Lieutenant Quintin was genuinely embarrassed as he said, "I assure you, Miss Waverly, Pelham embellishes the story— which is, in any event, hardly suitable as ballroom discourse, or for the ears of a delicate young woman."

"Don't forget, Quintin, I was there," Pelham said, sounding hurt at Quintin's reproof.

"Nevertheless—" Quintin started.

In jumping to Ensign Pelham's defense, Sydney also sought to help Lieutenant Quintin divert the discussion. "Oh, I see," she said in an overly bright tone. "It is all right for young men to live those horrors, but young women must not be exposed even to reports of such."

Herbert groaned. "Oh, don't let her get started on women's rights."

Lieutenant Quintin seemed to welcome a shift in topic, for he assumed a tone of mocking shock. "Do not tell me we have a follower of the scandalous Mary Wollstonecraft in our midst!"

Mildly surprised that he so readily sidestepped a topic that could only have shown him in a good light, Sydney responded to his gambit by saying, "I will concede that her lifestyle was—uh—less than orthodox, but heavens! were we to judge the ideas of others by the way they conduct their private lives, surely we would have little of interest to read—and very little from Parliament or the Prince Regent worth attending."

Lieutenant Quintin chuckled. "Fascinating. A woman whose opinions are not merely an echo of some treatise on 'How to Be Agreeable to the Male Half of the Species.'"

Before Sydney could whip out her response to this sally, a simpering female voice intruded. "La! If it isn't Mr. Carstairs and his cousin. We never thought to see you here so soon after a tiring journey, Miss Waverly. You must be especially eager to sample the offerings of Bath society."

"We country girls are hardy stock," Sydney said to the speaker, a woman named Faith Holmsley who had also been a student at Miss Sebastian's school, but two years ahead of Sydney. That Miss Holmsley was accompanied by Elizabeth Kenmore came as no surprise, for the Kenmore girl had always shadowed Faith's every move. Sydney had never particularly liked either of them and she was fully aware that their interest now was not in an old schoolmate, nor in one of their Bath neighbors, but in the smart-looking soldiers. The two women had been visitors in her aunt's drawing room when Sydney arrived the previous afternoon. Miss Holmsley's conversation then had turned on her London debut two years ago and how utterly superior London society was to what one found in Bath, but Grandmamma insisted on her annual sojourn to take the waters and Grandmamma was, after all, supplying the wherewithal for a handsome marriage portion. Miss Kenmore's contributions seemed limited to an occasional "Oh, my, yes."

The gentlemen all scrambled to rise to greet the newcomers.

"Oh, goodness. Please do not get up, gentlemen," Miss Holmsley said after they were all on their feet. "We would not put England's wounded soldiers to such trouble."

Herbert offered to procure extra chairs for them.

"Don't bother, Herbert," Sydney said. "They may have our seats as we need to find Aunt Harriet. You know what she said." Then she added with a polite nod at the two soldiers, "If you gentlemen will excuse us—"

Herbert looked bewildered but joined her in taking their leave of the two soldiers. As they left, Miss Holmsley was gushing. "Lieutenant Quintin, I am especially pleased to see *you* here this evening. You simply must tell me all about your brave stand at Badajoz—or was it Salamanca?" She giggled. "Oh, dear, those foreign places all sound so strange."

Sydney and Herbert drifted out of earshot as she prattled on.

"What was that about my mother?" Herbert asked.

"Oh, nothing. I just wanted to escape those two females. They were in school with Celia and me."

"I know. Celia likes them well enough, though."

"Celia is more tolerant than I. I did not want to listen to any more of the 'Bath-is-so-provincial-and-London-is-so-exciting' chit-chat such as we heard from them yesterday."

"So we left Pelham and Quintin to endure it?"

Sydney felt a twinge of conscience at this. "I think they will manage. Most men love to talk about their exploits." She said this just as though she actually knew what might fascinate "most men."

"That has not been my impression of those two—especially Quintin," Herbert said.

Any response Sydney might have made was lost as they encountered another of Herbert's friends, Baron Anthony Whitfield, a fashion-conscious young dandy who had also been a visitor in Aunt Harriet's drawing room yesterday. He promptly asked Sydney to dance, and Sydney was further chagrined to find him every bit as self-absorbed as Faith Holmsley. *Serves you right*, she told herself.

Lieutenant Quintin was annoyed. Miss Waverly had simply dismissed him and Pelham out of hand with a lame excuse, and not ten minutes later she was whirling through the forms of a country dance on the arm of that fop Whitfield!

Even with this ugly scar slashing across his face, Zachary Andrew Quintin was not accustomed to being treated with indifference. In fact, in the last few weeks, he had found that the scar, along with the limp which he hoped to be rid of sooner rather than later, had given him a certain cachet with the fair sex. And now this slip of a girl—whose expressive gray-green eyes, light brown hair, and very kissable lips had set his senses to humming—this slip of a girl had first intrigued him, then left him to endure the usual pointless ballroom chatter. Still, he thought her suggestion that they all sit had come from her sensitivity to his and Pelham's injuries, so she was not so concerned with herself as many other young women seemed wont to be—like the two with whom she had left them.

Miss Waverly's virtually snubbing you did you a favor, he told himself, his natural sense of humor winning out over the annoyance. *Talk about self-absorbed! Too full of yourself by half. This sojourn into civilian life is making you soft and complacent. Next you will be worrying about such momentous matters as how many folds you can manage in a cravat—like that coxcomb, Whitfield.* At least an army uniform protected one from that extreme.

On a very practical level, however, Zachary was aware of—but deliberately chose to ignore—his worth on the social scene, though it was very well known by hopeful misses and their avaricious mamas. As a civilian, Zachary Quintin was just a plain "mister," but his mother was Lady Leonora, daughter of the sixth Earl of Paxton, and Zachary was the principal heir to the immense fortune his father had amassed in the last century during service with the East India Company. But Zachary himself dismissed these attributes, for they had not come from *his* efforts.

He might have commanded a good deal of attention for his status as a war hero, but so far he'd not been tempted to play that card—and did not anticipate ever doing so. The very idea was repugnant, disrespectful to men who were real heroes, whereas he had merely been in a particular place at an opportune—or perhaps inopportune—time.

Within a few weeks he fully intended to be on his way back to the Peninsula. By then the leg should have fully mended, and he would have got through his cousin Henry's wedding. His mind drifted to Cousin Henry, eighth Earl of Paxton, who seemed to Zachary to be inordinately indifferent to the whole idea of his upcoming marriage.

Henry, returning via Bath from a hunting expedition in the Highlands, had stopped, along with two companions, in Bath a week ago "to discuss a bit of business." Zachary had been surprised to receive Henry's letter, for, despite only two years' difference in their ages, the two had never been close. Zachary's mother had been estranged from her family after her marriage. As youngsters, the two cousins had attended different schools—Henry at Harrow, Zachary at Winchester—and they shared few interests.

In the past week, they had spent three days attending sporting events—horse races as well as a pugilists' match and a dog fight in a neighboring town. Henry bet heavily on these affairs with little care about how much he won or lost. Zachary tagged along because he was genuinely glad to see his amiable, devil-may-care cousin—certainly not because he felt a burning need to watch men and animals tear each other apart. God knew he had already seen enough of that sort of brutality on the Peninsula, and likely faced a good deal more. Enough to last a lifetime. The four of them—their numbers often augmented by Pelham, Harrelson, and Carstairs—had also consumed an incredible amount of alcohol. Enough to float the proverbial ship, Zachary thought.

Only when Henry and his hunting companions were about to leave Bath did Zachary learn the purpose of his cousin's side trip to England's most famous spa. He and Henry were at breakfast; the others had not come down yet.

"So, Henry, what was this 'business' you mentioned in your letter?" Zachary asked as he made selections of bacon, sausages, kippers, eggs, and muffins from the sideboard. He sat, poured himself coffee, and laced it with a liberal splash of cream.

Henry looked with disgust at the pile of food. "Good God! Are you going to eat all that?" He himself nursed a cup of coffee laced not with cream but with brandy if the bottle in front of him was any indication.

Zachary grinned. "I surely am. We champions of freedom and protectors of the realm must gain sustenance when we can."

Henry snorted, but his tone was amiable. "Champions and protectors be damned. I never have understood your insane fascination with the military."

Because the comment seemed born of genuine interest, Zachary answered seriously. "I suppose the attraction was romance and glory for a young boy. Alexander the Great. The Crusaders. Achilles and Hector. Later, it seemed a natural progression from sporting contests at school."

"Surely you have outgrown all that nonsense by now."

"Yes. Now it's more a matter of duty, I think. Doing something worthwhile—to give back. I'll not inherit a title and a seat in Parliament like some I could name." He took a swig of coffee. "Your 'business,' cousin?"

"Ah, yes. Two things, actually." Henry ran a hand distractedly through his hair. "I'm to be married a few weeks from now. I'd like you to stand up with me."

"Good God! You mention this only now? And—and as sort of an afterthought?" Zachary shook his head in wonder, then quickly recovered himself. "I do wish you happy, cousin. What lucky damsel managed to capture your heart?"

"It isn't like that, Zachary. As with many alliances in the *ton*, ours is an arranged marriage. Her father is our vicar. He and my father were lifelong friends from school days on. Her family is distantly related to the Howards. There's a duke on the family tree somewhere. Some sort of 'Fitz,' though."

"Poor relations?"

"Something of that sort. But it's not like I need to hang out for an heiress now, is it?"

"No, but I cannot believe you just accepted this—this 'arrangement'—as a *fait accompli*."

Henry shrugged. "Why not? I cannot marry Louisa—ever—no matter how much I want to. Eventually I must marry. Bella is good looking. Comes of good stock. Gently reared. I've known her for ages. We'll rub on well together."

"I take it Louisa is your latest venture into the demimonde."

"Not at all. Louisa is received in the highest circles."

"So, why do you not marry her then?" Zachary reached for the carafe to refill his coffee cup.

"She's already married. To Baron Ryesdale."

"Oh. I can see where that might be a problem. Still, divorce is not unheard of. We have the example of the Prince of Wales to confirm that. Is he not seeking to divorce the Princess Caroline?"

"In Louisa's case, that is not an option."

"Why? She could not face the ostracism?"

Henry sat up straighter and clenched a fist on the table. "No. That's not it. For one thing she is not royalty. And because her husband is quite literally mad—confined to one of those exclusive asylums for the very rich who have lost control of their faculties. He cannot bring a suit. Nor can she—largely because she's a woman. But both her husband's family and her own oppose her."

"I see. That truly is an untenable situation." Zachary felt a surge of sympathy for his cousin.

"She has a son," Henry went on. "Three years old. If she does anything to upset the social apple cart, her husband's family will take her child—the Ryesdale heir."

"But they turn a blind eye to her liaison with you?"

Henry nodded glumly.

"Unbelievable," Zachary said. "Not to mention hypocritical."

Henry shrugged. "You know how it is when a title and money and property are involved."

"Does your prospective bride know about Louisa?"

"Oh, God, no."

"Is she not likely to find out?"

"Perhaps. But men have mistresses and wives pretend they do not exist. That's the way it's done."

"If you say so." Zachary shook his head again. "Sounds to me like a disaster just waiting to happen." He paused. "Does Louisa know you are marrying?"

"Not yet. I'm actually on my way to London to tell her. I doubt it will come as a total surprise, though. She knows it had to happen sometime. I must have a son—a legitimate heir—or all of Paxton will be lost."

Zachary chewed thoughtfully on a piece of bacon; Henry replenished the brandy in his cup. Then Zachary said, "From a vicar's daughter to a countess? That's quite a leap, isn't it?"

"I suppose so, but Bella is very capable. She will be able to handle it—and handle Anne and Amy as well," Henry said, naming his much younger half siblings.

"Seems a lot for a new bride to take on," Zachary said.

"Well, it isn't as though she won't have sufficient help," Henry said. "My God, we must have a staff of fifty or more in Paxton Hall alone, what with footmen, maids, a governess, and so on."

Zachary raised an eyebrow, but decided not to pursue a topic that was, after all, none of his business. "As I said, I wish you happy and I shall be glad to witness your wedding."

"Thank you." Henry lifted his cup, drank, and said, "There's more."

"More?" Zachary paused in the act of shoveling a forkful of egg into his mouth and returned the fork to his plate.

"When Father died last year and I became the earl, my solicitor drew up all the necessary legal documents, including a new will for me."

"A will seems a bit premature."

Henry rushed on. "And I've named you as executor-trustee and guardian of all property and persons for which I am responsible until my heir is of an age to be so."

"What? You did this without even asking if I would be willing to take on such a huge responsibility?"

"You were in the Peninsula. Takes weeks—sometimes months—to get word back and forth. And, frankly, you are the only one I'd trust. Bertie Cummings is too stupid and Percy Laughton is always up the River Tick with gambling debts—there'd be nothing left of the estate for an heir."

Zachary rested his head in his hands. "Oh, Good Lord."

"You'll do it, won't you?" Henry sounded anxious. "Phillips, the solicitor, will help you. If it should come to that. But of course it won't."

"From your lips to God's ears."

"So, is it all right? Will you do it?"

Zachary nodded. "If you insist."

"I intend to be around another forty or fifty years. In less than half that time, my heir—surely I will have a son—will be able to handle things himself. So you see? It's just a legal formality."

"From your lips to God's ears," Zachary had repeated.

He brought his mind back to the Assembly Rooms and tried to focus on the meaningless chit-chat around him. *Better appreciate seeing pretty girls in stylish gowns while you can*, he told himself.

CHAPTER 4

Half an hour later, having managed to fob Miss Holmsley and Miss Kenmore off on men eager to dance, Quintin and Pelham made their way about the crowded ballroom not nearly as aimlessly as Pelham perhaps thought. Finally Zachary spotted his quarry. She stood—quietly for the moment—with her cousin Herbert and his mother.

The two soldiers greeted the Carstairs party, then Zachary said, "Miss Waverly, if you are not engaged for the next set, perhaps you'd care to stroll about a bit with me?" He leaned closer to say for her ears alone, "You owe me, you know."

She looked a little chagrined, but he liked that she did not try to dissemble and pretend she did not know what he meant. She placed her hand on the arm he offered and they began to circle the ballroom. She looked up at him, her eyes dancing. "I—uh—suppose I owe you an apology?"

"You do. But I shall forgive you if you will go out driving with me tomorrow—weather permitting, of course."

"D-driving?"

"An open carriage and only about town and through the park. Nothing in the least improper."

"Such an outing would be lovely."

"It's settled then. I shall call for you at, say, two o'clock?"

She nodded, but he thought he detected a certain reluctance in her demeanor. Then her expression brightened, almost as though she deliberately brushed away a concern, and she introduced a new topic. "Have you been in Bath long, Lieutenant Quintin?"

"A little over a month. The mud baths were recommended therapy for my type of injury."

"Is the treatment working?"

"I think so. I am certainly walking better. Not dancing yet, mind you, but I haven't fallen in the last day or so." He said this with a deprecating laugh. "What about you? Are you in Bath for long?"

"Only for three weeks."

"Three weeks! That is hardly sufficient time—"

"For what?"

"To see the sights." He found himself becoming strangely serious. He'd meant this to be an idle, light, teasing exchange. "To establish a friendship, fix one's interests, make an impression." The words were out before he'd had time to plan them. He paused and held her gaze for a long moment.

Finally, she looked away. "Please let us not engage in meaningless flirtation," she said softly.

"I am not doing so."

"I don't mean to be rude," she said, "but I now have less than three weeks here, and then I must return home to face a—a deal of responsibility."

He smiled. "Then Cinderella returns to her chimney?"

"Something like that."

"I shall be returning to the Peninsula about the same time. Seems Fate is being decidedly unkind to both of us. So—shall we make a pact, Miss Sydney Waverly?"

"What sort of pact, Lieutenant Zachary Quintin?"

"We shall endeavor to enjoy our time here in Bath and not allow considerations beyond to intrude."

She smiled and said, "I quite like that idea."

But that smile, along with a light perfume that was both flowery and woodsy, already threatened his resolve.

"You know," she said, "I rather disagree with what you said earlier."

"What I said—?"

"About time for making an impression. I think first impressions are often instantaneous—and accurate."

"I would say they are mostly hasty and often downright wrong," he said partly just to challenge her.

"Do you not find yourself responding to people and even things—like food, or art, or books—with a positive or negative view within minutes of encountering them?"

"Well, yes, but all too often I then must revise that initial opinion as I become more familiar with that person or object."

"But finding things that support your initial reaction comes more naturally, more easily, than searching for those that contradict it, would you not agree?"

"Perhaps," he conceded. "But I at least try to be open-minded and give an artist or writer the benefit of doubt. For instance, I'll grant an author a few paragraphs or pages before I put the work aside."

"Oh, generous man!" she scoffed. "And people?"

"I hope I am not unduly harsh with people. I withhold an opinion until I feel I know the person reasonably well, but generally I find that once an impression is established, it does not change."

"Never? Nothing—positive or negative—changes your mind?"

"Rarely," he temporized. "But I will agree that an event or given behavior might well change one's view of another."

"That is good to know," she said. "I may now view our drive tomorrow as my act of redemption."

He laughed and their conversation drifted to other topics as he identified for her such persons as he could among the dancers and they were companionably amused by the high shirt points of a dandy that made turning his head difficult, or by the outlandish ostrich feathers on the headdresses of certain of the women. Zachary felt genuine regret when her partner for the next dance came to claim her, but comforted himself with thoughts of the morrow.

That night Sydney pleaded a headache to forestall the bubbling Celia who wanted to rehash the evening. Sydney needed to be alone, to examine, if she could, precisely what had come over her. Never had she experienced such a visceral reaction to a man as she had toward Zachary Quintin. That tightening in her chest when their eyes first met had been as nothing to the overwhelming thrill that surged through her body when she'd put her gloved hand on his arm. Heavens! What would it have felt like had it been bare skin touching bare skin? What would it be like to kiss him?

This thought did not shock her, but it did make her feel somewhat ashamed. After all, in a mere four weeks she would be marrying Henry. As a betrothed woman, she had no right to these feelings about another man.

Besides, it was probably just pre-wedding nerves that had her engaging in such nonsensical imaginings. She took refuge in clichés: the die was cast; there was no going back now. Too much and too many depended on her following through with the plan two fathers had hatched between them many years before. She had accepted this marriage wholeheartedly as a solution to the problems the Waverly family faced. She had given her word.

"What's done is done," she told herself, then smiled at the absurdity of applying Lady Macbeth's famous line about murder to the happy occasion of a marriage that would resolve so many difficulties.

The next morning Sydney arrived in the breakfast room to find only her aunt Harriet there before her. The older woman had finished her breakfast, but sat enjoying yet another cup of tea as she sorted through the mail. Aunt Harriet was of an age with her brother, Sydney's father. With graying auburn hair, she was an attractive matron who had been widowed some ten years ago. Sydney had always liked her for her "live and let live" approach to life and for her sense of humor. Aunt Harriet had always listened intently, and non-judgmentally, as children and then young adults explored and experimented with even the most outlandish ideas.

"Celia and Herbert are not down yet?" Sydney asked.

"Oh, goodness! Those two slugabeds won't be down for another hour, I am sure," her aunt replied. " 'Tis just as well. I have wanted a private word with you. But get your food first, my dear."

Sydney selected bacon, eggs, and a muffin from the sideboard, then poured herself a cup of tea and sat.

"I have been thinking of your proposed outing with Lieutenant Quintin, my dear," Aunt Harriet said.

"You disapprove?"

"Um—not exactly. He seems a fine young man. However, I am concerned that he may be under the impression that you are an eligible *parti* when, in fact—according to your father's letter—you are not."

"Oh." Sydney considered this for a moment, then said, "I assure you, Aunt Harriet, I have no intention of engaging in a flirtation during my stay here. I find the lieutenant to be an interesting person—as a possible friend, nothing more. In any event, I am quite sure he is not looking for a match. He intends to rejoin Wellington's army in a month or so."

"Still, I cannot help but think it would be wise to make a public announcement of your betrothal."

"Perhaps it would, but Henry—Lord Paxton—wished to keep it very simple and not draw undue attention—and, frankly, Papa and I agreed with him. It's not as though ours is a great love match, or one of those lavish *ton* weddings that intrigue the gossips for weeks before and after the event."

Aunt Harriet shook her head and sounded reluctant. "Well, I suppose you and his lordship know what you are about. I will honor your wishes. I have not mentioned it to Celia or Herbert."

"Thank you, Aunt Harriet."

Privately, Sydney conceded that her aunt made sense, but, since there was no way of discussing the matter with Henry at this point, she simply shrugged it off and determined that she would make the most of these days her father had so generously given her. It crossed her mind that Lieutenant Quintin was the most interesting person she had met in years. Such a friendship might well prove one to cherish.

Soon after breakfast a florist delivered two bouquets to the house on Queen Square. Celia received a dozen pink roses. Sydney received a nosegay of violets with a card reading "Carpe Diem." She smiled, for "seize the day" was, indeed, her plan for this sojourn in Bath.

Later she went shopping along Milsom Street with her aunt and Celia. She would not enter the married state with a lavish new wardrobe, but her father had assured her a few new day dresses and a ball gown or two would not do irreparable damage to the family budget. Paxton might not expect his bride to set fashion trends, but he would expect her to be presentable in the loftiest of *ton* circles. Once they eventually removed to London, she would have to be outfitted with a traditional court dress, but that could come later—and at Paxton's expense. Sydney had never equaled her female friends and relatives in their zeal for that time-honored female pursuit: shopping. One perceived a need for a particular item; one searched for and found it; one purchased it or arranged to have it made. And that was that.

Thus it came as a surprise to her that she entered into this shopping expedition with such enthusiasm. She experienced a moment of downright shock when, as she was trying on a pert little straw bonnet, the vision of a certain soldier admiring her in it popped into her head.

"Oh, good heavens!" She hastily removed it.

"Sydney!" Celia protested. "It's perfect for you. You simply must have it. And it will go splendidly with the green print you saw at the dress shop. Never say you will pass it by."

Torn, Sydney put the offending hat back on her head. "What do you think, Aunt Harriet?"

"Celia is right. You should have it."

As the shopkeeper put the hat in a box, Sydney turned her mind resolutely to imagining how *Paxton* might view it. But she had no idea how much interest her future husband might take in women's clothing. His compliments had been of a very general nature.

Vanity won out later in the day as she wore the new bonnet for the drive with Lieutenant Quintin. He had arrived punctually and, after polite greetings with her relatives, handed her into his curricle. He placed his cane on the floor of the vehicle and somewhat awkwardly hoisted himself into position beside her to take up the reins.

"I've not quite mastered my technique for getting into and out of a vehicle with grace," he apologized.

"I thought you did very well," she said, feeling again that strange but not unpleasant physical sensation that had so astonished her the day before.

He glanced at her, smiled, and said, "I'm told on good authority that ladies like to be complimented on their headgear. And I must say you look very fetching in that bit of straw and ribbons."

"Why, thank you, kind sir." She was glad she had given in to temptation and worn it.

Both were silent as he maneuvered the carriage through the worst of the city traffic. Then he said, "Alexandra Park is on a hill and affords a very nice view of the city. Gives one perspective."

"That would help get me oriented," she said. "I was in Bath once before, several years ago, but I was too young to appreciate what I was seeing."

"There is much to see and your time is short. However, a good deal of the city is best seen on foot—the Roman Baths, Pulteney Bridge with its shops, the Abbey."

"And I do want to see it all," she said.

"Perhaps you will allow me the pleasure of being your tour guide."

"Oh, but you just said much is best seen on foot," she blurted, then blushed with embarrassment at drawing attention to his infirmity.

He gave her a rueful smile. "I am not so lame as all that, Miss Waverly. As a matter of fact, I am encouraged to walk as much as possible. So, you see, you would be doing me a great favor."

"Oh, well—if you put it that way—"

"That's settled. Now what shall we talk about? The terms of our agreement last night put the future out of bounds."

"Hmm." She pretended to be puzzled. "I suppose there is always the weather . . ."

"'Tis a fine day. Let us hope it does not rain." He paused. "Now what?"

"The royal family? No. Some of that would not be quite proper."

"And is Miss Sydney Waverly—that champion of women's rights—always so very proper?" His tone was teasing, but she thought there was sincere interest in the question.

"Oh, my. How does one answer a question like that without seeming either pompous or hoydenish?"

He laughed. "With the truth?"

"The truth, then." She thought hard for a moment. "I suppose the truth is that I am, indeed, 'proper' in terms of behavior, but somewhat unorthodox in my thinking."

"And you do not see that as being hypocritical?"

"No. Merely practical. One must live in the real world, even though it is not ideal."

"A thought definitely worth pursuing," he said, "but here we are." He reined in his team to position the carriage to allow a panoramic view of the city. "See? All the major landmarks lie before you."

"It is like having the world at your feet."

"Yes, a peaceful, serene world."

She thought she heard a sense of longing in his tone, so she said lightly admonishing, "No future now."

"Right," he agreed heartily. He leaned close to point out sights to her. "See the Royal Crescent there? It was the work of John Wood the

Younger. His father built the Circus—just down the street, there. And way down there is the Abbey."

She was intensely aware of the warmth of his nearness and the subtle spicy scent of what must have been his shaving soap. "It's beautiful," she said and turned to him. "You were right. This view gives one wonderful perspective."

He held her gaze for a long moment and she thought he might be going to kiss her, but she forestalled that by lowering her lashes and turning back to the scene below them, feeling confused and somewhat bereft as she did so.

"Yes, indeed, very proper," he murmured almost inaudibly, then in a more forceful tone, "I suppose we should be getting back. I would not have Mrs. Carstairs think I had spirited you away."

She laughed nervously. "Thank you for sharing this with me."

They chatted amiably of weather and traffic and Bath history until he handed her down at the Carstairs door.

Zachary made no specific assignation with Miss Waverly as he bade her good-bye, but he was confident she would be in the Pump Rooms the next afternoon, for her aunt had mentioned such earlier. In any event, he knew everyone was likely to be in the Pump Rooms several times a week, if not daily. Not only did one "take the waters" of the medicinal fountains there, but the accompanying tea rooms were the social center of the spa community.

He had been shaken by that moment in the park with her. He had wanted to kiss her, had been on the verge of doing so, then sensed reluctance or conflict in her and the moment was gone. He found her intriguing—and that bothered him. He could not afford the sort of commitment of time and attention a woman like Sydney Waverly would require—would deserve. In a month he would be back on the Peninsula, slogging his way to and through the Pyrenees.

Three weeks, Quintin. Enjoy them while you can. Don't waste time and energy on what could have been or might have been. After all, that was what she wanted, too.

CHAPTER 5

In the next two weeks, Miss Waverly visited the usual tourist attractions in the city of Bath—always on the arm of Lieutenant Quintin, for he proved to be as good as his word in acting as her guide. The two were invariably in an open carriage, a crowded public place, or accompanied by others—Sydney's cousins, the lieutenant's fellow soldiers, or a combination thereof, along with other young men and women. But just as often, the two might be seen in company somewhat separated from others, engaging in private conversation, though the gossips found little to criticize in their behavior.

A keen observer, or a particularly snide one, might have pointed out that the lieutenant was always quick to seek Miss Waverly's company in the tea rooms or at a ball, and that he was a more frequent caller at the Carstairs home on Queen Square than he had been before her arrival in Bath. If the observer were especially astute, he or—more likely—she would see how their eyes lit with pleasure on seeing each other. He—or she—might observe innocent touches occurring more often than one might expect and glances that suggested shared opinions and amusements.

For her part, Sydney welcomed his company. As they became better acquainted, she found him an easy companion. Their "pact" kept the relationship casual, free, on the surface at least, of the usual extremes of tension between a young man and a young woman attracted to each other. They argued vehemently, albeit amicably, about the relative merits of two modern landscape painters. Mr. Constable's scenes of the English countryside pleased Lieutenant Quintin, while Sydney praised Mr. Turner's experiments with light. They were equally strong in considering the place of women in public life. Here, their disagreements were just as vehement, but considerably less amicable.

Lieutenant Quintin and Ensign Harrelson, calling at the Carstairs home one afternoon, were invited to stay for tea. As befitted the modest home of a navy widow, the drawing room sported furniture chosen for comfort rather than showy style. Sydney found the colors—maroon, mauve, and gray—relaxing. The Carstairses and their guests occupied two couches and two upholstered chairs arranged around a low table on which was a large tray with tea paraphernalia. The conversation had turned to stories of school-day escapades and Lieutenant Quintin casually mentioned having studied Greek during his days as a university student at Oxford.

"Oh, how I envy you that opportunity," Sydney said wistfully.

"To study Greek?"

"To go to university."

"Why? University is no place for women."

"Why not?" she challenged.

"Because there is simply no need for females to have such training. Men are the ones destined to play the major roles on the world stage."

"That is largely because men refuse to recognize the talents and abilities of half the human race," Sydney said.

"Uh-oh. You're in for it now," Herbert said to Quintin.

Quintin merely glanced at Herbert and went on in what Sydney perceived as a condescending tone. "Come now, Miss Waverly. You cannot possibly believe women as capable as men in—say—statecraft."

"Why not? History tells us one of our greatest monarchs was a woman named Elizabeth."

"But she was an anomaly," Quintin said.

"Only because women are generally not allowed to realize their potential."

"I suppose you would also have women donning uniforms and fighting wars."

"Why not?" she said again. "Boadicea led an English army to defeat the Romans. Joan of Arc was rather successful."

Others in the room observed this exchange with a good deal of interest, though Aunt Harriet looked as if she would like to change the subject as she pointedly passed around a plate of tarts and offered refills of tea.

Lieutenant Quintin, however, seemed reluctant to let the subject drop. "Your examples, Miss Waverly, are from ancient history and have little relevance to modern times."

"He has you there, Sydney," Herbert said, biting into a lemon tart.

"Perhaps the men of our time are less enlightened than those of former times," Sydney said and they all laughed.

Celia then deftly turned the discussion to the musical selections on the program for a concert they would all attend that evening.

When the Carstairs party arrived at the concert that night, the audience buzzed with news from London. Perhaps a hundred people already were seated in padded straight-back chairs and another hundred milled about. Gas lamps in wall sconces provided soft light. Over the noise of a small orchestra warming up and tuning instruments, the atmosphere was charged as people shared the news: Two members of the House of Lords had been involved in a duel.

"A duel?" Sydney asked, taking a seat next to Lieutenant Quintin who, with Pelham and Harrelson, had arrived earlier and saved places for their friends. She felt that now familiar thrill of just being near him, but tried to ignore it as she said, "Whatever in the world was so important as to result in a duel?"

"Lord Ackerman took offense when Lord Feldson criticized a bill Ackerman had proposed to continue the government's oppression on the Catholic question."

"They dueled over a religious issue?"

"Yes. Apparently an ongoing dispute."

"I hope they are both all right."

"Ackerman is. He's a skilled marksman. Feldson had never fired a pistol before."

She stared at him. "Good heavens! But he agreed to a duel. So—"

"Feldson was wounded in the thigh. Guess he'll join Pelham and me in the ranks of cane-bearers."

"Men!" she muttered. "What a childish and dangerous way to settle a dispute. Women would be far more likely to *discuss* the issue."

He laughed. "You never give up, do you?"

Pelham offered, "However, there might be more to this dispute. Rumor has it that Feldson had a—uh—liaison with Ackerman's wife."

Feeling a response to this information might be improper, Sydney was glad that the director chose just this moment to signal the first musical selection, a number by Handel.

Two days later, the same group met during the morning at the Pump Rooms. Zachary was feeling in especially good spirits, for he had just two hours earlier given up use of the cane. He still walked with a limp, but his mobility was improving rapidly. He had mixed feelings about that fact, for the sooner he mended, the sooner he would leave England again. Even as he dreaded what he knew he would face on the battlefront, he wanted to be there—in the thick of things. But damn! He had just met the most intriguing woman he had ever known!

He spotted Sydney at a large round table with Mrs. Carstairs and Herbert. He made a show of waving both hands at her and was delighted to see her eyes light up with pleasure.

"Show-off," Pelham muttered in mock disgust at his side, for Ensign Pelham still required his cane.

They made their way through the crowded, brightly lit room. After an exchange of greetings, Sydney said, "Congratulations, Lieutenant Quintin, on abandoning your cane."

"I am thinking of celebrating by building a bonfire and burning the infernal thing."

"I ain't burning mine," Pelham said. "Saving it for when I get to be in my dotage."

"The frugal one among us," Zachary said.

At a signal from Mrs. Carstairs, a waiter brought more tea, and cups, along with a plate of sandwiches and assorted cakes and tarts.

"So where is the third member of your triumvirate?" Sydney asked.

"We encountered Miss Carstairs as we came in, and she insisted Harrelson take the waters with her. They will be along soon," Zachary said, helping himself to an apple tart.

Herbert snorted. "I'm sure he will find the waters very tasty."

Pelham laughed. "If Miss Carstairs offers it, Harrelson will treat it as nectar of the gods."

"Now. Now," Mrs. Carstairs admonished, then said, "I think I shall leave you young people to your banter. I promised to meet the Crowleys and I believe they are in the next room."

As she stood, so did the three men. Herbert looked about the room and said, "Pelham, there's Robert Hansen just come in. Now would be a good time to ask him about that black mare. Come, I'll introduce you."

When they had all gone, Zachary sat down and exchanged a rueful look with Sydney. "I think we have been deserted."

"So we have. Alone in a crowded room," she said with a laugh. She gestured at the plate of food. "But we shan't starve on this desert island."

Neither said anything for a few minutes, but Zachary noted that it was not an uncomfortable silence. Nor was it entirely silent. There was the hum of conversations at other tables and a single pianist played softly in the background. He liked that she was not one of those people who must fill every moment with idle chatter.

After a while, he said, "I want you to know that you sent me off to a circulating library this week."

"*I* sent you—?"

"Yes. You. Or, I should say, the views you were espousing on women. I assumed they came at least in part from Mary Wollstonecraft's famous essay on the rights of women. So I read it, though I did note that the essay is nearly twenty years old. Surely, she must have tempered her ideas later."

"Something that is universally true is not tied to a given period of time," she said, lifting her chin.

He grinned, relishing the sparkle in her eyes. "Universal? Does that mean men and women are absolutely equal?"

She leaned forward in her chair and sounded very earnest. "No, of course not. But she—and I—would argue that certain abilities and their related rights are or should be equal."

"For example?"

"The ability to learn, the right to an education."

"Do you not think the respective roles of a husband and wife require very different kinds of education? The role of housewife and mother do not require university training. Managing business and government does."

"What if she wants to work in business or government? In our society—and I daresay in most societies—a man has options in what he may do with his life. A woman does not."

"God—or Mother Nature—has fixed the roles of men and women in the human community," he said firmly. "Besides, she has the protection of the husband she serves." He lifted his cup to take a swallow of tea.

She arched an eyebrow. "He protects. She serves. Does that sound equal to you? Not to mention the moral restrictions to which she must adhere while he may go his merry way."

He nearly choked on his tea. "Good grief. Do you mean what I think you mean?"

"If you perceive that I think husbands and wives should both respect the sanctity of their marriage vows, yes."

"My dear Miss Waverly. Sydney, that is not the way of the world for much—some would say most—of society."

"I know. And isn't that sad?"

"Don't you two look inordinately serious?"

Celia approached with Ensign Harrelson.

"Did you enjoy taking the waters?" Sydney asked, and Zachary thought she welcomed the interruption.

Harrelson made a face behind Celia's back, but she turned in time to catch him and they all laughed at his chagrin.

The general conversation took a much lighter tone as Celia said, "Do watch for Mrs. Moseby. She is wearing a hat made with peacock feathers. I vow every time she turns her head, it's like that creature in Greek mythology with all those eyes staring at you."

"The Cyclops?" Harrelson offered.

Celia laughed. "No, no. Cyclops had only one eye. Even I know that."

"You mean the hundred-eyed giant, Argus," Sydney said.

"Yes! That's the one."

That afternoon, Zachary discovered yet another dimension to the character of this woman he was finding so intriguing, despite her bizarre ideas on the role of women. When an excursion to the Abbey was proposed, others begged off. Celia had a fitting at a dress shop; Herbert and Pelham had arranged to look at a horse; and Harrelson announced that he was not interested in some moldy old church.

"That leaves you and me to uphold the group's aesthetic interests," Zachary quipped to Sydney.

"I am sure we will prove equal to the task," she said. "My father would never forgive my not visiting the Abbey."

Out on the street, he offered his arm, which she readily took. He delighted in even this slight physical connection with her. The day being overcast, but not yet threatening rain, they took a long, circuitous route to the Abbey Church which, in fact, was not far from the Pump Rooms. Zachary hoped she relished their just being together as much as he did.

They chatted amiably about Bath history, making up personalities for Roman generals whose troops must have ousted the earliest natives to commandeer this spot and build the elaborate system of hot and cold baths. In the piazza in front of the Abbey, they found street vendors and musicians vying with each other for sightseers' attention. Zachary and Sydney admired the stone angels climbing Jacob's ladder on the exterior, then moved within to appreciate the serene quietness of the interior.

They took an equally circuitous route as Zachary escorted her home to Queen Square. Traffic on the streets was rather heavy as people ventured forth to see and be seen. Hearing a sudden shout, Zachary and Sydney turned to behold a horrifying scene that he thought seemed to pass before them in almost suspended motion.

A small yapping dog dashed under the clashing feet of a team. Right behind the dog was a little boy of four or five years screaming, "No! Scotty! No!" The driver sawed at the reins. The horses neighed and reared. The child fell and lay prone on the cobblestones, apparently clipped by a horse's hoof. The carriage came to a wobbling standstill.

The driver shouted, "Oh, my God! They come outa nowhere."

A woman's querulous voice called from within the vehicle, "What on earth—?"

Instantly, Sydney was kneeling over the child's body, dangerously close to the team's prancing hooves. The little dog took a stand at the boy's head, wagging its tail. Zachary sprang to grab at the harness of a lead horse's head to try to calm the team.

Oblivious to gathering onlookers, Sydney put her head to the boy's dirty, threadbare, and torn shirt over a pitifully thin chest.

"He's alive," she announced. She gently felt along his arms and legs. "Not broken." She carefully felt along his head and pulled back to see blood on her glove. "We need a doctor," she shouted at the crowd even as she took the child into her arms.

Zachary turned his hold on the team over to a bystander and joined Sydney, taking the child from her arms into his own.

A woman wearing a shabby man's coat over a thin cotton dress pushed through the crowd, screaming, "Tommy! Tommy! My son!" As she came closer to reach for him, she said, "Oh, my God! Oh, my God! He's bleeding."

Sydney grasped the shoulders of the nearly hysterical woman. "He's all right. He has a cut on his head. He was knocked unconscious." She shook the woman's shoulders. "Do you understand me?"

Slowly the woman focused her gaze on Sydney and nodded. Sydney released her and Zachary placed the boy in his mother's arms just as the doctor arrived. Having taken in the state of the clothing of both the mother and child, Zachary pulled a card from his pocket.

"Send me your bill, doctor."

"Thank you, sir."

The crowd parted, then closed around the departing trio of mother, son, and doctor. Several voices spoke at once.

The driver of the vehicle: "'Twasn't my fault. Happened in a flash, did."

His passenger: "Come along, John. I am late already."

A male bystander: "Quick thinking there, soldier."

A female bystander: "Oh, miss. Your clothes. Them stains will never come out."

Zachary saw Sydney look down at the light green pelisse she wore over a light cotton dress, the flowery print of which bore the same shade of green. There was blood on her chest, a sleeve, and her gloves, as well as street dirt on the hem of her dress. Zachary had thought earlier of how that shade of green intensified the gray-green of her eyes. Her bonnet had been knocked askew. He thought she had never looked lovelier.

He noted movement at her feet.

"Oh. The puppy." She reached to pick it up, thus getting even more street filth on her garments.

"Here. I'll take it," a young woman in the crowd said. "Tommy will be lost without that mutt."

Sydney turned it over, straightened her bonnet, and she and Zachary finally managed to extricate themselves from the group. Zachary felt her hand on his arm trembling in the aftermath. He put his other hand on hers.

"Do you always go around rescuing street urchins and puppies?" he teased.

"No-no." She quickly regained control of herself. "This was my first street urchin. My second puppy."

"You were quite heroic there. You may well have saved that little boy's life."

She smiled up at him. "You were not so bad yourself. I daresay you may have saved both that child and me."

He merely patted her hand as they walked on, but he stored the incident away as providing more insight to the enigma of Miss Sydney Waverly.

CHAPTER 6

Zachary was finding it harder and harder to adhere to the rules of the pact he and Sydney had made. She fascinated him as no other woman ever had. He responded as he supposed any virile male would to her physical attributes: shining light brown hair that his fingers itched to touch, eyes that seemed truly to be "windows of the soul," a smile that dazzled, and a figure that was both trim and enticing. But what really intrigued him were her quick wit, her readiness to smile or laugh, her lack of hesitation in responding to ideas.

It had been his experience that most women waited to find out what *he* thought, then they agreed with him—or pretended to do so. No, that applied mostly to younger women. Certainly, his mother and her friends did not demur at offering their opinions on anything and everything—nor did they hesitate to admit that they occasionally read a newspaper or a book. So why did they encourage their daughters to be empty-headed flibbertigibbets? Thank God that description did not apply to his friend Miss Sydney Waverly.

His friend. Yes. She had become that. But he often found himself wanting more. *Hold on!* he told himself. *Stop right there. You have no right to "more" from any woman at this point. The war is likely to go for a long while yet—a year or probably longer. Nor can you violate the "rules" by intruding into Sydney's personal life.*

Nevertheless, he treasured what he did know of her personal life. He knew that her mother was dead and that, since leaving school,

Sydney was in charge of her father's household. She was fond of her younger brother and sister and talked of them much more often than of herself. Her father, a clergyman in Devonshire, was something of a scholar and had encouraged her in similar pursuits. Had her father actually encouraged those unorthodox ideas about the role of women? Well, never mind. Once she was a wife and mother, that nonsense would fade away.

For some reason that she had not shared, Sydney seemed worried about her father. And, yes, he thought of her—as *Sydney*—for they had agreed early on that they would be "Sydney" and "Zachary" in private. Zachary did not feel she was deliberately hiding information from him, but he sensed that the future weighed heavily on her mind and he was determined to honor her wishes in putting off facing it just yet. God knew he felt the same way about his own immediate future.

So they would go along as they had been. Enjoying this time and this place, tacitly agreeing to concentrate on the here and now.

Then he kissed her.

Well, to be honest, they kissed each other.

It happened just the day before she was scheduled to leave Bath. Zachary had called alone and invited Sydney for a stroll in the small park that formed the center of Queen Square. It was one of those crisp September days when the temperature lets one know winter is knocking at the door, but summer is not yet giving way. There were only a few other people in the park, mostly older people sitting on the benches, feeding birds or dozing in the sun. Sydney and Zachary paused within a grouping of young trees that seemed to be trying to shed the leaves of summer.

"This is my favorite time of the year," Sydney said. "Don't you just love the colors?"

He smiled, thinking that at the moment the colors he admired most were in her cheeks and eyes, but what he said was, "Right now the trees are putting on quite a show for us, but soon enough they will become 'bare ruined choirs.'"

"'Where late the sweet birds sang.'" She finished the line. "I love that sonnet, though it does have a sad, melancholy tone."

"Yes. Well, it *is* about parting." Recalling the last line, he was sorry he had alluded to this particular Shakespearean sonnet.

Just as though she had read his mind, the words came tumbling from her lips. "'To love that well which thou must leave ere long.' Oh, Zachary—" She turned to him, her eyes suddenly filled with despair.

And that's when he kissed her.

He simply drew her gently into his arms and settled his lips on hers. She'd had time to protest, to withdraw. But she did not do so. No. She had hesitated for the barest moment, and then her lips were responding to his with equal passion. It was the sweetest, most earthshattering such experience of his entire life. He felt a fierce surge of desire and sought to deepen the kiss, but she pulled away slightly and lifted her hand to caress his cheek.

"Please, Zachary. We must not—I must not—I am so sorry."

"No. No. It was my fault. 'Had we but world enough and time.'"

She smiled weakly. "More poetry?"

He shrugged. "Why not? The poets always seem to have something for every situation."

"Even ours."

He thrilled at the word *ours*. It told him, as a thousand others could not, that she shared his longing, the fervent wish for circumstances to be otherwise.

He still had his arms loosely around her. "Sydney, when this war is over—"

"No," she said sharply, then more softly, "no." She pressed a finger against his lips. "It cannot be—ever."

Suddenly, it hit him. This whole three weeks made sense now—this need to live as though tomorrow did not exist. "You are promised to another." It came out as a statement, not a question.

She nodded.

"Do you love him?—I'm sorry. I had no right to ask that."

She disentangled herself from his embrace and they continued to stroll along the pathway just as though the whole world had not turned topsy-turvy. He thought she intended to ignore the question.

"I don't know," she said quietly. "I care for him and I intend to make him a good wife. It is the least I can do."

"I—see. And I truly am sorry. It seems our timing has been woefully off."

"Rather."

He was proud of himself for having mustered such a casual tone as he suddenly realized the extent of his sense of loss. Until this moment he had not realized how deeply he cared for her. And he knew full well that, given her character, she would not jilt the man to whom she had given her promise.

For several minutes, they walked along in sad quietness, not looking at each other. Finally, he said, "I think I will not come to bid you good-bye in the morning."

"Perhaps that would be best."

He stopped and gripped her elbow to force her to look at him. "Sydney—I—" His voice caught. "I do wish you well."

Her eyes were watery. "I know," she whispered. "And I, you."

All the way back to Windham village, Sydney only half listened to the conversations of her aunt and cousins who were accompanying her. Last night, she and Aunt Harriet had shared with Celia and Herbert the news of Sydney's impending marriage.

"Married?" Celia squeaked. "You are to be married and—and you have not mentioned it until now?"

"Must have had her reasons," Herbert said.

Sydney explained the circumstances and Lord Paxton's desire for a simple affair with a customary announcement after the fact.

"But you did not see fit to tell *us*?" Celia sounded hurt.

"Aunt Harriet knew," Sydney said. "And—and I thought it best to—to limit the number of people—"

Herbert interrupted. "She knew you'd blab it all over town, Celia. And you know you would have. You never could keep a secret."

"I can too," Celia said with a slight pout, but it was obvious that she recognized the truth of his accusation. "Besides, good news should be shared."

Sydney smiled; Herbert rolled his eyes; and Aunt Harriet said, "Never mind, Celia. You know now and you have to contain yourself only for this evening."

"Celia, I'd like you to be my bridesmaid," Sydney said.

"Really? Me?"

"Really. You."

"Oh, I'd love it. But you must tell us all about him! An earl! Aren't you the sly one? Faith Holmsley will be positively green with envy."

Herbert grinned at Celia. "And that, dear sister, is why you did not know earlier."

"Well, neither did you."

"But I'm not getting my feathers all ruffled over it."

"Nor am I." Celia made a show of dismissing her brother by deliberately turning to Sydney. "Here I thought you and Lieutenant Quintin—but never mind. I want to know all about this secret romance. You must be so very much in love."

Sydney laughed at Celia's dreamy tone. "Henry and I are both very practical people—it will be a good marriage."

She had fervently hoped this would be true as she dealt with the dozens of questions and comments her cousin threw at her.

Now on the journey home, she replayed on her mind's stage that scene in the park. She was absolutely sure that Zachary cared for her and she hugged that knowledge to herself. He was right: their timing was woefully off. She wished their circumstances were different. She wished she had met him six months earlier. She had wanted to lose herself in that kiss. In fact, she had done so—if only for a moment. But it was a moment she would remember—cherish—for the rest of her life.

She could not help comparing Zachary's kiss to Henry's. She had welcomed Henry's kiss; it seemed born of genuine regard and affection. But Zachary's kiss, born of longing and passion, had stirred her very soul.

Stop it! she told herself. *You are not being fair to Henry who is, after all, saving the Waverly family. He deserves better of you.* As she had informed Zachary, she had every intention of making Henry a good wife. And she would do so, this interlude in Bath notwithstanding. Thus did she put the last three weeks firmly behind her as she was caught up in plans for the wedding, her removal to Paxton Hall, and helping her father entertain their guests.

"Will you have to live at the Hall all the time?" Marybeth asked. The little girl had perched on Sydney's bed as her big sister was packing away some mementos of her own childhood. Eight-year-old Marybeth sounded wistful. Sydney knew that, like most children, her little sister was wary of change in her life.

"Yes, darling. But I will see you every day. It won't be like it was when I was away at school and we did not see each other sometimes for weeks."

"Oh. Well, I guess it will be all right then."

Sydney laughed. "Good. I am so glad to have your approval."

"You will leave Brownie with us, won't you?" Brownie was the family's cocker spaniel and Marybeth was especially attached to the pet, though the dog had come into the family as one of Sydney's rescue projects.

"Yes, Marybeth. Brownie will stay here to protect you and Geoffrey and Papa."

Sydney recalled vividly Brownie's entrance into the vicar's household. Muddy, shivering, and starving, the bedraggled puppy had appeared at the kitchen door one day. When Sydney allowed it in, Mrs. Travers, the Waverly family's usually indulgent cook-housekeeper, had objected mightily to having it in the kitchen. Marybeth squealed with delight and Dora, the kitchen maid, squealed in shock when the pup shook itself, showering her with cold rain. Called to the kitchen by the commotion, the vicar had wanted Stanley, the stable hand, to take the animal away.

"Give the poor brute to one of Paxton's tenant farmers," he had ordered.

However, both Sydney and Marybeth had already succumbed to the appeal of the puppy's big brown eyes and wagging tail.

"Oh, Papa, no," Sydney pleaded.

"Sydney, you cannot rescue every stray that happens along," her father told her. "Two cats in the house. Heaven knows how many in the stable. And you do remember how devastated you were when that robin's wing mended and he flew away."

"But Brownie won't fly away," she said, observing how Marybeth held the small squirming body close to her. The puppy licked Marybeth's face and the little girl giggled.

"Good grief. You've already named this mutt?" He threw up his hands and returned to his study. The vicar knew a lost cause when he saw one. "Just see he stays outdoors."

"Yes, Papa," his daughters chorused.

Fed and cleaned, the puppy responded with unconditional love and soon wriggled his way into all the Waverly hearts. Geoffrey and Marybeth were known to sneak tidbits from the table to him and Brownie not only regularly slept on a rug near the vicar's bed, but also accompanied the churchman on his daily walks.

Marybeth's voice abruptly brought Sydney back to the present. "Did you see my dress?"

She jumped from the bed and skipped down the hall to her own room. Moments later she returned, clutching a bundle of blue silk. Sydney shook it out and examined it carefully.

"Papa had Mrs. Beck make it for me while you were gone," Marybeth said. "Isn't it pretty?"

"Indeed it is," Sydney agreed. "Mrs. Beck did a fine job and you will be the prettiest girl at the wedding and the breakfast afterwards."

"Oh, no, Bella—I mean Sydney." Marybeth's tone was very serious as she sat on the stool in front of Sydney's dressing table. "That would not be proper at all. At a wedding, the bride must be the prettiest girl."

"I see." Sydney assumed the same serious tone. "Then you will be the bride's prettiest sister."

Marybeth giggled. "That's silly. I'm your only sister."

Sydney knelt in front of her. "Once I am married, Lady Amy and Lady Anne will be my sisters too. You must think of them as yours as well."

"Really?"

"Really."

"Will they like me for a sister?"

"I'm sure they will love you just as I do." Sydney crossed her fingers and silently prayed this would be true.

Marybeth jumped from the stool and said in her best grown-up tone, "I must go and arrange with Mrs. Travers for tea for Rebecca and me. Would you like to join us?" Rebecca was her favorite doll.

"I should be delighted," Sydney said, silently thanking God yet again for this joyful child in her life—even though her birth had cost the life of their mother.

"We'll be in the playroom."

CHAPTER 7

Zachary watched from a secluded doorway as Sydney and the Carstairs family settled into a hired traveling coach. He chastised himself as a lovesick schoolboy, but he couldn't help himself. He had imagined all last night a number of melodramatic scenes in which he dashed in to rescue her from a dastardly devil who could not possibly appreciate her as he did. Common sense quashed that foolishness.

But he could not stay here in Bath where it seemed every site, every shop, every brick brought to mind something she had said or a certain expression in her face—a raised eyebrow, a dazzling smile. He returned to his quarters, ordered his batman Charlie to pack the few belongings he had there, left notes for Pelham and Harrelson, and he and Charlie set off for London to visit Zachary's parents. With luck the city would provide sufficient diversion until it was time to report to Devonshire for his cousin's wedding.

Devonshire. Sydney was from Devonshire. Might he find her after Henry's wedding and—and, what? Spirit her away? To where? The Peninsula? Ridiculous. Besides, he did not even know her direction and Devonshire covered a vast amount of territory. The Carstairs servants might know where she was, but in light of what he perceived to be Sydney's own wishes, he could not ask them. No. Best leave matters as they stood.

In time this pain, like that in his leg, would surely fade to a little regretted memory.

In London he visited with his family—his parents and his fifteen-year-old sister Julia. His two brothers were away at school. His other sister, two years older than Zachary, was about to present his parents with their second grandchild. His mother, especially, was preoccupied with this event.

He loved his family dearly, but he was finding the whole domestic scene somewhat oppressive. He tried to avoid doing so, but he kept imagining Sydney in this or that setting: Sydney at dinner with his family, Sydney riding or walking in the park. In unguarded moments images of Sydney intruded—her face, her laugh, the way she toyed with a lock of hair when thoughtful. Never had he been so obsessed by a woman. Good God! Was he in love with her? On three weeks' acquaintance? Ridiculous.

On his third night in town, he went first to White's, his father's favorite of the gentlemen's clubs, then to Brooks's. In each of them he encountered men he knew—old schoolmates and fellow military officers who greeted him warmly. He played several hands of whist at Brooks's, but in general found this night on the town less than satisfying. He told himself it was probably just as well that, immediately following Henry's wedding, he would report directly to Plymouth to board a ship back to the Peninsula.

Return to the war would shake this out of him.

He had intended to arrive at Paxton Hall in the early afternoon, but, having run into a rainstorm, he did not arrive until very late in the evening. The journey had not been a pleasant one, largely because of the weather. The coach had been stuck in mud at one point and Zachary and Charlie had to lend their shoulders to help get it unstuck. Apart from that, traveling gave him too much time to think. Even when he managed to doze, images of Sydney haunted him.

"I was beginning to think you weren't coming," Henry said as Zachary divested himself of a many-caped greatcoat and handed it to a footman.

"I usually manage to keep my word," Zachary replied, then was immediately contrite about being so testy. It wasn't Henry's fault that Sydney was lost to him. "Sorry. It was a hellish journey."

"Do come into the library. I have a really fine cognac here."

"Contraband, of course?"

"Of course."

Zachary accepted a crystal glass, inhaled the aroma, and sank into a comfortable leather chair. He looked around to admire the Paxton library. A painting on the ceiling depicted idealized scenes of a bucolic countryside. A large painting over the fireplace showed a fox-hunt with a Paxton ancestor in the foreground. And books. Hundreds of books—and Zachary doubted the present earl had read more than a handful of them. He assumed a tone of mocking censure. "You are aware, are you not, that you are supporting the enemy when you encourage the smugglers?"

"Hah! You know as well as I do that half our intelligence about what the infernal French are up to comes via smuggling operations."

Zachary laughed. "Trust an Englishman to turn his self-indulgence into a virtuous act of patriotism."

Henry shrugged and changed the subject. "I am sorry you were so late. You missed meeting Bella. She and her family were here for supper, but they left over an hour ago."

Zachary raised an eyebrow. "An inspection tour?"

"No. Just a visit, though I did ask her to look over the arrangements for the wedding breakfast to be held in the ballroom."

"I take it she approved?"

"Yes. Bella is not hard to please." Henry emitted a derisive laugh. "I will not face the sorts of problems in this marriage that plague our prince and future king."

"His troubles are largely of his own making. He never has treated his wife with the degree of respect a wife rightly deserves."

Henry gave him an oblique look. "Princess Caroline is not blameless, you know. Her behavior often has tongues wagging."

"I daresay she retaliates in the only way she knows how—or can—when he so openly flaunts his mistresses."

Henry laughed. "You're right. The prince is not a paragon of discretion."

Realizing that this conversation might veer into an area Henry could find uncomfortable, Zachary changed the subject to a safer area of public discourse: the ongoing conflict between the king's conservative Tory government and the Whigs, supported by the monarch's rebellious heir.

Well after midnight they finished the bottle of cognac and Zachary was feeling quite mellow as they said their good-nights. The drink had not truly worked its magic: His last thought before sleep overtook him was of Sydney.

The next morning Zachary donned his dress uniform and sat in Paxton's best carriage opposite his cousin who was dressed in the fashionable pantaloons and tailed coat of formal town wear. Zachary thought the care Henry had taken in his appearance might indicate a deal of respect for his Bella beyond what he demonstrated in casual conversation about his bride.

As the two cousins stood at the altar of the parish church, Zachary looked over the small group assembled to witness the ceremony. He guessed there were, perhaps, thirty people gathered here. Well, Henry had said it was to be a small, private affair. Then his glance fell on two members of the group on the bride's side of the church. Herbert Carstairs and his mother. What were they doing here? Was Sydney here too? Might he see her again? He looked more closely at the guests, but did not see her.

Suddenly it hit him. Sydney—his Sydney—had been promised to another before her sojourn in Bath. In one of those intuitive moments that suspend time, it occurred to him that Henry's Bella could be his Sydney. *Please, God, no!* Feeling as though some giant had dealt him a blow to the midriff, he sucked in a deep breath, but he had no time to adjust to that horrifying idea before he saw her. Sydney, preceded by her cousin Celia, appeared on the arm of a tall, thin man with a shock of white hair. But it was Sydney who commanded Zachary's attention. Sydney in an ivory silk gown, the style of which even he recognized as belonging to a bygone era. She was, quite simply, beautiful. As he looked closely at her face, he thought he detected signs of fatigue or stress—a tenseness about her eyes and mouth. Then her gaze went from Henry to him and he saw a wisp of a sad smile of recognition.

Had she known all along? Had Bath been a weird sort of game she played? Those trips about town? All those hours together? A grotesque joke at his expense? Just an adventure before settling into the hum-drum of married life? The interlude that had affected him so profoundly had been a charade to her. He recalled her response to his kiss. No. That at least had been genuine. Maybe.

Anger and doubt assailed him. So long as her future had been a vague unknown, he had accepted it. But now? His own cousin? He thought fleetingly of making a scene when the minister got to that part about "anyone who had objections to this union." He winced inwardly as her father placed Sydney's hand in Henry's. Zachary re-called clearly the feel of that hand in his own.

Then the bride's father stepped into place as the clergyman an-nounced the intention of this man and this woman, Henry Matthew Alistair Laughton and Sydney Isabella Waverly, to enter into the holy state of matrimony. Well, that explained the confusion over her name. Zachary struggled to maintain his composure, drawing upon years of experience in observing military decorum—of not flinching in seeing a man flogged, of fighting on, directing others even when a friend's death rattle seemed to drown out all other noises of battle.

He could do this. He would do it.

And somehow he did, even to the point of handing Henry the heir-loom ring at the proper moment and watching, fascinated, seeing only their hands as Henry slipped it on her finger. He stood stoically as Henry kissed her. Then the bridal party retired to the vestry to sign the church registry, first Henry, then his bride. As Sydney handed the pen to Zachary, their hands touched and, for just a moment, his gaze held hers. Was it regret or resignation he saw there? Or was that merely what he wanted to see? He signed quickly and handed the pen to Celia.

Then it was over.

But no. There was still the wedding breakfast. For the return trip to the Hall, he found himself in a carriage with Henry's younger sis-ters with whom he had only this morning become acquainted. They reminded him of his own sister, Julia, and he only half listened as the two girls giggled and gushed over the beauty of the bride and the cer-emony itself. They were polite in trying to include him in their con-versation and he was pleased to be able to respond in a normal tone.

Unlike Zachary, Sydney had been prepared for their meeting again—and the circumstances under which it would occur. She had spent a mostly sleepless night before that long, long journey down the aisle of her father's church. She had worked hard to school her emotions since her sojourn in Bath. Then yesterday, in an instant, all that effort had been shattered.

Along with her father, Geoffrey and Marybeth, her aunt Harriet and her cousins, she had visited Paxton Hall in part to check on seat-ing arrangements at the post-wedding breakfast. After showing the visitors the more public rooms of the Hall, Lord Paxton accompanied Sydney and her aunt to the ballroom, leaving the vicar and the younger visitors in the music room with his sisters. In the ballroom, they found a long table at one end of the room, with a number of smaller tables spread along the side walls, each providing seating for eight people.

The room itself was magnificent. One long wall had several large windows and two sets of double French doors leading to a large and well-tended garden. Opposite that wall were three large tapestries between which were large mirrors that would at night reflect the light from two large chandeliers. The other walls were covered in green and gold embossed silk; the painted ceiling, like the tapestries, depicted scenes from Greek mythology.

"What a beautiful room," Aunt Harriet exclaimed. "I remember attending a ball here soon after my brother moved to Devonshire. You have done a marvelous job of preserving it, my lord."

"My father had the tapestries cleaned and mended. They date from the fifteenth century. And, please, Mrs. Carstairs, call me Henry. We are to be family, after all."

"Why, thank you. Then I shall be *your* aunt Harriet as well as Sydney's."

Henry smiled and shook his head, but looked with affection at his fiancée. "I am forcing myself to think of her as Sydney. To me, she has always been Bella. I keep forgetting."

They all smiled at this, then Sydney, observing the linens, fine china, and table decorations, said, "I had not realized this breakfast would be quite such an elaborate affair. There must be a hundred places set here!" She felt a little overwhelmed and some of her trepidation must have shown in her voice.

"Never mind, my dear. Stevenson and Roberts, along with Mrs. Knight, have everything in hand," Henry assured her, naming his steward, the butler, and the housekeeper. "Besides, you know almost everyone—tenant farmers, Paxton Hall servants, village people, and so on."

With a gentle hand at the small of her back, he guided her to the head table and began to point out who would sit where. Sydney took it all in, but only half listened until he said "—my cousin Zachary, here, next to you—"

"Your cousin *who*?"

"Zachary. Zachary Quintin. His mother is my aunt. You will like him. Army man. With Wellington."

"I—I know him," Sydney said.

"You do?"

"We met in Bath," she said, trying to quell the surprise and panic she felt with knowing that Zachary would see her being married.

"What a small world it is," Aunt Harriet said. "Lieutenant Quintin is a particular friend of my son."

"Had I known you were going to Bath, Bella—uh, Sydney—I would certainly have made him known to you," Henry said.

"It happened very quickly," Sydney said, still trying to absorb this news. Zachary. He would be here. Tomorrow. Oh, dear God.

Aunt Harriet cast Sydney a questioning look, then launched into babbling about soldiers coming to Bath to convalesce from war wounds. Sydney was grateful for time to pull herself together and wondered just how much her keen-eyed aunt knew of what had passed between her and Zachary.

"Such a pity so many of them must return to the battlefields," her aunt was saying.

"But are we not lucky to have them performing as they do for our sake?" Henry said.

"Indubitably," Aunt Harriet said.

When the three of them rejoined the others, Sydney had herself under control and could marvel with the others about the coincidence of Zachary Quintin's being Henry Laughton's cousin.

"My grandfather, the sixth earl, disapproved of his daughter's marriage to a man he thought of a 'nabob' and because of that, my father was never very close to his sister," Henry explained. "Sad, isn't it, what happens to some families?"

Later that night—the eve of her wedding—Sydney had tossed and turned in her bed, beset by doubts. Was it right to marry Henry feeling as she did about Zachary? And, really, how *did* she feel about him? How did she feel about either of these men? Yes, there was this incredible chemistry between her and Zachary. That kiss in the park had shaken her to the very core of her being. She loved the fact they seemed to understand each other on some fundamental level she had never known with another human being.

But she had known Zachary only a matter of weeks—less than a month. With a seven-year age difference, she and Henry had never been close as children, but she had known him virtually her whole life. Yet what did she really know of this man she was to marry? She knew Zachary's taste in art and what books he liked; they shared an interest in history, even if they did not always agree on who were the positive and who the negative players on history's stage. Was Henry a reader? Did he even like literature—let alone was he able to quote well-known works?

Oh, do stop, she told herself. This was an exercise in futility. There was no point in considering what might have been. She had given her word. Under no circumstances could this well-reared vicar's daughter ever subject her intended husband, her father, her family, to scandal. Nor was it merely the threat of scandal that gave her pause. Henry could and would protect her, her father, Geoffrey and Marybeth—and he would do it now. Zachary was returning to the war for God alone knew how long. And only God knew how much time her papa had left.

Thus ran Miss Sydney Waverly's thoughts throughout the night before her wedding. By morning, she was sure she had gained firm control of herself and not only her future, but also those of Geoffrey and Marybeth.

Then she saw Zachary standing next to Henry and she faltered, but only momentarily. He looked splendid; his impeccable red-coated military uniform was a stark contrast to the conservative civilian wear Henry wore. She tried to read his expression, but couldn't. Her gaze shifted to Henry. She saw only friendly welcome in his eyes. Her hand trembled on her father's arm and he placed his other hand over hers.

"Courage, my love," he whispered. "It will be fine. You'll see."

And suddenly, it was. She repeated her vows in a strong voice and signed the registry with a steady hand, though she admitted to herself the familiar sensation she felt when her hand touched Zachary's at the signing. In the carriage on the way to the Hall, refusing to let herself consider what the rest of the day and night held for her, she sought diversion in small talk with her brand new husband.

With a gesture to the window, Henry said, "Happy the bride the sun shines on."

Was he nervous too? She smiled. "And the groom, I hope."

"We shall have decent weather for the drive and our stay at Tarrenton—perhaps it will even hold as we go on to the sea." Sydney knew Tarrenton, a manor house with extensive acreage, was another Paxton property located thirty miles from Paxton Hall.

"I shall enjoy it in whatever weather we find," she said. "I love the sea, especially when it is stormy."

"My wife—the consummate rebel." Henry took her hand in his and continued to hold it until the carriage swung into the driveway. Aware of and nervous also about the great changes the last hour had wrought in her life, Sydney clung to his hand, grateful for the reassuring contact.

The wedding breakfast, about which Sydney had previously harbored a good deal of apprehension, turned out to be rather fun for her. Henry had been right: she knew these people and they not only wished the bridal couple well, but did so with gusto. There were many toasts, but later Sydney remembered only the first one. Zachary's.

"To my cousin Henry and his delightful bride. May their trust in each other and fidelity to the vows they took today see them safely through any turbulence in the sea of life. May neither of them ever be tempted in any way to alter the regard they have only for each other and the honesty and integrity with which they begin their married life."

Henry, leaning back in his chair to speak to a guest on the other side of Celia who sat next to him, seemed not to have heard Zachary's toast. Sydney nodded and smiled and said all that was proper, but later she wondered if there was some double entendre to his remarks.

And much, much later, she was sure there had been.

Sydney gave herself up to enjoying this party, refusing to allow the disconcerting presence of one Zachary Quintin to deter her. She was aware of him seated next to her; she sensed the warmth of his body. Occasionally, their arms chanced to touch. There was an instant in which she caught the familiar scent of his shaving soap. There was so much she wanted to say to him, but this was neither the time nor the place. And, in truth, what *was* there to say? The meal and toasts over, the glasses were refilled again and again. Musicians had played softly throughout the meal and now played country dance tunes and many of the guests formed sets while others merely mingled and chatted.

Sydney was determined to make this an enjoyable occasion, not only for herself, but especially to assure her father that she was happy, for, after her return from Bath, he had seemed nervous about whether she would be content with her lot in life. Had he suspected something had happened to her in Bath? She and Henry led the first dance set and after that she took part in others as well. She was pleased to find herself able to meet Zachary in the twists and turns of one dance set with a cool detached demeanor—at least outwardly. She struggled to control her inner emotions.

During a lull in the festivities, Sydney sank into a chair next to her father. "How are you faring, Papa?"

"Quite well, my daughter. Quite well."

"You are not getting overly tired, are you?"

"No. No. I am thoroughly enjoying myself. I had a nice chat with Lieutenant Quintin. I met his mother years ago. Nice lad. He danced with Marybeth."

"He did?" It occurred to Sydney that she had never been his chosen dance partner. "So what did you and he talk about?"

The vicar chuckled. "Would you believe the relative merits of *The Iliad* and *The Odyssey*? I accused him of military prejudice in his preference for a war story. Fine topic at a wedding celebration, eh?"

Sydney laughed and kissed his cheek. "Oh, Papa."

He put his hand on hers and gazed into her eyes. "Bella, you *are* happy, are you not?"

She held his gaze, trying to project her sincerity. "Of course I am. Could any woman ask for more?"

It had been a rhetorical question, but he took it seriously. "Maybe—" he started, still holding her hand.

She leaned close and kissed him on the cheek again. "Do not worry yourself, Papa. It will be fine. I promise."

Sydney was also keenly aware that this was her first public appearance as the Countess of Paxton. It was important that these people, almost all dependent on the earldom to some degree, see her changed status as a positive factor in their lives. To this end, she made sure that she and her new husband had a personal word with everyone.

When she and Henry had changed into their traveling clothes, they returned to the party to bid their guests farewell and endure a good deal of merriment at their expense. They also had private moments with their family members.

"Zachary, feel free to stay here at the Hall as long as you wish," Henry said.

"My ship sails in three days. I shall leave in the morning," Zachary said as he shook hands with Henry. He then lifted Sydney's hand to pass an air kiss over it. She squeezed his fingers for a moment as he held her gaze and said in a husky voice, "I do wish you both every happiness."

"Thank you," she whispered.

There was a flurry of good-byes as the newlyweds settled into the traveling coach with a driver and two outriders to accompany them. Henry's valet and Sydney's maid had been sent on ahead an hour earlier.

As Sydney poked her head out the window for one last good-bye, she caught sight of Zachary standing behind the crowd. He leaned against one of the columns of the portico on the Hall, arms crossed over his chest staring at the ground. Her heart wrenched at the bereft expression on his face.

It was the last she would see of him for nearly four years.

CHAPTER 8

Determined that she would be a good wife to Henry, Sydney had few reservations about her coming wedding night. She knew essentially what to expect—had she not assured her father that she knew about "the birds and the bees"? Still, she was nervous; she did know the basics, but there were glaring gaps in this part of her education.

Maisie, who had helped her into and out of the wedding gown, then into her travel clothes, now helped her remove those and don a sheer silk and lace concoction that was intended as a nightgown. Sydney felt suddenly shy in front of the maid and tried to cover her embarrassment with small talk.

"I must say, Maisie, I do appreciate your help. Dressing is far more complicated for a countess that it ever was for a vicar's daughter."

"Aye, my lady. Fancier dress has more pins and tapes."

"You'd think people who could invent steam engines and construct huge bridges could devise simple closings for women's dresses." She knew she was babbling, for, now that the moment was upon her, she was increasingly apprehensive.

"Yes, ma'am." Maisie hung the traveling dress in the armoire, folded the other garments, put them away, then turned to dealing with her mistress's hair.

Sydney sat on a stool in front of the dressing table as Maisie combed out the upswept hairdo. "And that's another thing. It would seem I must now spend much more time on my appearance every day."

Maisie, who was only two years older than her mistress, smiled and said, "Married ladies of the *ton* generally do, I think." She finished brushing out the light-brown tresses which now hung below Sydney's shoulders and ended in soft curls. "Will that be all, my lady?"

"Yes. Thank you, Maisie." It occurred to Sydney that Maisie delighted in saying "my lady." After all, Maisie had, in an instant, gone from being a vicar's general purpose maid—doing whatever needed to be done in that understaffed busy household—to being a lady's personal maid in a great house.

As Maisie left, Sydney moved to a comfortable couch near the fireplace to wait for Henry. She reviewed what had surely been one of the most eventful days of her life, but she refused to dwell on Zachary's having been there. Should they ever meet again, it would be as mere acquaintances. She gazed about her, aware of the movement and muffled voices of her husband and his valet on the other side of the door to the adjoining room.

Her husband.

She looked about the room to avoid going where that thought was leading. It was an attractive room with pale blue and silver silk bed draperies and dark blue velvet drapes at the windows. The light gray marble fireplace and oyster-colored furniture showed the previous generation's obsession with Egyptian decoration. The colors here reflected those of the countess's bedchamber and sitting room at the Hall.

She was startled out of these musings by a knock at the connecting door to Henry's room. He entered dressed in a dark maroon robe, awkwardly carrying a decanter and two glasses which he set on a low table in front of her before settling himself next to her.

"I thought a bit of cognac would be in order," he said, splashing the liquid into the glasses. "Helps one relax." He handed a glass to her, then touched his glass to hers. "Here's to us, my dear."

She gave him a tentative smile, drank, and promptly coughed at the burning sensation in her throat. She felt her eyes watering at the fumes. "I—I'm not used to—"

He grinned. "Just sip it slowly."

She did so and felt warmth spread through her.

"Better?" he asked.

She nodded. "Much." She took another sip, not really sure she liked the taste, though she did appreciate the relaxing warmth the drink offered.

Henry shifted his position to put his right ankle on his left knee. She noted a small tattoo on the ankle, a pair of crossed swords. He saw her looking at it and explained.

"Paxton heirs always have this mark."

"Why?"

"Tradition, mostly. Twins are rather common in the family—Amy and Anne, for instance. The first earl of Paxton had identical twin sons. To distinguish the first born from his brother, the earl—a great swordsman, by the way—had him immediately tattooed. Thereafter, we've all had it."

He finished off his drink, then gathered her into his arms and kissed her. It was a long, deep kiss that tasted of the drink. He moved his mouth to nibble at her earlobe and then trailed kisses down her neck to the swell of her breasts. She drew in a deep breath as his hand caressed her breast and she felt her body relaxing and responding. His lips sought her mouth again and she opened to him. He drew back, breathing hard. Then he stood and extended his hand. As she rose, he stepped back to survey her. She felt naked in the filmy gown and held her breath for his approval.

He sucked in a long, whistling breath. "My God, you're beautiful. How did I get to be so lucky?"

She merely blushed and allowed him to lead her to the bed. She slid under the covers and watched as, loosening his robe, he bent to blow out the bedside lamp. She was disappointed. Other than statues and drawings, she had never seen a completely naked man before, let alone a fully aroused one. She had—wantonly—looked forward to doing so. Nevertheless, light from the fireplace allowed her a peek— a peek that gave her pause. Good heavens! However would her body be able to accommodate *that*? As he lay next to her she felt the hardness pressing against her.

He shoved her nightgown above her waist and stroked the soft flesh between her legs. Again recalling her intent to be a good wife, she tried to adjust to him.

"Ah, Bella," he murmured. "This may be painful the first time, but I cannot wait any longer."

"I—I—all right . . ."

He positioned himself between her legs and pushed slowly, gently into her. She felt searing pain and cried out sharply. He covered her cry in a cognac-flavored kiss. They both lay still for a very long moment, his face buried against her neck.

He raised his head. "Are you all right now?"

"I—I think so." The pain had subsided.

He began to move inside her, his strokes becoming more and more intense. Then he uttered a long, satisfied moan. Suddenly, it was over. He rolled to her side, held her close, kissed her tenderly, and within seconds, it seemed, he was breathing the deep breaths of dream-filled sleep.

Sydney lay staring at the underside of the bed canopy. Was that it? *That* was what married women whispered about and virginal girls could hardly wait to experience? Somehow she had expected more. Much more. She gave herself a mental shake. Ah, well—

Finally, she, too, slept.

The next morning she woke to an empty bed. Sometime in the night, Henry had returned to his own room.

That became the pattern of intimacy in her marriage. In time she achieved a degree of enjoyment and comfort from their couplings, but never the sheer ecstasy of whispers and dreams. The ever-practical Countess of Paxton consigned that notion to the stuff of fantasy, and she went on with her life, determined to ignore any foolish longing for "more."

As with most lives, the next few years of Sydney's vacillated from the ordinary to the extraordinary, with elements of both tragedy and farce, dreams realized and dreams quashed—or altered at least.

That first year had been a year of learning and loss. In midwinter the new Countess of Paxton traveled with her husband to London for the opening of Parliament and the social season. The former vicar's daughter was presented at court—Queen Charlotte insisted on maintaining her traditional receptions despite the king's bouts of ill health. Lady Paxton acquitted herself well in the entire social milieu, even hosting a large dinner party for members of her husband's Tory faction, though some whispered that her ladyship was rather quick to voice her own opinions on Parliamentary matters—and—*gasp!*—that those opinions often seemed to have Whig overtones of reform.

With her husband's compliance—nay, his encouragement—she made two visits to Windham to alleviate what she recognized as bouts of homesickness.

Her father, having given up his duties as vicar just after Christmas, moved, along with Marybeth and Geoffrey, to Paxton Hall. As long as he was able, he tutored his son and oversaw his younger daughter's education. He also discussed with Sydney his wishes regarding further schooling for them: Harrow and Miss Sebastian's, of course. The Laughton twins, Lady Anne and Lady Amy, would also go to Miss Sebastian's when Marybeth went, for the girls had become fast friends. Meanwhile, a governess saw to their training. Sydney regretted the time in London, time away from the family back at the Hall.

In London, Henry was attentive to his new wife, though he made it quite clear they should not expect to "live in each other's pockets." He frequently spent long evenings away from home, presumably at his club or out with his male friends. Though he tried to be quiet, Sydney would hear him come into his room next door sometimes even as the city's delivery people were starting their rounds. Still, he performed his marital duties with alacrity, pronouncing "this business of getting an heir to be quite wonderful indeed."

But it did not happen.

When the season ended in June, Sydney welcomed the return to Paxton Hall, but she found her father's health far weaker than his letters had led her to expect. She was so preoccupied that summer and autumn with the increasingly imminent loss of her beloved papa that she scarcely noticed Henry's prolonged absences. He was often off to oversee the earldom's far-flung interests, which included Welsh coal mines, Irish estates, and sundry other enterprises. He announced his latest departure during one of his frequent visits to her bed.

When Sydney commented on the geographical diversity of Paxton holdings, he explained, "My ancestors made interesting acquisitions in their marriage settlements."

"Unfortunately, the present earl did not," she said, aware of just how little of material value she had brought to this union.

He pulled her closer and murmured, "Do you hear me complaining?"

Not yet, she thought. But so far she had not fulfilled her primary obligation of getting an heir.

Her father died in late autumn, over a year after performing her wedding ceremony. Sydney had mixed feelings about his passing. She had selfishly exulted in every moment he stole from the inevitable, but his last weeks were so fraught with pain that she—and he—welcomed the release.

"Oh, Papa," she said on visiting that grave next to her mother's, "I am going to miss you so very, very much."

She had shared one spot of joy with him before he died, though: She was four months pregnant.

Christmas was a subdued affair that year and Henry later journeyed to London alone for the opening of Parliament. Sydney, with few regrets, missed the London season of 1813 entirely, for by the time the official six months of mourning for her father were over, she was too near her confinement to journey to the city.

In late March Henry managed to make it home in time for the arrival of his son and heir, Jonathan Alfred Henry Laughton, named for his two grandfathers and his father. His cries as he was promptly given the Paxton heir tattoo fairly broke his mother's heart.

A week after his birth, she still could not bear to be away from him for long. "Isn't he beautiful?" she cooed, as she sat in her bed, bolstered by pillows, and held him close.

Henry, dressed for travel, had popped in to say good-bye. He laughed softly. "Beautiful? Red and wrinkled as he is? If you say so, my dear. If you say so."

"But just look at this shock of dark hair—that comes from you. His eyes are from me—and my father. I do hope they won't change. Mrs. Hatfield, the midwife, says they often do. And he has such spirit!"

Henry grinned at his wife and touched a forefinger to his son's cheek. "I assume by 'spirit' you mean he has a healthy set of lungs. He does that."

She cuddled the baby closer and said, "Pay your father no mind, my son. In time, he will learn to appreciate all your attributes and achievements."

"Just as soon as they manifest themselves." Henry rose and kissed her on the forehead. "I must be off, my dear."

"For how long did you say?"

"A fortnight. Maybe longer. I will write you."

"All right." As the door to her bedchamber closed behind him, she turned her attention back to the baby.

*   *   *

Life settled into a comfortable routine. Sydney refused to be one of those society mothers who relegated total care of their children to nursery maids. She was also determined that, though she had not brought a great estate to this marriage, she would have something of value to offer. She worked closely with the housekeeper, butler, and the head gardener to ensure that the Hall itself was operated efficiently and smoothly.

Then one day, she took on a new role—one outside the conventional duties of a countess. Henry was away and Sydney was just finishing breakfast with the twins and her own brother and sister, when Mr. Roberts, the butler, appeared to announce that Mr. Stevenson, the estate steward, wanted to speak with her.

"He says it is rather urgent, my lady."

She found the steward, a man of perhaps forty years, pacing in the library, his hands behind his back, a worried expression on his face.

"Good morning, Mr. Stevenson. Won't you sit down and tell me what the problem is?" She gestured to a chair in a nearby grouping and took one of them herself.

The steward sat, his hands splayed on his knees. He seemed nervous. "I am sorry to trouble you, my lady. Not a matter for a woman, don't you see. Ordinarily, his lordship would handle this, but he is not here and you having grown up in Windham and all—well, it just seemed logical to at least ask you about it."

"And what is 'it' exactly?" she asked.

"You know the farmers Davis and Newton?"

"Oh, dear." She knew immediately what the problem might be. "Those two have hated each other for years. Ever since Darlene Ryan chose to marry Tom Newton instead of Fred Davis. But—good heavens!—that was over twenty-five years ago."

"Their feud escalated this week."

"Not over that same plot of land again, I hope. I thought they were to share it as grazing land."

He nodded. "That was the plan, but Newton fenced off part of it and planted a garden. Davis's pigs got into it and destroyed it. Davis says it was an accident, that Newton's fences weren't well built. Newton, of course, says it was deliberate. Last night Davis's barn caught fire. He's blaming Newton. The Davis men were drinking and plotting revenge last night. I'm afraid someone's going to end up dead over this squabble."

"You may be right," Sydney said. "When we were children all those boys—Davises and Newtons—had tempers that were quick to flame. Many a black eye resulted. What to do? What to do?"

"Perhaps if we sent word to Lord Paxton," Stevenson offered.

"He is in Ireland. By the time we got word to him and he could reply or return, it would be another fortnight. No, we must handle this ourselves, Mr. Stevenson."

They sat in thoughtful silence for several moments, then Sydney said, "Send for the grown men of both families. You and I shall meet with them this afternoon."

"Here?"

"Yes. Uh, no. Someplace more neutral. The magistrate's chamber in Windham's town hall. That should lend an air of formality."

"You have a plan, my lady?"

"I will have. And I shall depend upon your support."

"You shall have it."

"Oh—and Mr. Stevenson?"

"Yes, ma'am?"

"Have those who are married bring their wives."

"Wives, my lady?"

"Wives. They may be able to talk some sense into those hot-tempered men."

Stevenson nodded and directed an admiring grin at her as he took his leave.

That afternoon, dressed in her most conservative no-nonsense, lady-of-the-manor style, Sydney met with the adult members of the Davis and Newton families. Other than her wedding ring, she wore no jewelry; the only adornment on her dark green gown was a lace fichu at her neck. She also wore a dark green bonnet with a single black feather.

"Do I look like a female Solomon about to pass judgment?" she asked Geoffrey, who accompanied her to the village.

"Most intimidating," he said.

At the town hall, she and Mr. Stevenson sat at a table facing the two families: two older couples in their forties flanked by the three Davis sons, two of whom had wives with them, and two Newton sons, of whom one was married.

"We are here to settle this dispute," Sydney announced in a voice that belied her nervousness. What if those Davis boys defied her as they had when they chased her with a snake when they were much, much younger?

The elder Newton, a slender man with graying brown hair, stood and said in an emphatic tone, "Begging your ladyship's pardon, but the fifth Earl of Paxton allotted the use of that land to my grandfather."

Immediately, Fred Davis jumped to his feet to yell, "And his son gave it to my father." Davis, whose bald head was pink and shiny, was shorter and heavier than Newton.

Other members of both families, some standing, began to voice loud agreement with their leaders.

Sydney rapped the magistrate's gavel. "Sit down, all of you."

Obviously surprised, they did so and silence ensued.

"Owing to a fire at the Hall some twenty years ago, it is impossible to verify either of these claims," Sydney began in a calmer tone. "The compromise Mr. Stevenson and Lord Paxton worked out previously is apparently not working. The fact is that that land is *Paxton* land—it belongs to the Earl of Paxton and is his to do with as he wishes."

She paused to allow this thought to sink in, then went on. "Both these farms are profitable and well tended. Both the Davis and Newton families have proved themselves valuable members of our community. However, neither of you is indispensable." Again, she paused for effect. "Elsewhere in England small holdings such as yours are being eliminated, sending farm people into factories and mines—if they can find work at all. It would be more profitable for Paxton to take that step."

She held the gazes of the two leaders for a moment then shifted her gaze to each of the other family members. The women, especially, seemed apprehensive, even fearful. These were not stupid people. They clearly knew the plight of tenant farmers in other parts of the country.

"Destroying families, a way of life, is not Paxton's way. But we cannot have this discord continue. So. I give you a choice. You can settle this between you amicably, or Paxton will require either or both of you to emigrate, either within the United Kingdom or perhaps to Canada, and we will absorb your holdings into the Paxton home farm." She stood. "And that, ladies and gentlemen, is that. Today is

Friday. You can let me know after church on Sunday what you have decided to do."

Back in the Paxton carriage, Sydney asked Geoffrey, "Well, what did you think as you sat there in the back?"

"I was quite proud of my big sister."

"Oh, were you now?"

"But more than that, I heard Mrs. Newton say, 'That little slip of a girl has a head on her shoulders.' I think you won her over."

On Saturday, Mr. Stevenson reported that the Davis and Newton men had shared tankards of ale the night before—an unprecedented event. On Sunday, they reported a simple agreement to divide the land with a stone wall and stile to allow access.

In the weeks and months following, Paxton people were as likely to seek advice and counsel from the countess as from the earl.

During school holidays, Sydney welcomed the fun and frivolity of Geoffrey and his friends, who readily accepted her company as they went riding, and they grudgingly tolerated that of the younger girls. In the evenings they all played card games, billiards, or charades. There were also picnics and family theatrics, as well as occasional assemblies in the village—and Windham's annual Harvest Festival in September appealed to people of all ages.

When he was in residence, Henry readily took part in these activities. He occasionally urged her to accompany him on his trips and, often enough, she did so, though with mixed emotions about leaving her son behind. Henry, like the steward, began to voice his concerns about this or that business enterprise to his wife. She was pleased that he confided in her so much and that he seemed genuinely to seek— and respect—her opinions on such matters.

Henry was often away on his own, though. She accepted the fact that he had far-flung duties associated with the earldom and that he was an avid sportsman. Young men of his class were known to spend an inordinate amount of time and money on racing, hunting, or sailing. Given the circumstances of her marriage, Sydney was in no position to object to those outings. He certainly denied her nothing and was seeing to the needs of her family admirably.

So what if she was sometimes lonely?

Even when he was home, other than estate matters, the two of them shared few interests. Henry devoured the sporting news, but took little interest in whatever else the country's journalists reported.

Sydney, on the other hand, read the newspapers voraciously. She was keenly interested in the labor unrest in the Midlands—the continuing activities of the so-called Luddites and their opposition to new technologies. She noted the ongoing conflicts between the king's Tories and the Whigs with whom his son and heir—now the Prince Regent—sided at the moment. She also followed the war in the Peninsula with sharp attention; she always scanned the casualty lists with apprehension. Twice she had noted Zachary's name in special dispatches. He was a captain now.

Henry's dabbling in political issues was superficial, born more of social obligation rather than sincere interest in what was good for the nation. As a peer, he was obliged to hold that seat in Parliament, but one needn't get carried away. He had no interest in literature or history. Religion was a matter of form rather than substance.

To counter her persistent sense of loneliness, she threw herself into estate matters in the country. In the city, she had become acquainted with Lady Allyson Crossleigh, daughter of the Earl of Rutherford. Lady Allyson quickly involved her new friend in one of her charity projects: a home run by a pair of spinster sisters who offered protection and comfort to abused and abandoned women and children. The Fairfax sisters were located near Spitalfields, one of the less desirable areas of London.

When he learned of her first visit to the Fairfax sisters, Henry had been alarmed. "It is downright dangerous, even during the day. All those out-of-work silk weavers. I should not like it at all were you to go there at night."

"We are careful to have adequate protection," she assured him. "Besides a coachman, we have one or two strong footmen accompany us. And often a maid as well."

"Don't see why it's necessary for you to go at all," Henry grumbled.

"*Someone* needs to care for these people," Sydney said.

"The poor are always with us. There's nothing anyone can do about that. But if it makes you feel better . . ." His voice trailed off.

"It does," she said, lifting her chin. And since he had not expressly forbidden her doing so, she continued her involvement with Lady Allyson and the Fairfax sisters.

All in all, she thought she and Henry muddled along quite well.

She considered herself luckier than many of her contemporaries. Her husband drank and gambled far more than she would have liked, but, so far as she knew, he was faithful. And that was important to her. Yes, she did wonder now and then about all those trips hither and thither, but she trusted him. She had to, did she not?

Later, she would remember this as her "head in the sand" period and wonder how she could possibly have been so obtuse.

Her awakening came very abruptly during "the little season" in the autumn.

CHAPTER 9

Sportsman that he was, Henry usually spent the months from August to November on various hunting expeditions—for quail, grouse, deer. However, this year his usual hunting companions were unavailable, so he opted to take the family to town for the "Little Season," which offered rounds of social activities during the autumn from September through November. Then the nation's political bigwigs and social leaders would retire to their country estates through Christmas, returning to town for the opening of Parliament in January or February.

After a whole year away from London, Sydney actually looked forward to removing to town, renewing her friendship with Lady Allyson, and just being in the social and political hub of the nation.

Geoffrey had, of course, returned to school after the summer holidays, but the twins and Marybeth, along with their governess, accompanied Sydney, Henry, and the baby Jonathan to London. The Paxtons' traveling party included four coaches and drivers, six footmen, and two maids—besides the butler, Roberts; his lordship's valet, Brewster; and her ladyship's maid, Maisie. Plus luggage. And the family pet, Brownie, the cocker spaniel.

Henry settled into the seat next to Sydney and said, "I must say, travel to London was a far simpler matter when I was a bachelor." Their three sisters occupied the opposite seat at the moment. Baby

Jonathan traveled in one of the other carriages so that his sleep would not be disturbed by the chatter of his young aunts.

"Oh, but think of all you missed," Sydney said with false brightness. "Companionship, conversation."

He snorted. "Noise, confusion, delay."

Sydney patted his hand. "We do appreciate your sacrifice, my dear. Don't we, girls?"

They chorused their concurrence.

"As you should," he said with a smug grin. "And, Amy and Anne, not another word about the menagerie in the Tower."

"But we are *so* looking forward to seeing a real elephant," the irrepressible Amy said.

"You may see it only if I do not have to hear about it incessantly."

Amy and Anne ignored him and went on babbling about seeing the menagerie and other sights of the city. "And shopping," Anne added dreamily. Sydney looked forward to seeing her aunt Harriet and cousin Celia who would arrive within the week.

Several days later the girls did see the elephant and a tiger and some exotic birds housed in the Tower of London. Sydney, who had accompanied them while Aunt Harriet and Celia shopped, was more interested in seeing the rooms where Queen Elizabeth and Sir Thomas More had been held prisoners—and the spot where Anne Boleyn had lost her head. Marybeth pronounced the animals "pathetic" and wanted Sydney to rescue them as she had once rescued Brownie.

Both family life and social activities in the city settled into a comfortable routine. Then in early October, Lady Paxton's careful complacency abruptly ended.

She and Henry, along with Aunt Harriet and Cousin Celia, attended a ball at which Lady Bessborough achieved every hostess's dream: a veritable "crush." Sydney, having danced three sets, chose to sit the next one out. The room was hot, crowded, and noisy. Her partner delivered her to a chair near one of dozens of huge potted trees placed strategically about the ballroom. Sydney sat quietly watching the dancers. She saw Henry executing the steps of a country dance with that pretty Lady Ryesdale. Sydney had met her a few days earlier and learned her sad story of a husband who was confined to a mental facility. Lady Ryesdale did not go out much in society, but she was related to Lady Bessborough. Hence her presence here tonight.

Sydney suddenly became aware of a conversation behind her and behind yet another of those gigantic potted plants. She recognized the voices immediately. Faith Holmsley and the ubiquitous Elizabeth Kenmore. She shrank into the fronds of her own potted plant, not really wanting to spend the next half hour engaging in small talk with those two.

After three seasons, Faith Holmsley had finally managed to bring a certain viscount up to scratch and she was now the Viscountess Ellsworth. Elizabeth Kenmore had married a knight named Fullerton a year later, for it would never do, Sydney thought, for the acolyte to aim higher than her idol. She immediately chided herself for the pettiness of that thought. Their voices broke in.

"Can you believe that?" Faith asked with a gasp.

"Believe what? What did I miss?" Elizabeth whined.

"Paxton is dancing with Lady Ryesdale."

"No!"

"They are usually much more circumspect. Too many trips to the punch bowl, I suspect."

"Do you think his wife knows about them?" Elizabeth asked in a conspiratorial but still very audible voice.

"Good heavens, Liz, how could she not know?"

"Well, she was in the country all last season."

"But that affair has been going on for—for *years*—long before that mismatched marriage of his. Everyone knows Paxton settled for Miss Waverly only because he could not have his Louisa."

"I did not know that."

"Really, my dear, you simply must keep up," Faith said scornfully. "I suppose you also did not notice that Lady Ryesdale was significantly absent from society in the spring?"

"No, I did not. But so what?"

"Oh, Liz. You are such an innocent. And this is so delicious! The story is that Lady Ryesdale was in an interesting condition."

"Oh, my goodness."

There was no mirth in Faith's laugh. "Isn't it rich? Paxton's wife and his mistress gave birth within weeks of each other. Both boys."

The rest of the conversation was lost to Sydney, who sat in stunned silence, not daring to move lest they notice her and witness her utter humiliation. Was it true? Oh, dear God, could it be true? Inanely, it occurred to her that eavesdroppers rarely hear good of themselves. Her immediate reaction was anger—no, fury. How could he do this to her? How could he be so false to his own vows?

She waited until the other two left, then she found her way to the ladies' withdrawing room, feeling slightly nauseated. There, she gulped a glass of water and calmed herself enough to send a maid to locate her aunt.

Aunt Harriet arrived shortly. "What is it, my dear? Are you unwell?"

"I—I—yes. I wish to go home immediately."

"I'll go and get Henry for you."

"No." She spoke more sharply than she intended and now modified her tone. "No. Just tell him I have gone home and I shall send the carriage back for the rest of you."

"I shall come with you. You are definitely looking unwell."

Half an hour later Sydney and her aunt were safely returned to the Paxton townhouse. Sydney had not spoken on the way, afraid she might burst into tears.

Having disposed of their cloaks, Aunt Harriet followed her up to her sitting room and closed the door behind them.

"What is it, Sydney? You look as though you've received a terrible shock."

"I—I—heard some—something very disturbing." How much could she bring herself to divulge to this woman who was like the mother Sydney had missed for over a decade now?

"About Henry?"

Sydney stared at her, knowing full well this awful pain must show in her eyes.

Aunt Harriet cleared her throat. "I—uh—saw him dancing with Lady Ryesdale. It—it was not very wise of him."

"Then it is true? And you knew? Everyone knows?" Sydney did not sob, but she could not stop the tears streaming down her face.

They had been standing in the middle of the room. Aunt Harriet put an arm around Sydney and steered her toward a couch. "Sit down, my dear, and I'll ring for some tea."

Sydney sat and buried her face in her hands. Now a sob did escape her. "I feel like such a fool."

"You are not the one who has behaved foolishly here. Do not even think that. Now, tell me what happened."

Sydney did so and was surprised that merely saying the words aloud was helping her gain control. She had barely finished when a footman delivered a tray with not only tea but also a decanter of sherry. Sydney kept her tear-stained face turned away and the discreet footman quickly left.

Sydney smiled tremulously. "Tea?"

"And a little something else. Sherry has marvelous medicinal properties."

"If you say so," she said dully. "Tell me, Aunt Harriet. You knew?"

Aunt Harriet poured both tea and sherry and handed Sydney the sherry glass first. Then she nodded. "I was in town last year, too, you know."

"And you did not tell me? Why?"

"My dear girl. This simply is not a topic one brings up out of the blue. Often as not a wife already knows and chooses to overlook the matter. Calling her attention to it is hurtful."

"But I did not know." This came out in a soft wail. She drank from the sherry glass, then set it down. "And—and—is it true? There is a child? Henry has another son?"

"I think so. That *is* the rumor."

Sydney twisted her hands in her lap and said bitterly, "And I suppose there are jokes and bets in the clubs."

"That, I do not know." Aunt Harriet leaned close to pat Sydney's shoulder. "Now, my dear, the others will be returning very soon and you need to think about how you will handle this matter."

Sydney's first inclination was to pack her bags and return to the Hall with her son. But of course she could not allow her problems to spill over to other family members. Besides, running away was a coward's solution—and, in the end, no solution at all.

However, she did take the coward's way out that night in order to gain time to think. She pretended to be asleep when Henry looked in on her. He was gone from the house all the next day, so it was late in the evening before she could have a private word with him. Later, she wondered how she had made it through that day. But she had done so—even entertaining visitors in the afternoon, many of whom were solicitous—or merely curious—about her early departure from the ball. With Aunt Harriet's knowing help and Celia's unknowing help, she managed to fob off their questions.

That night Henry came to her room apparently totally ignorant of her real trauma of the previous night. Dressed in the familiar maroon robe, he seemed ready to assert his customary rights as a husband.

"We need to talk, Henry."

She gestured for him to sit on the couch as she took a nearby chair.

"Oh? I hope the baby is all right."

"He's fine. We need to discuss you and Lady Ryesdale."

She saw him go very still. Finally, he clasped his hands on his knees and said, "So. You know about Louisa."

"Yes. How long, Henry?" She was surprised at her own calm demeanor.

"Six years."

"So why—why did you agree to marry me three years ago?"

He sighed heavily. "For all the usual reasons. It seemed like a good idea. I thought we would get on well together—and we have. I needed an heir."

"Well, now you have one."

"Yes, I do. A fine one he is, too."

"Rumor has it that Jonathan is not your only son."

He looked embarrassed and gave her a sidelong glance. "You know about that, too?"

She nodded even as she felt a lead weight where her heart should be. She had hoped this was not true.

He relaxed on the couch, stretching one arm along its back. "Louisa and her son have nothing to do with us, Sydney. In fact, you and I should not be having this discussion."

She sat up straighter in her chair. "You find infidelity meaningless? I do not." She folded her arms across her chest. "I will not share my husband with another woman."

"You dare to refuse me?"

"Only so long as you expect me to share your favors with another."

She saw anger flash across his face. She had never seen him truly furious before. His eyes narrowed to a squint. "I could force you, you know. The law and society would be on my side."

"Yes, you could. But I seriously doubt rape is part of your nature."

He stood and pulled his robe tightly about him. His tone dripped acid. "Try not to be crude, my dear. And do let me know when you come to your senses."

CHAPTER 10

After seeing Henry and Sydney off on their wedding journey, Zachary returned to the Hall, but not to the ongoing party in the ballroom. He ordered Charlie to see that all was readied for them to leave at dawn, then he shut himself in the library with a full bottle of Scotch whiskey and drank himself into oblivion—or tried to.

He was beset by a profound sense of loss. "'I look upon myself and curse my fate,'" he muttered. The quotation immediately conjured up an image of Sydney in the Bath park, smiling sadly. Would he ever again be able to read a Shakespearean sonnet without thinking of her?

Her touch, her kiss, the feel of her in his arms, the scent she wore—all haunted him. Earlier images of her in the arms of some unknown lover had been painful; now that he knew who the lover was, they were more vivid and more excruciating. He shifted position on a leather chair in front of the fireplace, leaned back and closed his eyes to shut out the visions. It didn't work.

His regret and despair were tempered by anger. Anger at an indifferent, abstract fate in which timing was all. Anger at himself for falling into this moonling state. And anger at her. Clearly his standing there at the altar had come as no surprise to her. She had known all along! He not only felt humiliated at being so duped, but also foolish for still wanting her. He sighed and refilled his glass.

* * *

His dark mood stayed with him during the long voyage back to the Peninsula. With winter hovering on the fringes of the world, the seas were often rough. Never one susceptible to seasickness, Zachary relished the stormy weather as a mirror of his own mood. In Portugal and then Spain, he was finally able to confine his pain to a less prominent place in his thoughts and memories. Dulled, but still plaguing him.

He quickly settled back into being merely one more soldier with the Allies on the Iberian Peninsula: those British and Portuguese forces supplemented by a German regiment and Spanish elements who opposed Napoleon's having installed his brother Joseph on Spain's throne. These were arrayed against the French, who sought to keep the incompetent Joseph on his seat of power, and such Spanish elements as had sided with the conquering French. In the north of Spain, the fiercely independent Basques added another ingredient to the often baffling mix.

"Just keep your head down and do your job," Zachary told himself and anyone else wondering about this political mish-mash.

In the months following his return, Lieutenant—now Captain—Zachary Quintin had made a name for himself. He thought "Zany Zack" was a bit of a misnomer. He did not consciously seek risky assignments and he never knowingly exposed himself or others to extreme danger. However risk and danger seemed to pursue him, and he admitted to himself a degree of indifference to his own safety since returning to the war. He distinguished himself in the major back-and-forth skirmishes of that first year after his return—Ciudad Rodrigo in January and Badajoz—again—in March. However, by the end of that year, routine military duties were anything but "routine."

At Badajoz, he had caught the attention of his commanding officer who demanded that he appear before a panel of three officers: Wellington himself and two colonels. The three senior officers sat behind a heavy, dark table in a room with whitewashed walls. There was a single dark wooden chair in front of the table.

"At ease, Captain," Wellington said and gestured at the empty chair. "Have a seat." He looked briefly at a paper on the table. "Since you seem intent on challenging both the enemy and yourself, we should like you to consider becoming one of our exploring officers."

"Sir? You want me to be a spy?"

"That *is* what it amounts to. Working behind enemy lines. Gathering information on enemy troop movements—and terrain. Our maps are woefully inadequate and we desperately need better information."

"You work with local partisans—and they are not always reliable," one of the colonels said.

"It is extremely dangerous," the other colonel cautioned. "You operate as a civilian, you know."

"Yes, sir. I do know."

"Then you also know that if you are captured, you may be summarily shot? No special treatment as an officer. No parole."

"Yes, sir."

"You speak Spanish, I'm told," Wellington said.

"Yes, sir. And French."

"Well enough to pass yourself off as a Spaniard or Frenchman?"

"I think so, sir."

"Good. Then you are the man for this mission—if you want it. It is strictly voluntary, of course. You may take some time to think about it."

"I'll do it, sir."

Wellington raised an eyebrow. "You do not wish to think about it?"

"No, sir."

"Very well. You may choose your own team. Small groups of five to seven men seem most efficient—but they must all be volunteers."

"Yes, sir."

Thus it was that Zachary and his small band of cohorts—sometimes four, sometimes six others—performed some of the most remarkable and dangerous exploits of the war in the Peninsula. Zachary had no trouble finding volunteers for his team, which soon came to be known as "Zany Zack's Rangers." His batman, Corporal Charles O'Brien, was the first to offer his services and Zachary welcomed him heartily. Charlie was famous for his ability to "find" things just when they were needed most. Ensign Trevor Harrelson, who had returned to the Peninsula on the same ship carrying Zachary and Charlie, was also welcomed with enthusiasm, for Trevor was one of the army's best sharpshooters. Other members of the group were chosen for special skills: Lieutenant Adam Richardson was an engineer with a fine hand at architectural sketches and map-making; Lieutenant Cameron McIntyre, like Zachary, spoke fluent Spanish and French, but he was also a genius at breaking French codes. The rest of the team consisted of Ensign Jack Gordon, who had had some medical training; Sergeant Arthur Whitten, who was an excellent horseman; and Corporal Owen Penryn, who had simply refused to take no for an answer when he requested permission to join the Rangers.

When Zachary presented his choices to the commander, Wellington emitted his famous whoop of a laugh and said, "You'd make a fine politician, my boy!"

"Sir?"

"These names appear to represent a cross-section of British peoples."

"Yes, sir. That just happened, sir."

"See to it that Harrelson and Richardson survive this venture. I do not want to be writing the Duke of Tyndale or the Marquess of Rodham to tell them I've lost one of their sons. Don't need them voting against us in Parliament."

"Yes, sir."

"Jack Gordon? Owen Penryn? Those names are familiar, too."

"Yes, sir. They have been mentioned in dispatches. As have the others. Good men, all."

Wellington nodded, approved the reassignments, and dismissed the team leader.

The French offered a tempting reward for the capture of any of the Rangers. There were some narrow escapes, but, besides truly fine mounts and their own cleverness in getting out of perilous situations, the explorers had the locals on their side—mostly. Portuguese, Spanish, Basque—even French—peasants knew that the English soldiers would pay for what they took—mostly. Wellington insisted on this— and that his own government see to proper supplies for men in the field. His expectations were met—mostly. French soldiers, on the other hand, were tossed into foreign lands and told to fend for themselves. Most were also peasants with few or no resources. So they stole, pillaged, looted—and left a sea of resentment in their wake.

In actual practice, Zachary and his lot were not continuously performing as spies or aiding partisans. They went out for a few weeks at a time—the longest period was ten weeks—to gather information and, most important, scout routes and draw maps. Then they would return to regular duties for a few days or even weeks until they were dispatched on another special mission.

At some point in those first months—he never knew exactly

when—Zachary realized he had to get on with his life. Sydney was lost to him forever, but he was still a healthy young man with the usual desires, needs, and dreams of that element of the human community.

Between battles, an army battalion or even a regiment would be encamped near a Portuguese or Spanish town or city with allied officers billeted in the metropolis itself. As they waited for suitable weather or supplies before taking up the campaign again, dinner parties and balls as well as theatrics and musical events helped alleviate the boredom. Such diversions might be sponsored by local dignitaries or by groups of officers. Wellington himself sponsored gala affairs to celebrate the anniversary of a battle he had won, or the king's birthday, or a holiday.

Women at these soirees, far outnumbered by men, were wives of English, Spanish, and Portuguese officers or wives and daughters of local officials and aristocracy. Zachary and his friends rarely had any difficulty securing dance partners. In an effort to put Sydney out of his mind, he engaged in several mild flirtations and even a month-long affair with a certain Dolores, widow of a Portuguese nobleman. Whenever a certain bit of music or a snippet of conversation brought to mind an image of Sydney, he forced himself to ignore it. Nevertheless, he counted himself lucky when a new assignment for his exploring team rescued him from the lovely Dolores's insistent demands on his time and attention.

There were, of course, many women among the long "tail" of the British army. Some were wives "following the drum" merely to be with their men. Officers were allowed to bring their wives—and servants, too—but at their own expense. Only a few did so. The army, recognizing women as useful to do cooking and laundry for the troops, allowed four women to ship out with each company of lower-ranking soldiers. These women, with no children, were chosen by lot. Zachary recalled with sadness the anguish of those who, having lost the lottery, were left behind on the dock at Plymouth.

Besides women legally following the army through Portugal and Spain and eventually through the Pyrenees and into France, there were hundreds of local females soldiers had picked up—and often abandoned—along the way. Many of these were whores who threw in their lot with a foreign army, but many were refugees with no other recourse. Zachary was especially touched by a group of seven nuns, aged fifteen to sixty, who had been driven from their convent by the French—but not before each had been repeatedly raped.

So female companionship was readily available to a rich young officer in His Majesty's Army, but after the Dolores episode, Zachary rarely availed himself of it—partly because of the erratic nature of the explorers' missions. And never did he allow himself to become involved emotionally.

Until he met Elena.

The Rangers were charged with two missions. Passing themselves off as local farmers and shepherds, they were to gather information on French troop movements and locate and map passes through the mountains. Zachary had sent the rest of the team into the mountains and he and Gordon and Whitten went to the small village of Segueros to meet with a partisan contact, a priest named Father Lorenzo.

Leaving their horses and two pack mules with Whitten in a copse of oak trees and low shrubs, Zachary and Gordon made their way along the dirt track of the main street to a small stuccoed church. Emerging from bright sunlight, they paused to adjust to the darker interior. Light came from open slits high on the walls and from two sets of candles before statues of saints. The walls had once been whitewashed; the altar was plain, with no intricate carving or gold leaf. A life-sized carved wooden crucifix was the focal point. About a dozen worshipers, two of them French soldiers, occupied the pews.

Zachary gestured to the soldiers and to Gordon, then pointed at himself and nodded toward the confessional set on the right wall. Gordon nodded and took a seat three rows behind the French. Zachary positioned himself near the confessional and waited for the low voices within to cease. A middle-aged woman dressed in shabby black and wearing a black headscarf stepped out of the confessional and Zachary stepped in.

He gave the password and asked in Spanish, "Is there any significance to those two soldiers being here, Father?"

"I don't think so. They came in only a few minutes ago." The priest chuckled. "It's cooler in here than outside."

"You have something for me?"

"This. Taken from a French courier yesterday." The priest shoved some papers through the crack below the wooden screen.

Zachary quickly tucked them inside his shirt and rose to leave. "Thank you, Father."

"You'd best wait a bit, my son." Zachary noted amusement in the priest's tone. "Unless you have been a very good boy indeed, it would take longer than this to recount your sins."

Zachary laughed softly and sank back down.

"Besides," the priest went on, "I have a favor to ask of you."

"A favor. Of course. We owe you that much."

"In my quarters I am hiding the partisan fighter who brought this message yesterday after an encounter with the French about twenty kilometers to the south. The situation is very dangerous here. I am sure I have come under suspicion."

"And you want us to—?" Zachary left the question hanging.

"Help get this person out of Segueros."

"Of course. When?"

"Tonight. Come after sunset. The moon is bright now, so you should be able to travel some distance before morning."

Zachary and Gordon rejoined Whitten, but instead of leaving the village, they moved their horses deeper among the trees to await nightfall. Over a cold meal of bread, cheese, and watered-down wine, Zachary explained the delay.

"Ye ken this is a good idea, Quintin?" Gordon asked in his amiable Scots brogue. The Rangers were careful never to refer to rank when they were in the field and Zachary had, early on, encouraged his men to share freely any doubts or concerns.

"Probably not," Zachary admitted, "but the partisans in this area have been very helpful to us. We can hardly refuse."

"Right," Whitten said with a yawn. "I'm for some sleep if we're going to ride all night."

Zachary looked at the pages Father Lorenzo had given him, but could not decipher the code. A job for McIntyre, he told himself, and followed Whitten's lead.

That evening they approached cautiously the rear of the priest's cottage. They noted a sturdy Spanish pony in the shadows, saddled and bearing a rolled blanket and full saddlebags. At Zachary's knock, the door opened immediately. The priest, a tall, thin man in his forties, filled the doorway, but the room behind him was dark. A small figure in a dark poncho, with dark trousers stuffed into boots, and wearing a floppy hat, darted out to mount the pony, achieving that feat somewhat awkwardly.

"Hurry," the priest said. "The French were here earlier. They will be back."

"Thank you, Father," the pony's rider said in a soft voice.

A female voice.

"Wha—" Zachary started to protest, but heard a commotion from the front of the cottage and quickly remounted his own horse.

"God bless you all," the priest said in a voice barely louder than a whisper.

They pushed their horses hard for a quarter of an hour, then slowed the pace when there was no immediate pursuit. Zachary moved his horse near the pony.

"Who are you?" he demanded in Spanish.

"Elena Ramirez." She seemed short of breath.

Both Gordon and Whitten emitted surprised gasps and Zachary felt his eyebrows rising.

"Your father heads the Ramirez band?" He knew that this group of partisans took a no-holds-barred approach to ousting the usurping French from Spanish soil, but he'd had no direct contact with them before.

She drew in a breath. "M-my brother." She paused. "Now, please, let us get on. My people are a day's ride from Segueros. Father Lorenzo insisted I not go alone."

"We'll see you there all right," Zachary said, slightly annoyed at her peremptory tone. "First we have to meet the rest of our team."

Sure now that they were not being pursued, Zachary called a halt before dawn in a small meadow near a stream. "Give the horses a rest, get some food and water," he announced, dismounting and grabbing a packet of food from one of his saddlebags. The girl just sat on her pony, seemingly unaware of her surroundings.

Zachary tossed his packet on the ground and walked around his horse to hers. "Señorita Ramirez? Would you care to join us?"

She leaned over the pony's neck, the reins lapped loosely over her wrists, her hand gripping the mane. Even in the dim predawn light, he saw blood on her left hand.

"Good God! Señorita!"

She swiveled her head toward him, staring rather vacantly. Then her eyes rolled upward as she fell into his arms, unconscious. He caught her and staggered back, but managed to remain upright.

"Gordon!" he yelled. "I need some help here."

Jack Gordon, the unofficial medical man of the Rangers, quickly spread a blanket on the ground and Zachary placed her inert body on it. They removed the poncho to see that the left side of her tan shirt was soaked with blood.

"A shoulder wound," Gordon said. "Gotta get the shirt off. Chemise, too. I'll get my kit."

Zachary removed these garments to find a blood-soaked bandage wrapped around her shoulder, covering her left breast and tied about her waist. He draped the cleanest part of the shirt over the exposed right breast and sat back to let Gordon do what he could.

"We need water," Gordon said, and Zachary hurried to fill a canteen.

He returned to find that Gordon had removed the bandage to reveal an ugly dark hole in the soft flesh below her collarbone. Both her breasts were now exposed and Zachary could not help appreciating their perfection.

"Good job she's unconscious," Gordon said. "She'd probably be embarrassed. I probed the wound, but whoever bandaged her got the shot out. She's lost a lot of blood." He poured water from the canteen onto a clean section of the bloodied chemise and used it to wipe away the blood around the angry-looking wound.

"What do we do now?" Zachary asked, gazing at the pallor beneath what appeared to be a normally golden complexion. Wavy midnight hair framed an oval face. *My God! She's beautiful,* he thought.

"Re-bandage and hope the fever passes," Gordon replied. "Could you see if she has extra clothes, then help me get her shoulder tied up again? We'll need to put her arm in a sling once she wakes up. That should have been done yesterday."

Zachary found a clean shirt, along with a little food, a pistol, and extra ammunition in her saddlebags. He and Gordon were both carefully impersonal as they dressed the wound and then dressed her, but he was sure Gordon found it as difficult as he did to ignore what was a mature, attractive female body.

Having watered the horses, then loosely hobbled them in grass, Whitten joined them. "How's she doing?"

"Still out," Gordon said. "She needs rest and, judging by those clouds building in the west, she's going to need shelter. We all will."

Zachary glanced at the sky and said, "It's some distance away yet. And we have to meet the others first. Maybe we can find a shepherd's hut. God knows we've seen enough of them when we were not looking for one."

They spread their bedrolls, ate some more bread and cheese and proceeded to rest themselves as well as their horses for a couple of hours. Zachary lay with his head near the girl's in case she should wake in a panic. With the typical soldier's ability to rest when opportunity presented itself, he slept. When he awoke, he found her staring at him, very alert to her surroundings.

"What happened?" she whispered.

"You fainted."

"I never faint."

"You fainted." He got to his feet and called to the others, "All right, lads. Up and about."

The other two groaned, but followed suit. Whitten and Zachary saw to the animals while Gordon fashioned a sling for their patient's arm. She was obviously still woozy; when she tried to stand, she quickly sat back down.

"Give me a moment," she said.

"Never mind," Zachary told her, leading his horse near. "You'll ride with me. Whitten will lead your pony."

She looked as though she wanted to protest, but ignoring that possibility, he lifted her onto his saddle and climbed on behind her. His saddlebags and bedroll were added to hers on the pony.

"Ready?" he asked in English, and, trying not to jar her injury, awkwardly took up the reins in front of her with one hand. At first she tried to hold herself stiffly away from him, but gradually he sensed that she was dozing off. Her body slumped against his and he wrapped one arm about her waist to keep her in the saddle. He found himself feeling inordinately protective.

Three hours later, they reached the rest of the Rangers at the rendezvous point.

"You're late," Adam Richardson called, then his eyes widened at seeing the fourth member of the arriving party. "Well, I'll be—Trust our fearless leader to find a damsel in distress."

Zachary glared at him. "That storm is coming on fast. I don't suppose you stalwart fellows who've been scouting this area for three days might have stumbled upon some place we might wait it out?"

His friends looked thoughtful, then Charlie O'Brien said, "Yeh. There's one o' them stone huts 'bout half an hour that way." He pointed north.

"Mount up and lead on," Zachary ordered. "We'll do a proper introduction when we get there."

"Aye, aye, sir," they chorused in slightly mocking tones.

It was late in the afternoon, the wind was blowing hard, and the first drops of rain were falling by the time they found the hut. Over her protests, Zachary settled Miss Ramirez on a blanket on the dirt floor, then went out to help with the animals. Soon, eight slightly damp people—along with saddles, saddlebags, packs, and bedrolls—were crowded into a living space meant to accommodate two.

"At least it's out of the rain," someone said as the storm unleashed its fury.

"And the wind," another offered.

The hut sported no usable furniture; a chair with a leg missing and a few pieces of wood lay about. It smelled of mold and rodents. The door hung at a peculiar angle on its one remaining leather hinge; there were no windows and Zachary thought the fireplace might produce more smoke than warmth. The men sat on the bare floor or on their saddles, staring in the dim light at the female in their midst. Zachary thought she looked as though she were terrified, but bravely fighting not to show her fear. He wondered if she had heard about the way the British army had gone berserk with looting and raping when they finally took Badajoz. He moved to sit next to her.

"Relax. You are safe," he told her in Spanish, then addressed the men. "Gentlemen, may I present Señorita Elena Ramirez?"

"Who?" Richardson asked in a wondering voice.

Owen Penryn whistled. "*La Belle Diable*. The beautiful devil. That's what the frogs call her."

Zachary looked at her to see her blushing.

"Well, she *is* a beauty," Richardson said appreciatively.

Penryn went on. "She and her brother and their gang have been playing bloody hell with French couriers and supply lines for months. Uh, sorry, miss."

Her blush had deepened and Zachary was sure she understood the gist of this conversation in English, if not every word.

"The bounty on their heads is as great as the one on ours," Richardson observed. This idea sobered them all for a moment.

Zachary turned to her and said in Spanish, "I'm sure you won't remember all these names, but allow me to present these boorish fellows to you anyway." He proceeded to point out and name each of them. She smiled and repeated the names as they were given to her, stumbling over the unfamiliar English syllables. She seemed pleased when McIntyre addressed her in her own language.

Zachary was glad to see her relax as the conversation veered away from her, but he also noted that she kept the saddlebag containing her pistol near her, even using it as a pillow when she slept.

The storm raged on, offering claps of thunder and hailstones the size of large peas at one point, then settling into a steady rain. As they ate sparingly of their remaining food, Zachary thought they'd have to find a goat or a couple of rabbits tomorrow.

Richardson sat near the doorway, sketching; Penryn and Harrelson played piquet with a well-worn deck of cards. When the sun set in some uncloudy part of the world, and it became very dark in the hut, two of them rummaged in their bags and produced stubs of two candles. McIntyre had moved near the girl and engaged her in seemingly idle conversation. Zachary listened, occasionally offering a question or comment. He was always amazed at the information McIntyre was able to extract when he interviewed anyone. Her father was a colonel in the Spanish army serving the government in exile in Cadiz; she and her brother—both of whom had been away at school—joined the partisans after the French kidnapped, tortured, and murdered their mother and two younger siblings; her brother had taken over the group when their leader was killed.

Still it rained.

Zachary assigned guards to serve two-hour shifts and the rest of them slept, lined up in the tight space like logs tied in a raft. He had Gordon check Elena's bandages, then he insisted the girl lie between him and McIntyre, partly to preserve body warmth and partly because he did not fully trust her. Stories abounded of explorers betrayed by supposedly friendly partisans.

It was well after midnight when the rain let up. Zachary woke and lay still, thinking it was too quiet. The guard was not near the door. Probably out checking on the horses. He heard an owl hoot and felt the girl stiffen next to him. She remained tense. He feigned sleep.

Suddenly, a human figure loomed in the gray rectangle of the doorway.

"Elena!" the man yelled.

Even in the faint predawn light, Zachary saw that the newcomer held a pistol and there were two other figures behind him, probably equally armed.

CHAPTER 11

Acting instinctively, Zachary jerked her saddlebag from beneath her head and drew his own always loaded weapon as he scrambled to his feet. He grabbed her good arm and pulled her close as he positioned the gun under her chin and drew back the hammer.

"Miguel!" the girl cried. "No dispares! No dispares!" Don't shoot.

The others were all awake now, probably surreptitiously reaching for weapons. Zachary knew his men would not be taken without a fight.

The hut faced east and the sun was rising rapidly. Zachary watched Miguel's face carefully as the man took in the situation.

"We seem to have a stand-off here," Zachary said in Spanish, his tone deliberately conversational.

The man nodded, but did not lower his weapon. "Elena?" His voice was controlled, but Zachary was sure his fear for his sister was very real.

"Inglés, Miguel. They are English. Put away the weapons."

She spoke in rapid Spanish, but she seemed calm. Zachary could not help but admire her cool handling of the situation. He watched the information register with the man in the doorway.

"Inglés?" he asked.

"Yes. English," she said.

"But you are hurt. Who did this to you?"

"The French," she said hastily. "They killed Fernando, but we got the courier and the message he carried. Two of them escaped. Jorge took me to Father Lorenzo. These English helped me. Now put the gun away."

Finally, the man in the doorway lowered his weapon and, lowering his as well, Zachary said to his own people, "It's all right, fellows. No shoot-out today."

There was a collective sigh of relief.

In the immediate aftermath, Ramirez apologized to O'Brien, the morning's guard who had been knocked unconscious when he'd gone to check on the horses. Miguel sat with his arm around his sister.

"We thought you were French," he explained.

"Why?" Zachary asked.

"We went to Segueros. We knew Elena would get that dispatch to Father Lorenzo. But when we got there, Father Lorenzo was dead and she was gone."

Zachary heard Elena's sharp intake of breath and saw her quickly make the sign of the cross.

Miguel went on. "The neighbors knew nothing of Father Lorenzo's guest—only that French soldiers had broken into his cottage. I knew the prints of Elena's pony. Once we picked up those prints, it was not too difficult for us to follow you—until the storm wiped out all signs of traffic." He grinned, a flash of white teeth against several days' growth of a very black beard. "We thought you'd look for shelter. We've been to every hut in a radius of fifteen kilometers or more. No easy task with the storm and darkness."

Zachary nodded sympathetically, then looked up at a sharp gasp from McIntyre, who had again this morning taken up his task of decoding the message Zachary had received from the priest.

"I've got it!" McIntyre said. "The peer needs to see this right away. Soult is on the move."

The peer of course was Wellington, who had been accorded that nickname when Parliament had first elevated the general to that status. Zachary thought it better than "ole nosey," which referred not only to the most prominent feature of the general's face, but also to his uncanny tendency to be anywhere and everywhere on a battlefield. Soult was the French commander at the moment. McIntyre handed his worksheet to Zachary, who read it and lifted a brow in surprise.

"Recode it and we'll send it off with Whitten. Harrelson and Penryn can go with him in case he runs into trouble. The rest of us will carry on—keep tabs on the frogs and find a passable route through these infernal mountains."

The Ramirez brother and sister had been conferring and now invited the rest of Zachary's team to their headquarters in a village even smaller and more remote than Segueros. On arrival, Zachary estimated this village's population at about fifty or sixty, half of them adult men with maybe fifteen women. The rest were children of varying ages.

The Ramirez village had started out in the middle of the last century as a rich aristocrat's hunting lodge with the necessary plethora of servants to cater to his and his guests' needs. These had been housed in smaller cottages, clustered around the lodge like chicks around a mother hen.

"Our great-grandfather was a favorite of the king," Miguel explained. He waved a hand in a sweeping gesture. "My family once controlled thousands of hectares of land here."

"What happened?" Zachary asked as he, Miguel, and Elena rode ahead of the others.

Miguel laughed. "Our grandfather was not such a favorite of the next king."

Elena explained. "They were both in love with the same woman." "And?"

Miguel emitted another hoot of laughter. "Grandfather always said she was worth every grain of sand he had lost."

Zachary grinned, and glanced at Elena, who merely smiled and shrugged.

Zachary and the remaining Rangers spent several weeks with the Ramirez partisans. They were housed in the lodge itself with the Ramirez family—Elena; Miguel; Miguel's wife, Pilar; and their two young children—along with the unmarried men of the Ramirez gang. The married men occupied the surrounding cottages. During these weeks, the Rangers would ride out for two or three days at a time, sometimes on their own, sometimes with two or more of the Ramirez people.

Often when they rode out together, Zachary would end up riding next to Elena. They shared stories of their childhoods and discussed a myriad of topics. If it occurred to him that she was as easy to talk with as Sydney had been, he quickly quashed that thought. Sydney had talked much about equality between men and women; Elena simply assumed it was so—or ignored that it was not so—and acted accordingly. He tried to dismiss Sydney as a fantasy, part of an interlude in life to be enjoyed only while it lasted, a pleasant memory from which one had to move on. His growing attraction to Elena was certainly helping him achieve this end.

The Rangers shared game and other foodstuffs they happened upon, so they were readily accepted into the partisans' extended family. No matter how sparse the fare on the table, Miguel, his wife, and his sister dressed for dinner, Ramirez in a semblance of formal evening wear, Pilar in a soft green gown, Elena in a fiery red one—both in a style popular four or five years before. Zachary conjectured that this practice was to remind them of what they came from and what they were fighting for: A way of life.

The other men, including the Rangers, made do with whatever clothing they had. Zachary and his men murmured admiringly on first seeing Pilar and Elena so elegantly gowned.

"Women are meant to be properly appreciated," Miguel said.

"Amen to that," Richardson said.

Zachary's usual place at the table was next to Elena. Often their hands, arms, or legs would happen to touch. And just as often, he wondered whether she might welcome more.

The third time the Rangers and members of the Ramirez band rode out together, Zachary was forced to face just how different their goals were. The mission of Zany Zack's Rangers was strictly reconnaissance: to identify and keep track of numbers and positions of elements of the French army, to intercept messages between those elements where possible, and to find and map alternate routes through the mountains. The Ramirez people were bent on engagement—and they were driven by revenge. Every adult member of their group had lost property, family members, or both to the marauding French.

By this time, Elena's wound had healed. Zachary admired her determination to regain full use of her arm. Even sitting quietly, she would alternately tense and relax that shoulder. Only during the first week did she forego riding out with the others. She was the only woman who did participate in this manner. The Ramirez men took great pride in her, even as they were intensely protective of her, and he suspected more than one of them to be half or wholly in love with her. As for that, the same might be said of his own men—and of himself.

Thoughts of Sydney still crept up on him when he least expected them, but Elena had managed to lessen their impact—at least during his waking hours.

Elena was beautiful, intelligent, playful, and generous with her brother and his family. On several occasions he saw her drop something she was doing to lend a hand in the kitchen or with the children, who adored her—as did their mother. She was gentle and sympathetic over a scraped knee or a loose tooth.

One afternoon he had been idly watching her from the veranda that encircled the entire ground floor of the three-story lodge. Elena was playing with the children on a swing in the yard. He had not noticed Pilar at his elbow until she spoke.

"You just see you don't break her heart," Pilar said just as though she were continuing a conversation.

Zachary started. "I have no idea what you mean."

"Oh, I think you do. I've seen the way you look at each other. Elena is not as tough as she wants people to think."

"I doubt any of us is," he replied, not wanting to encourage this discussion.

Pilar was not to be deterred. "Three years ago—she was only eighteen—she was hurt very badly. It must not happen again."

Zachary was appalled. "Someone abused her? Physically?"

"Her heart." Pilar touched her own chest. "They were to be married. He joined with Bonaparte and betrayed the Ramirez family."

Two days later, he saw an entirely different side of the fascinating Elena.

The four remaining Rangers had ridden out with about a dozen of the Ramirez people. They had been following what might have been a company of French soldiers. The Rangers were particularly keen on finding out precisely how individual French soldiers were now armed—new innovations in weapons, amounts of ammunition they carried, conditions of clothing and rations.

"Our orders are very clear," Zachary explained to all the others. "We are to avoid direct confrontation with the enemy. In no case may we betray the presence of British military in this area. Doing so would ruin the surprise Wellington is planning."

Miguel exchanged a speaking look with his sister, then said, "Luckily, we are not bound by such scruples."

"What do you mean to do?" Zachary asked.

"There's a ravine up ahead. Arroyo Robles. They are headed right for it. We shall arrange our people up above and pick them off as they pass through."

"Like ducks in a pond," exulted José, a young partisan standing next to Elena.

She wore a closed expression and nodded grimly.

"You can join us or not," Miguel said, "but do *not* try to interfere." His threat was clear.

Bound by their orders, the four Rangers hung back and watched, thinking the Ramirez people, opposing trained soldiers, might be in for more opposition than they counted on. Only then could the Rangers justify getting directly involved. It did not happen that way.

"My God!" Richardson said quietly when it was over. "That was not a fight—it was a massacre."

The Ramirez people were jubilant. They counted twenty dead Frenchmen with no injuries to themselves.

"Elena hasn't lost her touch. Even using her other shoulder, she shoots fine. Very fine," José chortled.

"My little sister does all right," Miguel said. "If you English had a battalion of soldiers like her, you'd make short work of this war!"

Elena seemed both pleased and embarrassed.

Despite deploring the tactics of this incident, the Rangers could not ignore the fact that they had, indeed, gleaned a good deal of intelligence from it. In war, Zachary admitted to himself, lines are not always as cleanly drawn as one would like.

He was also having a hard time trying to mesh his images of a gentle, caring girl to whom he was profoundly attracted with this fierce woman who could kill so coldly—La Belle Diable. He told himself he was being unfair. How could he know how life had shaped her? Therein lay the problem. He truly wanted to understand.

Several days later as they were returning from a short outing,

Elena, riding next to Zachary, directed a teasing question at him, her dark eyes sparkling with laughter.

"So—Inglés." She always referred to him as *Inglés*, though she addressed his men more formally. "I've been wondering. Would you really have shot me when Miguel found us?"

He held her gaze for a long moment, then shrugged. "Probably not. With that shoulder, you were no threat."

"And if Miguel had fired?"

"Luckily, we'll never know."

Her expression turned serious. "Yes. Lucky. I have much to thank you and Mr. Gordon for."

"We all do what we need to do."

"Yes. Still, I do thank you."

Miguel set guards around the compound night and day. All of the Ramirez men and some of the women regularly performed this duty. Zachary and his men took their turns at it too. That night, he sat beneath a huge old oak tree some distance from the lodge, waiting for his relief. A loaded rifle leaned against the tree at his elbow. He grabbed it on hearing footsteps approach, but relaxed when the moonlight revealed Elena's very female form. She wore the same tan blouse and leather split skirt she had worn earlier in the day.

"Sí, Inglés," she called softly. "Everything is all right, no?" She sat down next to him.

"Everything is all right, yes."

"You make fun of me, no?"

"I make fun of you, yes," he said, chuckling.

She leaned closer and he caught a faint whiff of the rose soap he knew she and Pilar used. "That is decidedly unkind of you," she said in a mocking reprimand.

He sucked in his breath and, without thinking at all, he grasped the back of her neck and kissed her soundly. Unhesitating, almost as though she had anticipated it, she responded in kind. He felt her lips part and he quickly accepted her invitation.

He pulled her closer and deepened the kiss, one hand caressing her back, the other moving to fondle a breast. He felt a hard nub; his own desire threatened to get beyond control.

He pulled away slightly, nibbling at her lower lip. "Ah, Elena. This is not wise."

"I know." She sounded reluctant in her agreement, but she pulled away and straightened her blouse. "You'd better go."

He slept only fitfully that night, but the next morning she greeted him in her usual cheerful manner as though nothing had happened.

A week later—a week of desire and uncertainty—he gladly welcomed her to his bed.

CHAPTER 12

As leader of the Rangers, Zachary had been given his own room, though others shared theirs. Four decades had faded the opulence of this comfortable guest chamber which boasted a large bed and two upholstered chairs, as well as other furniture—an armoire, dresser, and three small tables, all of dark polished wood. *That Ramirez great-grandfather provided well for his hunting companions*, Zachary thought and marveled yet again that this lodge was the most unusual partisan stronghold he had ever encountered. Definitely not the customary cave and campfire accommodations.

There were no modern amenities like gas or oil lamps, but he did have a branch of candles by which he was reading a well-worn copy of *The Iliad*. Zachary never traveled without at least one book and he had long since determined it wiser to stick with old friends when he could take only one volume with him. As a warrior himself, Zachary invariably found himself empathizing not with Achilles, the consummate Greek hero, but with Hector and Patroclus. He found these two, motivated as they were by duty and love, far more admirable than the glory-chasing Achilles.

His musings were interrupted by a soft knock. Having removed his boots and jacket, and loosened his shirt, he padded across the room in his stocking feet, fully expecting to find one of his men at the door.

"Wha—? Elena?"

She looked nervously about the hall and quickly pushed into the room. She was wearing the red gown she had worn at supper; it showed a generous view of her perfect bosom.

"Elena, you should not be here. Miguel will—"

"Oh, bother Miguel!" She closed the door and turned to place a hand on his chest. "Are you not glad to see me?"

"Of course I am, but—"

She put a finger on his lips. "No buts, Inglés. Just kiss me."

"As you wish." He pulled her closer and lowered his mouth to hers; her lips parted to invite him in. She smelled faintly of roses and tasted of the fruity wine they'd had at supper. She moved her body sensually against his.

He pulled back slightly. "Elena? Are you sure this is something you want?"

She laughed softly and caressed his cheek. "Ah, Inglés. Always so very proper. Do I seem unsure?"

Her arms around his neck, she drew his head to hers. Her mouth was sweet, warm, and oh-so-responsive. Zachary felt himself losing any semblance of control as her hands explored beneath his shirt.

He groaned. His hands on her luscious bottom, he pressed her closer to his own hard need. Common sense made one last effort. Even to his own ears, his voice sounded husky and reluctant. "Elena, if we don't stop now—"

"I've no wish to stop," she whispered. She pushed his shirt up and licked his bare skin. She touched the hardness at his groin. "Do you wish to?"

"Ah, God. Elena!" He pushed the top of her dress down to reveal her breasts and feathered his hands over her already pebbly nipples.

"Ah, Inglés," she said, mocking his tone. "You tease without mercy."

Suddenly the dress shimmied off her hips and pooled around her feet. Only later—much later—did it occur to him that she had arrived with the dress fastenings already loosened—and that she wore nothing under the red gown.

He nudged her toward the bed, hastily shed his shirt and breeches, and lay beside her to gather her close again. He kissed her, slowly, deeply as he caressed her body, exploring the tender flesh between her thighs. Then he nibbled and nipped and licked his way down and up her body until she was wet and writhing with need.

"Inglés, please—" She fondled and squeezed his erection until he thought he might explode.

He positioned himself between her legs and was surprised on entering to meet with resistance. He paused, breathing hard and cursing himself for an overeager, ignorant fool. He might have withdrawn, but her fiercely whispered "No!" and thrusting pelvis destroyed that insane thought.

Afterwards, they lay facing each other, both breathing hard.

"Oh, my. That was pretty wonderful," she said.

"You might have told me."

"Told you what?" He heard deliberate coyness in her tone.

"That you were a virgin."

"Would it have mattered?"

"Maybe."

She laughed. "I don't think so."

He was thoughtful for a moment, then asked, "Why me? Why now?"

"We do what we need to." He recognized his own words from a previous conversation. She went on. "I needed you—this—now. We live a very precarious life, you and I. Who knows what tomorrow will bring? Death, perhaps? Does even that matter?"

Half an hour later, when they came together again, nothing else mattered at all. Just before dawn, she returned to her own room while Zachary smoothed and washed away any traces of her having been there, even as he reveled in the memory.

Later, Zachary saw the next few weeks as crazy blends of days of hard riding and nights of soul-stirring bliss. On their forays out of the compound, everything proceeded as it had before, with Elena often riding between her brother and Zachary and keeping up a running, casual conversation. She joked and chatted with everyone as before, carefully not showing Zachary any special attention. If they were out overnight, she spread her bedroll near her brother's. Back at the lodge, she would come to Zachary's room long after all the others had retired, and always left before daybreak.

Human nature being what it is, Zachary was sure their relationship would not be a secret for long. Pilar, of course, was the first to suspect.

"Pilar warned me not to fall in love with you," Elena said as they lay chatting after making love one night.

"She knows?"

"She thinks she knows."

"And Miguel?"

"He knows nothing."

Zachary toyed with a strand of raven black hair on the pillow. "I cannot like this secrecy. We could marry, you know. There are many wives with our army."

She scoffed. "And then what? My place is here, with my people, fighting the French—not slogging along in an English baggage train."

"I see." He stopped fondling her hair and lay back.

"Ah, Inglés," she cajoled. "Do not ruin what we have."

She rolled on top of him and kissed and caressed and teased him into a repeat performance before she left for her own room.

Two days later Zachary and Adam Richardson were out trying to determine whether supply and baggage wagons might be able to negotiate what was little more than a narrow trail winding around a steep rocky mountain. A raging stream crashed through boulders some three hundred feet below.

"It's none of my business," Richardson said, "but I'd be careful if I were you."

"About what?" Zachary asked, afraid he already knew.

"You and Miss Ramirez."

Zachary merely nodded, unwilling to dissemble with such a trusted friend. "Is it general knowledge, then?"

"No. But I happened to see her leave your room one morning. The boy José keeps giving the two of you strange looks. And if Miguel finds out, he'll have you singing soprano."

"She refuses to leave here," Zachary said glumly.

"Take care, my friend."

A week later, the problem became moot, at least for a while.

Whitten and Penryn found the Ramirez village and brought orders that all the Rangers were to return to the main body of the army. Wellington was marching toward Vitoria to intercept Joseph Bonaparte, who was at last fleeing Spain. The Rangers who had been with the Ramirez band for so long said reluctant good-byes.

Elena was dry-eyed, having bade Zachary good-bye the night before.

"We'll be back," he had promised. "Vitoria will not be the end. God knows what else lies ahead before the French are firmly back on their own side of the Pyrenees."

"I know," she said sadly, "but let us not make promises we might not be able to keep."

Until Vitoria, the war had raged on between the Allies and their Spaniards on one side and the French and theirs on the other, with neither side gaining a sustained advantage over the other. Now, however, the Allies steadily pushed the French forces through and beyond the brutal terrain of the Pyrenees. Eventually, with the clear vision of hindsight, English military leaders would freely admit that the outcome might have been different in the Iberian Peninsula had Napoleon not drawn his best trained and most experienced troops off for a disastrous assault on Russia. Wellington's own forces also suffered shortages due to the war with the United States. Zachary was astounded that both France and England were waging war on two fronts, though that was not a fact of immediate concern to a mere captain in His Majesty's Army.

Meanwhile, on those occasions when they were back in camp, he and his Rangers would usually find mail and much-read newspapers from home waiting for them. Even in camp, they stuck together, sharing tents and pooling their foodstuff. One evening in November, long after their return from the sojourn with the Ramirez partisans, the team sat around reading and sharing news from the latest mail packets. On this occasion, with Wellington being hailed as a conquering hero in much of Spain, the Rangers were quartered in an inn on the outskirts of St. Jean de Luz, where Wellington had established winter headquarters—finally on the French side of the Pyrenees.

"Ay, Zachary," Harrelson called. "Celia—uh, Miss Carstairs—has some interesting news here."

Zachary looked up from sorting through a stack of letters of his own and grinned at his friend. "Celia, eh? You are writing her? Or at least she is writing you?"

Harrelson looked embarrassed. "Well, uh, yes. We have her mother's permission."

"Good for you. And what is her news?" Zachary kept his voice even, but instinctively braced himself for the twinge of pain likely to come with any news from Sydney's cousin.

"Her brother Herbert has joined the navy—following in his father's footsteps. He's assigned to the *Victory*, Nelson's old ship."

"I think I see Admiral Crowley's hand in that," Zachary said.

"She also says the Holmsley chit has married Viscount Ellsworth. Guess you lost out there, Quintin."

"My loss is Ellsworth's gain."

Harrelson read on silently, then said, "Her cousin Sydney had a baby boy. Celia says, 'The baby affords my cousin much joy as you may recall that she lost her father last winter.' "

Zachary grunted his acknowledgment, not trusting himself to comment. So Sydney had given Henry the heir he needed. He could not quell his regret. Sydney—his Sydney—had borne another man's child. *Careful, you are getting maudlin*, he told himself. *Besides, she was never yours.* He turned back to his own mail, where he was pleased to find several missives with updates on his family. He was surprised to find a rather thick letter from his cousin Henry; he had rarely heard from Henry in the past.

> *Paxton House, London*
> *October 1, 1813*

> *Dear Zachary,*
> *It is with a great deal of chagrin that I write you. You may recall that, at our meeting in Bath three years ago— just prior to my marriage—you suggested that my domestic arrangement was likely to prove disastrous. How prophetic! I do not wish to whine and complain about a situation of my own making, but should I unexpectedly leave this "vale of tears," you need to be informed. So, in strictest confidence, I share the following with you.*

> *As you may or may not know, the heir to the Paxton title was born in March: Jonathan Alfred Henry Laughton. He is a healthy and alert baby and Sydney came through the ordeal very well. I daresay motherhood has added to her already considerable beauty and she dotes on our son.*
> *Proud though I am of my wife and child, that is not my reason for writing you.*
> *Three weeks after Jonathan was born, Louisa also*

bore me a son. We have christened him William David. Needless to say, Louisa's family has demonstrated their extreme displeasure at the existence of this child. Although we tried to keep all this a secret, the rumor mill was grinding away and the Ryesdale faction have made it abundantly clear that if Louisa acknowledges William, she will never see her older son again. (The Ryesdale heir now has five years.) Louisa is truly torn between her two children—as, to a certain extent, am I between mine.

As if all this were not in itself enough of a headache, a month ago Sydney found out about Louisa and my other son. She reacted far more vehemently than I ever imagined she might. But that is another story. Eventually, I shall resolve this impasse with my wife. However, the crisis did prompt me to think somewhat more clearly and that is why I am writing you.

Mr. Phillips (my solicitor) has amended my will to provide for William, but I wanted you to know those provisions, especially as they regard his education. He is currently in the care of a vicar's family in Surrey. The direction is enclosed.

As I told you in Bath, I fully expect to see to all this myself, but having been launched into this business of fatherhood, I find myself somewhat more cautious—and I do trust you to see my wishes carried out.

Yours,
Henry

There were detailed instructions regarding the care and education of both sons. Zachary looked them over briefly and laid them aside, confident that Henry's last thought in the letter would prove true. He shook his head in a blend of disgust, resentment, and—yes—envy. He found Henry's basic attitude toward both Sydney and Louisa despicable. It was true that many a married man of Henry's class enjoyed the favors of a mistress—or those of a succession of mistresses. But Zachary doubted that they had wives like Sydney warming the marriage bed. Henry seemed to just accept this situation as his due—that the Earl of Paxton and his ilk need not be bound by the moral values that, in effect, provided restraints on the human animal, thus making civilization possible.

Oh, for God's sake, he chastised himself. *What gives you the right to be so judgmental? So sanctimonious? Given your liaison with Elena, you are hardly one to criticize. Would you even care if Sydney were not involved?*

Probably not, he admitted. But she was. He felt sorry for her. She had seemed so full of honor and so caring. He recalled her rescuing that child on a street in Bath.

He was also angry and resentful that just as he had been unable to come to her aid three years ago, he could not do so now. Besides miles and miles of distance that intervened, there were all those layers of social decorum. He quickly reminded himself that that oh-so-innocent bride had perpetrated a great hoax on him. Still, he wondered what these recent events might have done to that lively young woman who had argued so engagingly about equality between husbands and wives.

He heaved a long sigh.

McIntyre looked up from a ragged newspaper. "Bad news?"

"Not really. Legal matters that are largely irrelevant—and likely to remain so."

McIntyre gestured at the newspaper. "The *Times* says the Allies are amassing great forces near Leipzig."

"That ought to keep the little corporal out of our hair for a while," Richardson said as he put the finishing touches on a drawing.

Harrelson had been absorbed in his letter. "Celia says life in London is full of balls and routs. She says society takes its lead from the regent in virtually ignoring the king's illness."

"'Celia says—'" Zachary teased. "That girl is not married or engaged yet?"

"No." Harrelson wore a smug expression. "I guess she's waiting for something better than a town dandy."

Zachary worried about Harrelson's relationship with the charming Celia, so he now cautioned in a serious tone, "You watch yourself, Trevor. Girls like that do not stick around long."

"What do you mean 'girls like that'?" Harrelson challenged.

Zachary held up his hands in mock defense. "Nothing untoward, I assure you. It's just that proper young women need to marry—

especially proper young women of modest means—which Miss Carstairs is."

"I doubt Celia is husband hunting."

Richardson emitted a bark of laughter. "All women are husband hunting! If they aren't, their mothers are. And their mothers are very likely to take the traditional view that a bird in the hand is by far the wisest position to take."

"Celia ain't like that and her mother trusts her judgment." Harrelson sounded defensive.

Richardson shook his head in a show of despair. "Our friend appears to be a likely candidate for parson's mousetrap. I suppose he will just ignore the ladies at the ball tonight."

"You hope," Harrelson scoffed.

CHAPTER 13

In the weeks following Sydney's devastating discovery of her husband's infidelity, the atmosphere in the Earl of Paxton's elegant townhouse turned rather chilly. The servants went about their duties quietly and efficiently, and the principal parties of the house—all except the mistress—continued to attend the usual social affairs. However, a sense of subdued apprehension prevailed. The master and mistress of Paxton House maintained polite decorum with their servants and family members. Their communication with each other was merely courteous formality in front of others and mostly strained silence when they happened to be alone together.

Sydney spent a good deal of time privately warring with herself over the situation. She knew that pride—both hers and Henry's—was exacerbating matters, but she could not bring herself to make overtures to him. *He* was the one in the wrong. *He* was the one who had broken sacred vows. Indeed, he had taken those vows with no intention of living up to them! She recalled Zachary's toast at the wedding celebration. Good heavens! Zachary had known. Had made a joke of it. She felt so stupid, so betrayed by Henry, but also by Zachary.

Nevertheless, this estrangement was not the way she wanted to live the rest of her life. Henry was a major element in her life and would always be so. She simply had to come to terms with that fact. She was not the first woman to make such a heartbreaking discovery. But how—how did one go on from here?

As they had for some time now, these thoughts dominated her mind one morning. After visiting the nursery and playing with Jonathan until time for his nap, she sought futilely to escape in Mrs. Edgeworth's new novel. She sat on a comfortable couch in her private sitting room. Usually she felt relaxed and content in this room for which she had herself chosen the furniture, draperies, and wallpaper in soft blues and greens with touches of gold and yellow. She had reread the same paragraph three times already when there was a knock at the door.

"Come," she called.

Aunt Harriet entered. "Might I have a word with you, my dear?"

"Of course." Sydney was curious at the somewhat nervous tone in the usually unflappable Harriet Carstairs. She put her book aside and moved to allow her aunt room beside her on the couch.

Aunt Harriet sat and clasped her hands in her lap, then cleared her throat. "I—uh—I do not mean to intrude—but that is precisely what I am doing. I hope you will not be angry with me, but I wish to talk with you about—about you and Henry."

Sydney felt herself go very still. Embarrassed and apprehensive, she groped for a reply.

"Oh, dear. I have offended you," Aunt Harriet murmured.

"No. I could never take offense at frank talk from you, Aunt Harriet. I—I just do not know what to say. It is all so muddled, you see."

"I know, my dear. Many a woman has endured the neglect and indifference you must be feeling."

Something in her aunt's tone caught Sydney's attention. "Surely Uncle Charles never—"

"Had a mistress? In a sense, he did. My rival was the sea. And eventually I lost him to her."

Sydney reached to take the older woman's hand in her own. "I am so sorry. I had no idea you felt that way. So *that* is why you opposed Herbert's going into the navy."

"I held out as long as I could. He started pestering to go to sea when he was twelve. But, as they say, blood will tell. It seems my son has the same saltwater in his veins as his father had." She gave a rueful smile. "However, that is not what I came to say to you."

"Oh?"

"No. I simply wanted you to know that you are not without support—a shoulder to lean on, if you need it."

"I do need it," Sydney admitted. "I just do not know how to handle this. You know the circumstances of my marriage. I did so want to be a good wife to Henry. I thought he deserved that much from the Waverly family. But I did not count on a marriage that is such—such a—a *sham*."

Aunt Harriet, still holding Sydney's hand, squeezed it affectionately. "I know, my dear. You must do what others have done before you: carry on. Hiding away like this is not the answer."

"And I feel so stupid," Sydney went on, not heeding her aunt's words of comfort. It was as though, beginning to talk about it openly, she could not stop. "It has gone on for—for *years*—and I had no inkling." She stifled a sob. "Why, I even felt sorry for that—that woman when I heard her story. And all this time she was—they were laughing at me. The whole *ton* was laughing at me."

Aunt Harriet stood, placed her hands on her hips, and looked down at her niece. "That is not true. Were you not wallowing in self-pity, you would realize that people who are important to you do not waste time and energy on such affairs and others simply do not matter. *You* are keeping the tongues wagging by becoming a recluse." Her tone softened. "Come now, Sydney. You have never been one to run away from a problem."

"What can I do now? Everyone knows—"

"Very little. Celia and I have put it about that you have been seriously ill. A stomach problem. You were on the mend, then had a relapse, but we are sure you are doing much better now."

Sydney smiled weakly. "You did that for me? Lied?"

"We told a small falsehood. You have not been yourself lately. We will not have scotched all the rumors—servants do talk, you know—but I think we have controlled some of the damage."

"But—"

"No buts." Aunt Harriet extended her hand. "Come. You have indulged yourself quite long enough. You must join Celia and me in receiving callers this afternoon. A little rice powder will convince others that you are recovering from ill health."

Sydney rose and allowed herself to be led into her bedchamber, where she and Aunt Harriet chose a not very flattering puce-colored day dress to help reinforce the ruse of ill health. Sydney turned this way and that in front of the cheval glass.

"I may fool society," she muttered, "but what *am* I to do about Henry and—and—"

"Lady Ryesdale," Aunt Harriet supplied calmly from where she sat on a plush bench, her back to Sydney's dressing table.

"That Ryesdale woman. I just cannot bear the images that keep haunting me." She began to pace about the room. "What am I to do?" she wailed. "Just pretend nothing happened? Pretend she does not exist? Pretend that child was never born?"

Aunt Harriet rose, caught Sydney's arm, and steered her to the window seat. Sydney gazed, unseeing, as a soft, drizzly rain sent rivulets of water down the panes.

"Give yourself some more time if you need to," Aunt Harriet said in a matter-of-fact tone. "However, ultimately, you must arrive at some sort of compromise with your husband."

"*I* must compromise," Sydney said bitterly.

"Yes, you. Despite persistent rumors of divorce in royal circles, it is not an option in those you live in—even if Henry would consider it, and, frankly, my dear, he would not. Very few men would."

"I know—"

"But beyond that, as a divorced woman, you would become a pariah. You would certainly lose all contact with your son. I know how fond you are of Marybeth and Geoffrey—as well as Lady Amy and Lady Ann. You would be lost to them too."

Sydney took a deep shuddering breath and put her face in her hands. "Henry would never be so cruel."

"He *could* be. Who knows what measures a man with injured pride might take?"

They sat in thoughtful silence for a few minutes as Sydney digested these facts. None of this was news to her, but having it aired aloud in blunt terms was jarring. Then another thought occurred to her.

"Aunt Harriet? You have talked with Henry?"

Aunt Harriet nodded. "He asked to speak with me after breakfast when it was clear to all of us that you would—again—not be joining us."

"He told you he is willing to give up his—his liaison with Lady Ryesdale?"

"No. He did not say that. But he did voice genuine regret that you have been so profoundly hurt by his actions."

"And what happens when he tires of her and—and he turns to a new mistress and then another and another—and he brings some horrible disease home to *my* bed? That happens, you know."

Aunt Harriet shook her head in a gesture of impatience. "Yes, it does, but I doubt that is the case here. Face facts, Sydney. This is not about you alone. Try to see that this—this unfortunate situation—directly involves three basically decent people and two innocent babes—not to mention several others on the sidelines."

"I know," Sydney whispered. "In my head, I know, but—"

"But your pride has taken a serious blow." Aunt Harriet put a comforting arm about her niece's shoulders. "Still, I watched you deal in a very practical way with the consequences of your father's illness. I am confident you will come out of this a stronger person."

"I—I hope so."

"Then you will make amends with Henry?"

Sydney nodded. "In a few days. I need to think about it some more."

"Don't wait too long, my dear." Aunt Harriet rose. "Now—ring for Maisie and let us prepare to put the harpies of the *ton* in their place."

And that is precisely what the Carstairs ladies and the Countess of Paxton managed to do that afternoon and the next. The tension between the Earl of Paxton and his wife eased considerably, but they still had not talked things out.

Then, as so often happens, life intervened to make that matter far less important.

Sydney had taken special care in dressing for the evening meal the second day after her discussion with Aunt Harriet. She wore a teal silk gown she knew to be one of Henry's favorites and the diamond necklace and earbobs he had given her on the birth of their son. He stood and gave her an approving smile as she entered the drawing room. Aunt Harriet and Celia were there before her and sat sipping sherry. When it was just the family for the evening meal, Marybeth and the twins—twelve and thirteen now—were often allowed to join the adults. The three young girls had glasses of lemonade and chatted excitedly about a proposed boating trip on the Thames. Henry handed Sydney a glass of sherry and she deliberately chose a seat next to the one he had occupied when she arrived. He gave her a questioning look; Aunt Harriet gave her an approving one.

When Mr. Roberts announced supper, Aunt Harriet and Celia

shepherded the girls ahead of them with Sydney and Henry bringing up the rear.

Henry leaned close to murmur for her ears alone, "Does your appearance tonight hold special promise for me later?"

Feeling warmth rush to her face, she inclined her head and said, "I think it's time we talked."

"Yes. Past time," he said. "I must go out this evening—I promised Hoffman—but I shall make a point of returning early."

She nodded. Frederick Taunton, Viscount Hoffman, was a special sporting friend of Henry's.

The table conversation was amiable and forgettable. Afterwards, Henry excused himself and the six females of his house—along with the ever-present Brownie—retired to the music room, where Marybeth and the twins showed off their latest achievements on the pianoforte.

Before retiring to her own bedchamber, Sydney made her customary trip to the nursery to check on her son. She lingered over his crib, once again marveling that she had been so blessed with this perfect little human being. She could tell that she surprised Maisie when she chose a filmy nightgown and told the maid to leave her hair loose tonight. She settled down to wait for Henry.

She waited.

And waited.

It was after midnight when she heard a door open and close in the adjoining room. Then she heard it open and close again.

Still she waited for him.

Anxiety was replaced by annoyance, then anger. Finally, she charged through the connecting door to his room. It was empty. She closed the door firmly, crawled into her bed, and turned out her gas lamp. She was absolutely furious with him. If he came in this very moment, she would pretend to be asleep.

But he did not come, and eventually the sleep was not feigned.

Sometime before dawn she heard muffled male voices in the other room. Henry and his valet, Brewster. No. Three voices. What was going on?

Then she clearly heard Henry say, "We shall be back before she wakes up." This was followed again by a door opening and closing. She considered rising and confronting Henry, but was deterred by the presence of that third male voice.

Later in the morning, as Sydney sat in the library reviewing some papers the Paxton steward, Mr. Stevenson, had sent on from Windham, she heard a loud commotion in the foyer adjacent to the library. First, loud frantic knocking at the outer door, then loud urgent voices.

"Careful of his arm."

"Show us to his lordship's chamber. Now!"

"Y-yes, sir."

When Sydney opened the library door, the scene she beheld sent chills along her spine. Henry lay on a stretcher being carried above stairs by two men following a Paxton footman. He was covered by a blanket, but she saw blood on the part of his shirt that was exposed. Behind the stretcher was Henry's friend, Lord Hoffman, and an older man carrying a black bag—obviously a doctor.

"Oh, good heavens! What happened?" she demanded.

Hoffman paused on the third step, but waved the group on. "There's been an accident, my lady." He retraced his last steps and guided her back into the library, closing the door.

"An accident?"

Hoffman paused and ran his hand through his hair. "Oh, what can it matter now? It will be all over town by noon. Paxton has been shot."

"Shot? Why? How? What happened?" She tried to control her panic. Still standing, she leaned against the library's heavy oak map table.

Hoffman looked embarrassed. "It was a duel."

"It was *what*?" She could not believe her ears.

"A duel. With that hothead, Kingsley. Paxton *deloped*—sent his shot into the ground. Kingsley did not."

"Good heavens. H-how badly is Henry wounded?"

Hoffman's expression was grim. "Very badly. He took the bullet in his midriff. The doctor says it's—it's very serious."

Sydney closed her eyes and felt herself sway against the table as the impact of this message hit her. She knew such wounds were nearly always fatal. Hoffman stepped close and gripped her elbow.

"Come. Sit down, my lady."

"I—I need to see to Henry—"

"Allow the doctor to see to him first, then we shall both see him." With the ease of a long-standing friendship with the master of this house, Hoffman found a cabinet containing a well-stocked bar. He poured a measure of brandy into a glass and handed it to Sydney. "Here. Drink this."

Numbly, she did so, and the burning liquid cleared her head. Hoffman took a chair nearby.

"Better?" he asked.

"Yes. Thank you." She inhaled a long, shuddering breath. "Now. Please tell me what this was all about."

Again, Hoffman looked embarrassed. "It was a duel. Kingsley challenged Paxton. As Henry's second, I met with Kingsley's man, but Kingsley refused any terms." He raised his hands, then dropped them in a gesture of despair. "We honestly thought they would both *delope* and that would be the end of it."

"'The end of it,'" she repeated dully. "The end of *what*? What on earth was this about?"

Hoffman looked away, then sighed and returned his gaze to hers. "Ralph Kingsley is the youngest brother of Baron Ryesdale."

"Oh? Oh. Oh, dear. It was about *her*?"

Hoffman nodded. "Kingsley has tried to challenge Henry before. He gets drunk and starts ranting about family honor and berating Henry. Always before, Henry was able to defuse the situation and walk away. This time it was a very public forum—White's. Henry could not refuse a challenge."

"Well, he probably *could* have done so," she said sharply, still in shock.

"I'm sorry, Lady Paxton, but no gentleman could have done so."

She closed her eyes for a moment and refused to argue with him. Then she stood. "Let us see to Henry."

In Henry's bedchamber, they found the patient already changed into a nightshirt and lying in the middle of his oversize bed, attended by his valet and the doctor, who was introduced as Dr. Fisher. Perspiration beaded on Henry's face and he grimaced in pain, but opened his eyes when Sydney entered with Hoffman.

He looked at her briefly, then turned his gaze to his friend. "Kin-Kingsley?"

"He's already left England, probably. It will be many a year before he returns—if ever. Capital offense, you know."

Henry nodded, then groaned in pain.

"Doctor?" Sydney said, her voice steady. "Please be frank with me and tell me how I can help."

The doctor gave her an admiring glance, then drew her aside and spoke softly. "I am sorely afraid there is little to be done, my lady. This sort of mishap defies modern medicine." He shook his head. "All we can do is make him as comfortable as possible and wait. He is in a great deal of pain. I have given him a heavy dose of laudanum, which should take effect soon."

"Sydney—" Henry called. She rushed to the bed. "We mush . . . mus . . . t-talk," he said, fading on the last word.

"We shall." She patted his shoulder and touched her lips to his forehead. His eyelids fluttered, but she could tell he was no longer conscious.

"He will sleep for three or four hours," the doctor said, closing his bag. "Dehydration is a problem in such cases. See that he gets plenty of liquid. I shall come back later to check on him."

"Thank you, doctor." She turned to Lord Hoffman. "My lord, you are welcome to stay, but please do not feel you must."

"I think I will take my cue from the doctor and return sometime later today," he replied.

Sydney walked them to the door, where she found Aunt Harriet pacing the hall.

"Oh, my dear. I am so sorry. The entire house is distraught. What can we do to help?"

"Nothing." Sydney felt her tears flowing now that the initial crisis was stabilized. "Th-there's no hope, Aunt Harriet. No hope."

Aunt Harriet simply enfolded Sydney in her arms and held her for several minutes. Then Sydney gathered herself and told her aunt of the doctor's report and orders.

"I'll take care of household matters and see that you have what you need," Aunt Harriet said. "You stay with him for now and I'll join you later."

"Thank you." Sydney wiped her eyes and squared her shoulders before reentering the room even though she knew that, at the moment, Henry was insensible to anyone or anything. Feeling empty and bereft for herself, she was even more devastated by the thought of baby Jonathan's growing up fatherless.

She sat at Henry's bedside through the afternoon, wiping his brow with a cool cloth now and then and forcing spoons of water between his parched lips. He became more and more feverish and restless as the laudanum began to wear off. It was obvious that he was hallucinating. He was apparently reliving sporting matches and his days at school and university, flitting from event to event, with no regard for chronology. Most of his utterances were gibberish, but occasionally a phrase or a name was quite clear. He called her name once or twice, but it was the childhood *Bella* on his lips, not *Sydney*. Mostly the name he called over and over was *Lou*.

Sydney found herself strangely unmoved by the fact that her dying husband was calling for another woman. She wondered if she was herself suffering from shock. Yes, she was saddened by what she heard, but she managed in these few hours to face the reality of her marriage. Henry had treated her and her family well, but obviously the real love of his life had been Lady Ryesdale. And who was she—Sydney Isabella Waverly Laughton, Countess of Paxton—to complain? She had always been fond of her husband, but there had never been the sort of overwhelming need—the passion—the sharing she had once viewed as requisite to marriage. Clearly Henry had felt such passion, such need for Lady Ryesdale—while his wife had been denied such.

An image of Zachary Quintin standing next to Henry on her wedding day flashed across her mind. Zachary resplendent in his uniform. Zachary showing her the sights of Bath. Zachary's kiss.

Good heavens. Such schoolgirl foolishness, she chastised herself. Still, those images served to accord her some perspective later when Henry awoke.

CHAPTER 14

Others had been in and out during the afternoon, but Sydney was alone with Henry when he became truly conscious of his surroundings. She had drawn a comfortable barrel-shaped chair near the bed and sat reading when she became aware of a change in the sound of his breathing. She looked up to find him gazing at her, his eyes alert, seeing.

"Oh. You're awake," she said, feeling foolish at stating the obvious.

"Yes. For several—minutes now. You've—been here all this while?" His words came in short bursts, punctuated by grimaces of pain.

She nodded, then laid her book aside and reached for a glass of water. "The doctor said you must have plenty of liquid." She put her arm under his head to help him drink. The pillow was warm and damp with sweat. He drank, but also winced in pain and pushed the glass away, spilling a bit of water on his chest.

"I'm sorry," she said.

"No. I'm the one sorry. Sorry about—about this. Burdening you. The scandal. You did not—deserve this, too."

She put the glass aside and pulled the bedcover back over his chest. "Never mind, Henry. We can talk about it later."

He grabbed her hand. "No. Now. There's no time. I know. You know it, too."

"Oh, God, Henry—"

"Don't. Don't cry, Bella—Sydney." He loosened his grip on her hand, but still held it gently. "I need to tell you—never meant to hurt you—had to save Paxton from P—Per—" He coughed and the pain brought tears to his eyes.

"Percival Laughton, your cousin. I know." She disengaged her hand and helped him to another sip of water, then she drew her chair closer and patted his shoulder.

He sighed. "No, my dear. I doubt—you—you do know. Percy— truly evil—you—you—" He winced again.

"Henry, please. This isn't necessary."

"Yes. It is." His tone was fierce. "Now listen."

"All right." She did not want him upset any more.

He closed his eyes in a grimace of pain, then seemed to steel himself against the monster besetting him. "You must protect—protect J—Jonathan. Zac—Zachary—"

"Protect Jonathan? From Zachary?" This made no sense to Sydney. Was Henry hallucinating again?

His eyes flew open. "No. Trust—trust Zachary. He will help— help protect—"

"Zachary will help protect Jonathan?"

He nodded and seemed to drift off for a moment. Sydney thought about what he had said. So far as she knew, Percival Laughton had never been a guest in any of the Paxton estates. The Laughton family had been torn asunder some forty years earlier when the infamous Percival's father, one Robert Laughton, had tried to murder his cousin, Henry's father, in an attempt to gain the Paxton title and wealth. Historically, except for the first to hold the title, Paxton earls had each managed to produce the requisite heir, but then had had only girls or baby boys who did not survive beyond their third or fourth birthdays. The last one to produce a "spare" had been Henry's grandfather, and that spare had been the murderous Robert who had, in turn, spawned Percival, the nominal heir to the earldom—until Sydney had borne Jonathan.

She glanced at Henry to find him gazing at her again.

"Y—you understand?" he asked. "The danger—"

"Yes. Now you should get some rest."

"No. Can't." His voice was harsh, then softened. "More." He closed his eyes, then opened them again and held her gaze. "I—never meant—hurt you. Louisa and I—"

She touched his hand. "I understand." And, finally, she thought she *did* understand—at least a little.

"I—I thought perhaps you—you knew—"

"No. I did not." She wondered how she could have remained so ignorant for so long. But what did that matter now?

"Z—Zac—Zachary told me—said it would be—disaster. Didn't listen."

"Zachary told you?" Sydney closed her eyes but could not shut out the pain. Zachary knew—had known all along. His attentions to her in Bath—that kiss in the park—all had been meaningless to him. Some sort of game. What an utter fool that young girl had been as Henry and his cousin laughed behind her back.

Henry stirred and brought her attention back to the present. "Louisa and—I—loved—We never meant—Hopeless." He heaved a long sigh and lay still for several moments. Sydney had the impression he was gathering his strength. He gripped her hand again and said, "I want—I need—to—to see her. Please, Sydney." Henry Laughton was unused to asking favors of anyone.

"You want me to—"

"Invite her here—now. She—she cannot come—on her—her own."

"Oh, dear. Henry—"

"Please. She—she needs to know—not her fault."

But it is, Sydney thought. She put her head in her hands. *Oh, dear God.*

"Please." Henry reached toward her. Sydney was aware of the degree of pain of another sort that one word had cost him. She noticed increased perspiration on his brow. She busied herself wetting the cloth, wringing it out, and placing it on his forehead.

"The doctor will be here soon with some more laudanum for your pain," she said.

"No." He grabbed her hand again. "No more. Not 'til I—see Lou."

"All right, Henry," she said soothingly.

The doctor arrived a few minutes later and right behind him came Lord Hoffman.

"How's he doing?" the viscount asked in a hushed tone.

Henry glared at his friend. "I'm not dead yet, Fred."

"I can see that."

The doctor, having lifted the bedcovers to look at the bandage, now said, "If you will ring for his lordship's valet, he and I will change this dressing." It was a polite dismissal of the wife and friend.

"I need to speak with you," Sydney said to Hoffman, and led him two doors down the hall to her private sitting room. She gestured to a pair of chairs upholstered in a floral fabric sporting the room's dominant colors of green, gold, and blue—the room's cheery colors a direct contrast to her mood. When they were both seated, she explained Henry's wish to see Louisa.

"What? He wants her here? Highly irregular, don't you know?"

"Yes, I do know, but one can hardly deny the request of a man who is—is in his condition." She could not bring herself to say the word *dying*.

"No. I suppose not. Still—how is it to be done? Bound to be talk, you know."

"We can minimize it," she said briskly. She rose and went to her writing desk, where she quickly penned a note to Lady Ryesdale. Handing it to Lord Hoffman, she said, "If you would be so kind as to deliver this note and then escort Lady Ryesdale here—"

"Are you sure about this?"

"No. But I cannot refuse him. It is dark out already. I'll have Mr. Roberts rather than a footman answer the door, then you bring her directly up to Henry's chamber. Roberts is very discreet. So is Brewster. It will work. I'm sure it will."

Hoffman stood to take the proffered note. He shook his head. "You are quite a woman, Lady Paxton. Quite a woman."

"Henry considers you a good friend."

When they returned to Henry's bedchamber, they found the patient refusing the doctor's offer of another heavy dose of laudanum.

"Not yet," Henry said, glancing at Sydney, who merely nodded to him. "Leave it. My wife will give it to me—later."

"Very well, my lord." The doctor handed a vial to Sydney along with a small slip of paper with instructions. "Allow him as much as he feels he needs."

The doctor and Lord Hoffman exited Paxton House together.

Henry lay very still and closed his eyes for a moment; he seemed to be fighting a wave of pain.

"J-Jonathan?" he said. "Can you bring him—?"

"Of course."

Sydney tugged at the bell pull, then sent the footman who answered to the nursery. Within minutes, the nursery maid arrived with the squirming, babbling infant. Henry reached a hand toward his son and Sydney set the baby on the edge of the bed, keeping her own hand on him to prevent his falling. Henry smiled when Jonathan grabbed his index finger.

"He's a—fine lad," Henry said. "Strong. Thank—thank you."

"He is sometimes fussy nowadays," she said, reaching for trivia. "He's getting a tooth." Her heart ached not only at knowing Henry would miss all these milestones of his son's life, but that their son would grow up without his father.

Henry murmured appreciatively, but Sydney could see that the baby's movements were causing him discomfort. As she took Jonathan onto her lap, Henry reached to touch the baby's hair and cheek.

"Yes. Fine—lad."

After turning the baby back over to the nursery maid, Sydney took her evening meal on a tray at Henry's bedside and managed not only to eat half her meal, but also to persuade him to drink a cup of broth. Marybeth and the twins came to visit Henry, but Sydney shooed them away when she saw that they were tiring him. Aunt Harriet and Celia looked in briefly and Sydney refused their offers to relieve her.

"Perhaps later," she said.

Very late in the evening, when most members of the household were occupied elsewhere, there was a soft knock at the door of Henry's bedchamber. Sydney opened it to find Hoffman and Lady Ryesdale in the hallway. Lady Ryesdale, wearing a dark green traveling cloak and heavily veiled, was obviously apprehensive.

"Thank you, Lady Paxton. I cannot tell you what this means to me." The woman was already looking beyond Sydney to the figure on the bed. Sydney stepped aside.

Lady Ryesdale rushed to Henry's bedside, where she knelt and took his hand in hers. "Henry. Henry, my darling. My love. Oh, God. I am so sorry." She bent her head to the hand she held and sobbed.

Henry's eyes lit up at seeing her. "No, Lou—not to blame—your-self."

Sydney had felt rather numb ever since her earlier discussion with Henry. She gave Hoffman a rueful glance. "Will you join me in the drawing room for a glass of sherry? Or perhaps something stronger?"

"Definitely something stronger," Hoffman said.

In the drawing room they found Aunt Harriet and Celia sitting before a low fire in the fireplace. Aunt Harriet was doing some needle-work as Celia read aloud from a novel. Gas lamps on two end tables provided a pool of light in this part of the room. Sydney and Hoffman both murmured "Good evening" and the other two responded in kind.

"Is Brewster with Henry then?" Aunt Harriet asked.

"No. Lady Ryesdale is," Sydney said, going to the sideboard. "Cognac?" she asked Hoffman, who nodded.

"Lady Ryesdale?" Celia squeaked.

"Lady Ryesdale," Sydney said calmly, pouring drinks for Hoffman and herself. She had noted the tea tray on a low table between the other two. She handed Hoffman his glass and they both sat, Sydney on the couch next to Celia and Hoffman on an overstuffed chair matching the one Aunt Harriet occupied.

Sydney sipped her drink. "But that is not for public consumption," she said to Celia.

"I should think *not*," Celia replied in a shocked tone.

"It is what Henry wanted," Sydney said. "Lord Hoffman arranged it for us."

"I see," Aunt Harriet said with a look of understanding at Sydney.

"Roberts met us at the door," Lord Hoffman said. "We went directly up."

Aunt Harriet nodded. "Sounds discreet enough."

Sydney decided to change the subject. "Henry was quite worried earlier about Percival Laughton."

"That one is a nasty piece of work," Lord Hoffman said.

"I was introduced to him in the Assembly Rooms in Bath three years ago," Celia said. "Just after your wedding, Sydney. When I mentioned the wedding, he made a point of informing me that *he* was Paxton's heir."

"He *was* the heir. Now Jonathan is," Sydney said.

"But if something were to happen to Jonathan . . ." Celia let the statement fade.

"I think that is precisely what worries Henry," Sydney said, trying not to be overly fearful for her son.

"Don't worry, Lady Paxton," Hoffman said. "Percy Laughton has been out of the country for months. He is one of those on the fringes of the entourage of the Princess of Wales."

"Out of the country?" Sydney asked.

"Italy, last I knew," Hoffman answered.

Aunt Harriet shook her head. "One does hear the most dreadful things about that lot."

Hoffman shrugged. "Well, you know what they say: Where there is smoke—" He drained his glass and set it on the table between the chairs. He looked at the ormolu clock on the mantel and turned to Sydney. "It is time I returned Lady Ryesdale to the bosom of her family before they discover her missing."

Sydney nodded and rose as he said good night to Aunt Harriet and Celia. They found Lady Ryesdale again kneeling next to Henry's bed. She had removed the cloak and her veiled hat to reveal an amber-colored silk gown and dark auburn hair that Henry kept stroking. She turned deep blue eyes toward Sydney and Hoffman as they entered.

"Oh. Is it time already?" she asked in dismay.

"I am afraid so, my lady," Hoffman said. "It has been more than an hour."

Henry held Louisa's gaze and said, "Remember—what I—said. Zac—Zachary—"

"I will remember." Louisa rose and looked apologetically at Sydney, then bent over Henry and kissed him on the lips. "Good night, my darling. I'll—I'll come tomorrow if I may." Again, she looked at Sydney, naked anguish showing in her tear-filled eyes.

Sydney merely nodded, tears of her own threatening. Hoffman helped Lady Ryesdale with her cloak and Sydney handed her the veiled hat. Louisa touched a finger to her lips, then to Henry's. "Tomorrow," she murmured.

Sydney walked them to the door, where Lady Ryesdale said softly, "Lady Paxton, you have been far kinder than I deserve, and I do most sincerely thank you."

"It was Henry's wish," Sydney replied, sounding somewhat stiff to her own ears.

"And I may come tomorrow?"

"Yes, of course. Henry *is* still the master of this house."

When the door closed behind the pair, Henry seemed to shrink into himself, but gestured feebly at the chair near his bed. As Sydney sat, he said, his words ravaged with pain, "Thank you. I needed—thank you. Not easy—for you. You—more than I—I deserve."

She was struck by his echoing the words of his mistress, but all she said was, "We shall talk tomorrow."

He nodded. "Yes. I'll have—laud—have it now."

She shook the powdered dose into a glass of water, stirred it, and held his head as he drank it.

"Good night, Sydney."

"Good night, Henry."

She sat at his bedside until she was sure the drug had worked its magic and he slept soundly. *What a bizarre day this has been,* she thought. She recalled Henry's final words to his mistress. *So Louisa knew Zachary?* Sydney could not shake her feeling of betrayal.

It is not just the day that is bizarre, she told herself as she slipped into her own bed, exhausted. Knowing Henry would be unconscious for a few hours at least, she had called on Brewster to sit with him, but to rouse her the instant he awoke. *The entire situation is bizarre*, she went on mentally. But, really, did she have cause to complain? Had the Waverly family not benefitted profoundly? Henry had not been wholly honest, but he had behaved with far more honor than many others of his class and his generation. She and Henry had, indeed, developed a genuine friendship of sorts. She must be sure to reassure him of that tomorrow.

On the morrow, though, Henry Matthew Alistair Laughton, eighth Earl of Paxton, died shortly before noon without ever fully regaining consciousness.

CHAPTER 15

Henry was, of course, to be entombed with his ancestors in the family vault in Windham church—and this needed to be done as quickly as possible, but there were practical matters to be dealt with prior to the funeral journey, so Sydney refused to allow herself to give way to either grief or despair.

She was a widow. Widows in general were allowed a good deal more freedom than other unmarried women, but a very young, very rich widow would be a ready target for scandal. Any stigma attached to her would extend to members of her family. With three young sisters who would make their debuts in the next few years, she had to take this issue seriously. She needed a companion to deflect untoward gossip about the way she lived and behaved. The obvious person to fulfill that role was already in residence: Aunt Harriet.

The morning after Henry's death, Sydney invited Aunt Harriet into her private sitting room and laid out the problem and her solution.

"Of course. I will be happy to take on that role, my dear, so long as I may have Celia with me."

Sydney smiled and nodded. "It is settled then. I shall have not one but two chaperones. That ought to quiet the tabbies."

"I should hope so." Aunt Harriet rose from the couch she had been sharing with Sydney. "I must go and tell Celia of our new status."

"Which is hardly new at all. But I am grateful to you both. Perhaps you would be so kind as to be with me to receive a gentleman visitor this afternoon?"

"Of course, dear."

The gentleman visitor, coming at Sydney's request, was Mr. Walter Phillips, Henry's solicitor. Dressed in somber black, Sydney met with him in the library, where the two of them occupied wing-backed chairs in front of the fireplace, while Aunt Harriet sat in another corner of the room reading. Sydney was surprised to find this man of law to be only eight to ten years her senior. He had sandy hair and deep blue eyes.

He offered his condolences, then said, "I am sorry that you must deal with mundane matters of business at such a time, my lady, but your message indicated that you are returning to the country quite soon."

"Yes. We leave tomorrow morning."

"Since the executor of Lord Paxton's will is unavailable at the moment—"

Sydney interrupted. "Pardon me, Mr. Phillips, but I was under the impression that Henry's solicitor had served his father and his grandfather." She left her obvious question unstated.

The visitor smiled. "My father is Walter Phillips, Senior. He is semi-retired now and has turned over most of the firm's business to me. I have handled Paxton affairs this past seven years and more."

"Oh. I see. As you were saying—"

"The executor of Lord Paxton's will is unavailable at this time and it is highly unusual to have a woman involved in such matters at all. However, his lordship insisted that in the event of his death or if he were incapacitated, you were to be consulted and that, wherever possible, we should abide by your decisions—subject, of course, to final approval of the executor-trustee when he becomes available."

Sydney merely nodded as she tried to absorb what the lawyer was telling her. She knew Henry had respected her suggestions on certain estate matters, but here was confirmation of her husband's trust in her judgment.

Phillips continued. "So, I would have to defer any major matters to him—sale of unentailed property, large investments, that sort of thing—but a number of lesser matters need attention from time to time. Lord Paxton was quite clear in his wish that you be consulted. As I say, most unusual, but he reaffirmed that stipulation very recently."

"How recently?" Sydney asked, mindful of the estrangement between her and Henry the last month or so.

Phillips looked uncomfortable. "I received the note the day after the—uh—incident. It had a date and time of the night before and was witnessed by Lord Hoffman and his lordship's valet. It is quite legal, my lady."

"I am to have a say in matters of the earldom?" she asked in a disbelieving tone.

He nodded. "Actually, a great deal of authority, my lady. Until the trustee of the estate is able to take over that responsibility. All is to be held in trust for your son, of course. However, you may act only with the concurrence of the trustee, who is also the legal guardian of the new earl—until he comes of age. The trustee is also now the guardian of those minors for whom your husband was heretofore responsible: Lord Paxton's sisters and your own siblings." He cleared his throat and said softly, "And of you, my lady, until such time as you may remarry."

"G-guardian?" The implications of this idea knifed into her. Why had Henry never shared this with her? Why had she never considered even the possibility of having all control of her life fall into the hands of some unknown, perhaps autocratic man? "Who?" she asked weakly.

Phillips consulted a small notebook. "His lordship's cousin, Captain Zachary Andrew Quintin."

Sydney sank back into her chair, stunned. "Z-Zachary—Oh, my heavens."

"You know Captain Quintin, then?"

"Yes. I know him." She did not elaborate. She wanted time to digest this news.

He produced a thick folder of papers from a black leather case he had leaned against the leg of his chair when he sat down. "Here are copies of the relevant papers, my lady. The originals, all properly signed, are in my office safe. I have sent copies to Captain Quintin, but given the circumstances of communication between London and the Peninsula, there is no telling when—or even if—he will receive them, let alone act on them."

"Was no one named as an alternate?" She reached to take the folder.

"Yes." He paused. "I was. But I would be most reluctant to take any substantive action regarding the Paxton earldom without written concurrence from Captain Quintin—or until such time as I have proof that he is dead. Actually, I could not do so legally."

"That leaves us in a state of limbo, does it not?"

"To some extent, but perhaps only temporarily. This war cannot last forever. Meanwhile, I am assured that you have a trustworthy man in the steward, Mr. Stevenson. Should you have any questions once you have had time to examine these documents, do not hesitate to contact me. Luckily, communication between Windham and London is easier and more reliable than that between London and Spain."

The next day Sydney closed the townhouse, leaving only a caretaker staff. Accompanied by the remaining members of her family, including Aunt Harriet and Celia, she made the sad journey to Windham. Mr. Stevenson and the vicar had already arranged the funeral for the following day.

Defying custom, Sydney and the other females of her family attended the ceremony. Other mourners, most of them tenant farmers and locals with ties to the earldom—and mostly male—seemed to accept the countess's presence without much ado.

As she listened to the testimonies to her husband's character and prayers for his salvation, she tried to achieve some perspective about her own feelings. Yes, she mourned the loss of a friend she had known—well, forever, it seemed. He had been a part of her childhood and youth, albeit on the fringes much of the time.

He had lived up to the letter of their arranged marriage, though not the spirit of marriage at its best. He had not loved his wife. But, in all honesty, had she loved him? She decided that yes, she had. However, she had not been *in* love with him. Might that have been the way he felt, too? Henry had been capable of great love; that much was evident in his relationship with his Louisa. What if he had truly expended the time and effort to court his own wife? Had he done so, she might have long forgotten that silly schoolgirl *tendre* she had had for Zachary Quintin. Or would she have done so? At this point, it no longer mattered.

These thoughts preoccupied her off and on for a few weeks. She dealt with routine issues as they came to her attention—settling disputes, spending time with her son, overseeing the household. But mostly during these weeks, she avoided thinking about the future, choosing to drift from day to day, leaving matters to Mr. Stevenson or Mrs. Knight, even Aunt Harriet. After all, her hands were tied: Any decisions she made might be instantly undone by one Zachary Quintin. Why bother?

She went out riding or walking every day, often with Celia or one or two or all three of the younger girls or with Geoffrey while he was home over Christmas. Sydney insisted that the rules of mourning dress be relaxed somewhat for the others here in the country, though she faithfully observed the conventions herself. Wearing black all the time and foregoing jewelry suited her mood well enough.

One evening after the others had retired, Sydney and Aunt Harriet sat talking in the family drawing room. Aunt Harriet had earlier shared with the family her most recent letter from her favorite navy man.

"I do hope Herbert's waxing on so about how wonderful his life is will not lead Geoffrey astray," Aunt Harriet said. "Perhaps I should not have read the whole letter."

"Geoffrey has two more years of school, then university. He will have ample time to decide what he wants to do with his life." Sydney sighed. "At least he has a choice."

"Men always do," Aunt Harriet said as she stuffed the letter into her knitting basket. "But women have choices too. That is what life is truly all about: a series of choices."

"Yes. I suppose you are right," Sydney said absently.

Later as she lay staring at the underside of the canopy of her bed, the word came back to her. *Choices.* Yes, her choices could be circumscribed by others—by society's restraints, for instance. Also by the legal restraints of Henry's will. She wondered to what extent Zachary Quintin would exert his authority? This thought gave her pause, but she shrugged it off. Captain Quintin was hundreds of miles—and who know how many months or even years—away? She was forcing herself to think of him in more formal, distancing terms. Doing so seemed to mitigate her sense of betrayal at his having known all along not only of Henry's impending marriage, but also of Paxton's relationship with Lady Ryesdale.

Maybe she had needed these last weeks—living in a state of limbo. But no more.

The next day she set about truly examining the papers Mr. Phillips had given her. She sat at Henry's huge mahogany desk in the library and read page after legalistic page of meticulous instructions. She was gaining new insight into—and respect for—the husband she had often thought too preoccupied with sport and other pastimes. She noted, and grudgingly accepted as proper, his bequests to his mistress and his other son. *That* business she could certainly leave to Mr. Phillips and Captain Quintin. It needn't involve her at all.

She found Henry's stipulations on other money matters intriguing. He had always accorded her a very generous personal allowance. This would continue—subject to approval by the trustee—until such time as she should remarry. "I cannot conceive of that happening," she muttered to herself. There were vast sums set aside for land improvement and building maintenance and construction—again subject to approval by said trustee.

She reread certain portions of the documents. Perhaps Henry had built in more flexibility than he might have intended. If one divided a huge project into its component parts, might she not be able to do whatever she wanted? What could her "overseer" do if he were faced with a *fait accompli?*

A great deal, she answered herself. He had absolute authority—drat the man! He could reduce or eliminate her allowance. He could forbid her use of or access to any of the Paxton properties. He could—God forbid!—limit her access to her own son. He might even—should he be so inclined—have her confined to some remote place. Her mind leapt to an English king's having once locked his estranged wife away in a castle.

Oh, good heavens, she chastised herself. *You are borrowing ideas from some gothic novel. The fact that something is possible does mean that it is therefore probable!*

On the Peninsula, the object of much of this speculation was totally unaware of the obligations fate had tossed at him. Zachary's first inkling came in a letter from his mother, telling him of his cousin Henry's death a good six weeks after the fact. Then he read the lurid newspaper accounts.

His first thought was of Sydney. My God. Widowed at—what? Twenty? One and twenty? He tried to imagine her in widow's weeds but his mind kept dredging up the vision as she walked down the aisle on her wedding day. Sydney was free now! But what might that mean for one Zachary Quintin?

Probably nothing.

Three years—and how many more? People change and life goes on like a tree with branches extending and growing in random directions.

And one of his branches included Elena.

Belatedly, he thought of Henry. Poor Henry. Life had not dealt kindly with the Earl of Paxton. 'Twas little wonder he had spent so much time and effort on escaping his problems.

It did occur to Zachary that, as his cousin's executor, he had certain duties connected with that role, but he dismissed them as largely legalistic. The lawyer, Phillips, could handle matters—at least for now, and probably forever. He knew Phillips to be a man of integrity; the lawyer had been a fellow student at Trinity College, though three years ahead of Zachary.

The next packet of letters brought more details. Phillips had dutifully sent documents pertaining to Paxton affairs along with two letters, one from the lawyer himself and one in Henry's distinctive script. He read the lawyer's missive first.

> *Dear Captain Quintin,*
> *I feel certain that by now you have learned of the death of your cousin, Henry Laughton, Eighth Earl of Paxton.*
> *I have informed his widow of the precise details of his will and your authority over all that is now to be held in trust for her son. She also understands the full implications of your guardianship over the young earl and other persons for whom Henry Laughton was legally responsible.*
> *The Eighth Lord Paxton placed an unusual degree of trust in his wife's abilities to handle financial and legal matters of the earldom.*

Zachary silently snorted. *You mean she apparently learned to manipulate her husband,* he thought. He read on.

> *Having met her ladyship only briefly, I feel that despite her youth, Lord Paxton's trust was not misplaced.*

Zachary shook his head at this. *Did she charm you, too, Phillips?*
He picked up where he had left off.

> *Lord Paxton reaffirmed his confidence in her in a note*
> *written and properly witnessed the night before that duel.*
> *Therefore, I would suggest she be allowed a good deal of*
> *latitude in making decisions until such time as you are*
> *able to see to matters on a regular basis.*
> *I enclose a letter for you from the late earl. I assume it,*
> *too, was written the night before the duel.*
> *Yours, etc.*
> *Walter Phillips, Esq.*

Reasoning that he had little control over Paxton affairs so long as
the British army was stuck on the Peninsula, Zachary immediately
decided he would take Phillips's advice—for now. He could sort it all
out when this bloody war was over. He turned to Henry's letter, feeling
somewhat strange at reading some of the last words of a dead man.

> *Dear Zachary,*
> *If you are reading this, you know that worse came to*
> *worst in a confrontation with Kingsley, Ryesdale's*
> *youngest brother. It probably goes without saying that I*
> *did try to avoid this turn of events. Phillips has assured*
> *me that my previous communications to you sufficiently*
> *outlined temporal matters. The rest is up to God.*
> *I am sorry to burden you with this, but I feel sure you*
> *will look out for my sons and their mothers. When he*
> *hears of my demise, Percival Laughton is almost certain*
> *to try to make mischief for them, especially Sydney and*
> *Jonathan.*
> *Henry*

CHAPTER 16

Zachary took part in the usual attempts to stave off the boredom of winter quarters before the coming spring campaign, but he did so only half-heartedly. What he *wanted* to do was return to the Ramirez village, which was now hundreds of miles south through some incredibly difficult terrain. He needed to see Elena again, to shake some sense into her, to see whatever this was between them to some sort of conclusion. He hated this uncertainty, this doubt, this feeling of something unfinished.

Her last words to him—"Let us not make promises we cannot keep"—kept echoing in his mind. *Ah, Elena,* he replied silently, *there is always from that first kiss an implicit promise for men and women who truly care. And promises of any sort are meant to be kept.*

For now, however, he was stuck north of the Pyrenees. The army as a whole might be temporarily standing down, except for minor skirmishes here and there, but the Rangers' mission of gathering intelligence continued, especially for Zachary and Cameron McIntyre, whose language skills in both Spanish and French allowed them to blend in among villagers near the border and even among French soldiers. In February a major battle at Orthez brought Wellington's army ever closer to achieving the goal of defeating the Emperor Bonaparte in southern Europe.

Finally, on April 10, Easter Sunday, came yet another major battle:

Toulouse. One of the fiercest battles of the entire six-year Peninsular campaign, it ended with more than eight thousand Allied and French dead—and thousands more wounded, including one Major Zachary Quintin.

As an officer, he was mounted and charging around from one area of the battlefield to another, directing the firepower of foot soldiers, slashing his saber at any French uniform that materialized in front of him. He and his horse were ready targets for a French rifleman. The horse, the larger target, was hit first. The faithful Nestor—named for a Homeric hero—screamed and reared, upsetting his rider. Zachary felt a searing pain along his left side, then a jarring clunk as his head hit the edge of an artillery wagon, knocking his headgear askew. He fell into oblivion, his last conscious awareness the continued sound of booming artillery, rifle reports, sabers clashing—and the cries of men and horses dying around him.

When he regained consciousness, his head, his chest, and his left arm all ached abominably. The arm felt heavy and hurt as he tried to lift it.

"Unh." He groaned and opened his eyes. Walls. Indoor walls. A ceiling. A branch of candles. A bed. He lay on a real bed.

"Ah, you have decided to rejoin us after all." It was Jack Gordon's voice.

"Where—? Wha—?"

Gordon, occupying a wooden chair near the bed, said, "Toulouse. A shopkeeper's house. You have been out for"—he dug into a pocket for his watch—"nearly thirty hours."

"We took Toulouse?"

"Soult withdrew last night. Terrible losses all around."

"Our lot?"

Gordon's expression turned grim as he nodded. "Penryn and Whitten. Harrelson took saber slashes on his back and one leg. Lost a lot of blood, but he will make it. McIntyre stepped into a rabbit hole and sprained his ankle."

Zachary managed a feeble grin. He closed his eyes for a moment, then said softly, "Penryn and Whitten. Good men. We'll surely miss Penryn's jokes and Whitten's off-key singing. Hard to replace men like them."

"Well, as to that, it won't be necessary."

"What do you mean?"

"It's all over. Been over. Boney abdicated on the sixth. The peer got the news today."

Zachary was not sure of what he had just heard. "Napoleon ab—?"

"Abdicated—on the sixth."

"Oh, my God!"

"Right." Gordon's tone was bitter with impotent rage. "Penryn. Whitten. All those others. Totally unnecessary."

They shared in silence the sense of futility and loss. Then Zachary asked, "My horse? Nestor?"

"He will be all right. I dug a bullet out of his shoulder. Gave him some extra feed, too. He was how we found you. He was standing over you—on guard, you might say."

Zachary shook his head in wonder, the action increasing the pain in his head. But pain served to remind him that he was still alive.

As if to confirm this, Gordon stood and said, "You took a blow to your head—concussion there. Broke two ribs and your arm. I set the arm and bound the ribs. Bandaged a flesh wound above your waist, too."

"Lucky, eh?"

"I'd say so." Gordon headed for the door. "Better tell the others you are back. Get you some food, too."

Soon the remaining Rangers had crowded into the room, Trevor Harrelson taking the chair Gordon had vacated, leaning forward and stretching his leg out awkwardly. Others squatted, sat on the floor, or leaned against a wall as their leader wolfed down a bowl of stew and some crusty bread along with some watered-down wine. They rehashed their parts of the battle, each paying proper tribute to the fallen Penryn and Whitten.

During a lull in the conversation, Zachary said, "Hard to believe it is over."

"Six years. But we made it. Most of us," McIntyre said.

"Now what?" Richardson gave voice to the thought uppermost in all their minds.

"Home!" Harrelson said.

"That is the rumor," McIntyre said. "In a month there will be no more Brits on the Peninsula."

"Well, now . . ." Zachary allowed his voice to fade away.

"You thinking of staying on?" Harrelson asked in a disbelieving tone.

"I have to," Zachary said simply.

They were all quiet, accepting his statement at face value, for they all knew that Zachary's relationhip with Elena Ramirez had gone far beyond a mere wartime romance. Nobody talked about it, but in the way of families, they just knew.

Finally, McIntyre said, "You are not going anywhere for a day or two. Doctor's orders, you know. By then we should know the peer's plans, too."

"Toulouse town fathers are plannin' a celebration," O'Brien said.

"That so?" Zachary could not stifle a yawn and his men took the hint and left. He slept for another twelve hours, then still felt shaky, but definitely on the mend.

The five remaining Rangers were all present two nights later at a local theatre when Wellington's appearance literally stopped the show. The English commander, in a show of solidarity with the French who had opposed Napoleon, wore the white cockade of the Royalists; on seeing this, the locals gave him a standing ovation lasting a good ten minutes.

Word had also trickled down from on high that the triumphant Peninsular army was, indeed, to return home and demobilize, their services no longer needed. After the evening's celebrations on the town, the Rangers met for a nightcap in the living room of the home the shopkeeper had graciously—and for a fee—turned over to them. Zachary thought the others, too, felt this was a farewell of sorts.

McIntyre lifted a glass of a very fine cognac. "I propose a toast to what's left of Zany Zack's Rangers."

"Hear! Hear!" Harrelson said.

"And to absent friends," Zachary added.

"Absent friends," they all echoed.

Quiet ensued for a few moments, then Richardson cleared his throat noticeably. "Now, Captain—oops, forgot—*Major* Quintin. We have been discussing this madcap plan of yours to return to Spain."

"Do not even think of trying to dissuade me," Zachary said.

"Wouldn't dream of it," Richardson replied.

"We are going with you," Harrelson said.

"Oh, no."

"Well, like it or not, we are not letting you go alone," McIntyre said flatly. "God knows what a lone Englishman might encounter down there. It was chaos before. Probably on the verge of civil war now."

"Posssibly. But I need to go. You do not. So the rest of you just get on that troop ship next week and be done with it. Consider that an order."

"I do most sincerely beg your pardon, *sir,*" McIntyre said with exaggerated courtesy. "Perhaps you missed that part about the army being demobilized? That lends new meaning to the idea of *orders.*"

"Look," Zachary said. "I appreciate your willingness to put yourselves out for me, but I doubt I need a keeper. And I happen to know, Trevor, that you and Adam, especially, have family matters that require your attention." He knew he was ignoring his own obligation to his cousin Henry's concerns, but surely those could wait until he had dealt with the matter of Elena. How much difference could another month or two make?

"They can wait," Harrelson said and Richardson nodded.

"But they need not do so," Zachary argued. "Besides, a whole herd of us trooping back over those mountains would be hard to manage and could draw unwelcome notice. The fewer the better."

They all fell into grudging silence as this argument sank in.

"All right," Richardson said, "but we really cannot see you doing this alone."

"I could do it," Zachary said, "but it does make more sense to have company. "O'Brien?"

"Yes, sir."

"And me," Gordon said. "You are still my patient, you know. With that crippled wing, you'd be at a real disadvantage if you ran into trouble."

Seeing the logic of this, Zachary nodded.

"Now just a minute," McIntyre said. "Neither of these thatch-gallows speak anything but English—and even that none too well."

Gordon snorted. "Well, la de da."

Zachary held up his good hand. "All right. You three. The Irish-Scots contingent. But that is it. Period."

"Notice how he just ignores his own countrymen?" Harrelson said in an aside to Richardson.

"Give my regards to your families," Zachary said. "And to the fair Celia, Trevor."

As they were calling it a night and seeking their beds, Zachary said, "O'Brien. A word, if you please."

The others excused themselves.

"Sir?"

"Charlie, you have been my batman for some time now."

"Yes, sir. Goin' fer six years now."

"I want you to know that I have appreciated your service."

"Oh, Lord, Major. You ain't lettin' me go, are you?"

"Not at all. But it occurs to me that with the war over and your army duties finished, you might have plans of your own."

"Uh, nothin' to speak of, sir."

"Once I return to London and set up my own establishment, I will need someone to keep me in line. The job is yours, if you want it."

"Thank ye, sir. I don't mind tellin' ye, I was hopin' fer jus' that."

"Good. And I thank you, O'Brien." Zachary offered his hand, which Charlie eagerly clasped.

With so many officers selling extra mounts and pack animals, Major Quintin and the remains of his team had no difficulty outfitting themselves for the trek south. The night before their departure, Zachary wrote letters to his family and to the lawyer Phillips to inform them of the approximate time they might all expect his return to England. Harrelson was charged with the task of seeing these missives delivered. Zachary thought about writing a note to Sydney, but what was there to say to her? He had written his condolences when he heard of Henry's death and received a perfunctory thank-you in response.

And just what else might you have expected? he asked himself scornfully. *Besides, considering the nature of this new Spanish venture, you'd best let Phillips handle any business with the grieving widow.*

The journey south was surprisingly uneventful. Spring had arrived with fresh greenery and rushing streams. Some of the towns and villages they passed through had been all but totally destroyed by the war; others seemed scarcely touched. In the mountain villages, people simply carried on with their lives, tending their sheep and small garden plots.

As they left the Pyrenees and headed through mountains farther south, they found more and more devastation. They were also increasingly aware of danger from wandering bands of marauders.

Some of these were former partisan groups who seemed to have lost sight of their goals of the recent past. Others were vicious groups of deserters from both armies who formed into outlaw bands to prey on villagers and travelers.

Zachary was now immensely grateful to his companions, especially after an incident one night in which an outlaw band sought to surprise the Rangers and relieve them of their horses and goods. The desperados, perhaps deceived by earlier, easier successes, had not reckoned with the military discipline and expertise of their intended victims on this occasion. Gordon, as the guard of the moment, had quietly alerted the others to the presence of "visitors" just before dawn. The fight that ensued ended with the bandits fleeing, leaving behind the horses, weapons, and bodies of three dead companions.

"I doubt the others will be back," Zachary said, as they finished burying the dead. His friends nodded their agreement. Nevertheless, they were especially vigilant all that day and night.

Following Richardson's maps and their own memories of the terrain, they completed in ten days a journey that had taken Wellington's army a year to achieve. Finally, late one afternoon, they approached the Ramirez compound. Zachary was nervous. Would Elena be here? Would she welcome his return?

It was eerily quiet as they neared. No guards on the perimeter. No laughing, screaming children. No dogs barking. No chickens in the yards of the cottages. No smoke from cooking fires in the cottages. One of the cottages had been destroyed by fire, its roof gone and only stone walls remaining. The door of another hung askew.

"Careful," Zachary warned unnecessarily.

They arrived at the door of the lodge without being challenged. Zachary surmised that the place was deserted. Then he caught a flash of movement in an upstairs window.

"Hello," he called as he dismounted and motioned the others to stay put. He knocked on the door and heard someone struggling with the latch. A boy of about seven years opened the door. Zachary recognized Miguel's son. Behind him stood Pilar, holding a pistol. Zachary noted instantly that the weapon was old and rusty. He thought if it could even be fired, it was likely to do more damage behind than in front of it.

"Señor Quintin!" She lowered the weapon. In a worn black dress, her gray-streaked hair loosely bound behind her head, the attractive matron he had known little more than a year ago looked old and haggard. Her eyes, once invariably smiling and friendly, were flat and defeated.

"What happened here?" he asked.

"Banditos. Four—no, five months ago."

"Elena? Miguel?"

"Dead." Her eyes were glazed with pain.

Zachary sucked in a sharp breath. He felt as though he had taken a solid punch to his midriff. Pain shot through his chest where his ribs had not yet mended. "Both?" he gasped.

She nodded. "Many others, too. Put your animals up and we shall talk. The barn is still standing. Empty, but standing."

He stumbled back down the steps and directed the others to the barn in the rear where they took care of their horses and pack mules, supplementing remnants of hay they found with the feed they had brought with them. He told his friends as much as he had so far learned.

"Ah, God, Quintin. I am so sorry," McIntyre said.

"Rotten news, that," Gordon said.

O'Brien merely shook his head in sympathy.

"We will stay here for tonight at least." Zachary could not bring himself to say more, so they worked in silence, then carried their packs into the drawing room of the lodge where they found Pilar and nine other women, all in very sober dress. Another woman entered from the kitchen bearing a heavy tray with a large kettle and stacks of cups. McIntyre quickly took the tray from her and set it on a low table.

"Tea," Pilar said. "Not real. From local herbs."

The visitors, seated now along with the women on an assortment of chairs and couches, murmured appreciation and there was silence in the room for a few minutes, broken by the sounds of clinking cups and voices of children playing in a room above stairs.

Zachary set his cup down, impatient with this delay. "Señora Ramirez. I am sorry for the pain it must bring you, but—please—tell us what happened."

She sighed and set her own cup down. "The pain is easing. Five months now. You know Arroyo Robles? Yes?"

The conversation was taking place in Spanish with McIntyre

translating for Gordon and O'Brien as necessary. Zachary glanced at McIntyre and saw that he, too, recognized the name of the ravine where Miguel's partisans had taken out a company of French soldiers. "Yes, I know it."

"Miguel and—and others were ambushed there. Killed. All but my brother José. He was injured and they must have thought him dead too. They stole the horses. It took José two days to bring us word."

"Brave lad," Gordon said.

She went on as though she had not heard, as though having started, she could not stop. "Then they came here. Maybe twenty of them. K-killed our guards. Stole most of our livestock and much of our food. Tore up what was left of the gardens."

"Tell them the rest," one of the younger women said bitterly.

Pilar closed her eyes. Her voice was a fierce whisper. "Th-they, they raped us. All the women and girls. Some of the boys, too. Horrible. Horrible."

The same young woman finished the tale. "They found the wine cellar. Many were drunk and laughing as they rode off, promising they would be back."

Zachary and his three men sat in stunned silence. It was a familiar wartime tale of rape and pillage, but what could one say to women who had been so abused?

A baby's cry broke into this bleak musing. A baby. It almost seemed a sign: Life does go on.

"I'll get him." One of the women hastily left the room and returned carrying a still fussy baby. The young woman who had retrieved him handed him over to Pilar, in whose arms he soon quieted. Zachary judged the child to be several months old. He had a good deal of black hair and very dark eyes.

Zachary smiled at the madonna-like image Pilar and the baby presented. "Miguel's son?"

"No," Pilar said. "Elena's. And yours."

"Wha—?" For the second time in less than two hours Zachary felt like he had been dealt a resounding punch to his midsection. He barely heard the sharp intakes of breath of the other men; nor did he notice the women in the room openly staring at him.

"He is your son," Pilar repeated.

He had not yet had time to absorb the idea of Elena's death. Now this. An unreasoning anger bubbled up in him and it needed a target. "Are you telling me Elena abandoned her baby to ride off on a partisan expedition?"

"No, Inglés," Pilar said gently, using Elena's name for him. "Elena was not at Arroyo Robles with Miguel. She died in childbirth two months before. The baby came early."

Another punch. Would they never stop coming?

Pilar went on. "Miguel was very distraught at losing his sister. They were very close, you know. Had you been here, he might have tried to kill you."

With due cause, Zachary thought, but held his tongue, unable now to take his eyes off the baby.

"In the end, Elena knew she was dying. She made us promise to find you. Miguel would have honored her wish, but—" Pilar waved one hand in a gesture of despair.

Reeling inside, Zachary rose and touched McIntyre's shoulder. "See—see to them," he mumbled and stumbled out the door. He leaned against a pillar of the veranda as he gazed unseeing at the yard where he had watched a laughing, carefree Elena playing with her brother's children. He made no effort to control the sobs wracking his body. He felt every breath in his sore ribs.

CHAPTER 17

Having gained control of himself, Zachary sat on a bench on the veranda for a long while, grateful that the others were allowing him this time alone. The sun was setting, bathing the deserted cottages and surrounding trees in a rose-gold glow. As the light faded even further, he became aware of the door opening.

Pilar emerged, holding the baby, and sat on the bench next to him with the child on her lap facing him. The baby emitted an unintelligible gurgle and reached toward Zachary with a crust of bread in his hand. Zachary smiled and touched his cheek.

"He's beautiful," Zachary said. "W-what do you call him?"

"Lucas. He has brought much light into our lives." She seemed thoughtful for a moment. "But he is so young, you can change it—make it more English if you wish."

"You mean me to take him?"

"But of course. A child should be with his own parents. And it was Elena's wish. That is why she made Miguel promise—"

"I see." He longed to hold the baby, but was somewhat fearful of this little bundle of squirming humanity. He could not remember ever having—or wanting to have—a baby in his arms before.

Pilar broke into this thought. "There is something else, señor."

"What?" What more could this day throw at him?

"Elena's father—the colonel—he did not approve of her—of us, really."

"Elena told me Miguel had married against his father's wishes."

"Yes." For a moment she seemed to dwell on a memory. "He denounced us. Then he denounced Elena when she supported us. He disowned her entirely when she joined us—the partisans. A woman must not do such things—and a good daughter must not defy her father."

"He disowned her? She must have been very hurt by that."

She shifted the babbling baby on her lap. "She was. I think his rejection hurt her even more than her Arturo's betrayal."

He looked at her questioningly.

"The boy she was to have married."

"Ah." He was silent for a moment. "So—?"

"So. Colonel Salvatore Federico Ramirez is an ambitious and narrow-minded man. He will not welcome such a grandson. Not in Spanish society."

"Oh, my God! This beautiful baby—his own flesh and blood—"

"Is illegitimate," Pilar said sadly.

He was distracted now as Lucas reached two chubby baby arms toward him. Zachary knew instantly that he was lost forever to this son of his.

Pilar smiled. "See? He likes you already."

She thrust the baby forward and Zachary caught him gingerly, holding him close with his good arm and bracing the infant with the hand of the arm still in a sling.

Pilar laughed. "He will not break, Señor Quintin."

Lucas gazed solemnly at this new person in his life. The child had a fine head of very black hair, like that of both his parents, and, for a baby, unusually well-defined dark brows. His eyes were brown, but the softer brown of Elena's rather than the near-black of Zachary's. Zachary felt a surge of unadulterated, unconditional love. He recalled feeling just such protectiveness toward the injured Elena as they escaped the village of Segueros so many months ago.

He felt his eyes fill with tears as he whispered to Pilar, "Thank you for caring for my son. For giving him to me."

She rose and touched his shoulder. "He is Elena's gift. You must treasure him." She stepped toward the door. "I will see to our supper. Such a feast we shall have with the fresh meat you brought."

The supper was pleasant enough, though a more subdued affair than had been the case when most of the people at this table were the single men of the Ramirez band. The children—about a dozen of them, the Rangers were told—had been fed earlier, so conversation at the table was freer than it might have been. Having suffered terrible losses of their own, the women were sympathetic to Zachary's plight. He was glad to find that none of these devoutly Catholic women seemed judgmental of him or Elena. He conjectured that in this regard, they took their cue from Pilar, who had been very fond of her sister-in-law.

He looked around the table and finally thought to ask, "Where is José? Did you not say he survived the ambush?"

"Yes, he did," Pilar said. "But he was very weak."

"None of us thought he would make it," one of the others said.

"He has that same stubborn Guzman will as his sister," another said with a teasing look at Pilar, before going on. "He had a broken arm—like yours, Señor Quintin. And a terrible cut on his thigh. He had lost much blood in that long walk back here."

"Then the infection," another added. They all seemed eager to sing José's praises.

"A miracle he survived."

"God's will."

"But where is he?" Zachary asked.

Pilar answered. "I sent him and Sarita—you remember Sarita? Pedro's wife?" Zachary nodded, and she continued. "I sent them to locate our father. He, too, was with the loyal Spanish government, but we have had no word for many months, so he will be difficult to find perhaps."

"When?" McIntyre asked. "How long have they been gone?"

"Three weeks."

McIntyre exchanged a look with Zachary. "Too long. God knows where they might be. Guess we just wait, eh?"

Zachary was pleased that McIntyre, Gordon, and O'Brien all just assumed they would help these people. Before everyone retired for the night, Zachary made a point of looking in on the sleeping Lucas. He could not resist just touching him again. When the four Rangers were alone, sharing one of the lodge's rooms that two of the women had given up, he tried to thank his men for their support.

"Ah, God, Major. What else could we do?" Gordon said, as he and O'Brien laid out their bedrolls on pallets on the floor. They had lost the coin toss for the bed.

"So you plan to take baby Lucas back to England?" McIntyre asked as he removed his boots.

"Yes."

"You sure that's a good idea?"

"What else can I do?" Zachary echoed Gordon's earlier comment. Then his tone hardened. "I say—you do not mean to imply that that baby is not mine?"

"Not at all. The shape of those ears—those dimples in his cheeks. You must have looked like that at his age."

Zachary nodded. "As did *both* my younger brothers. Mother always said we looked just alike as babies."

"What I meant was how do you plan to explain his existence? Single men don't go around adopting foreign babies."

Zachary was aware that the other two were listening intently for his reply. "Hmm. Well—the truth, I suppose. *And* a lie—if I can enlist your aid."

"Our aid?" O'Brien sounded mystified.

"I just freely—and truthfully—claim my son." The words were still new to him, but he felt a touch of pride in saying them. "Then— I lie and have everyone believing Elena and I were married." He was warming to the story. "A Catholic ceremony. You all were witnesses, but agreed to keep it a secret."

Gordon said, "That could work—but what about Harrelson and Richardson—the whole British army, in fact? They might already be telling war stories in London drawing rooms."

"Trevor and Adam will support whatever we come up with," Zachary said.

"That they will." McIntyre, having stripped down to his underwear, was quiet for several minutes after crawling into bed. "All right. Some more truth and another lie." He paused again.

"Well—?" O'Brien prompted.

"Out with it," Gordon demanded.

Zachary merely waited as he took the other half of the bed, making sure his still healing arm would be on the outer edge.

"Everyone knows the Horse Guards have strict rules against English soldiers marrying foreign women," McIntyre said.

"Yeh. So?" Gordon said.

"So it had to be a secret. Against the rules and all. Had to be secret from her family, too, because they would never approve her marrying a foreigner and a non-Catholic at that."

"Actually, that is very close to the truth," Zachary said. "Pilar tells me her father-in-law would never have condoned his daughter's marrying an Englishman."

"Canna blame a mon for that," Gordon said, exaggerating his Scottish brogue.

"So—we just have to keep our mouths shut," O'Brien said with a yawn. "Don't see as that's a problem. Should work right well."

"It has to," Zachary said. "I do not want my son needlessly ostracized."

Long after the others were creating a symphony of snores, Zachary lay awake, his mind replaying images of Elena—of the years since his return to the war, but especially of Elena. Had he been in love with her? He thought he *could* have been—had not the image of another kept intruding—the image of a woman with light brown hair and marvelous gray-green eyes. Sydney.

Yet he cherished the easy camaraderie—the warmth, the laughter, the passion—he had shared with Elena. He treasured this baby. Her baby. A God-given wonder to be cherished for himself alone. He silently vowed that Elena's son would always know his mother.

For nearly two weeks Zachary and his men stayed with what was left of the Ramirez partisans. The Rangers supplemented the women's remaining food with game—and with what could now, with transportation available, be procured at a distant village. Zachary spent much of this two-week interval at the pleasant task of getting acquainted with and learning to care for his son.

One of the women, with a baby just three months older than Lucas, had been serving as a wet nurse to Elena's baby.

"That is going to be a problem when we leave here," Zachary said, only half joking.

Pilar emitted a soft snort of laughter. "Yes, but not impossible to solve. You must get a goat. In the village. Both these babies are taking solid food now." She was spooning mashed potatoes and carrots toward Lucas's mouth and some of it actually went in.

"That mess does not look very 'solid' to me."

"You'll learn, Papa."

On the fifth day, many of the inhabitants of the lodge were still sitting at the table after the midday meal when one of the women, named Almira, dashed into the dining room looking distraught. Her eyes full of fear, and her breath coming in gasps, she cried out, "They're here. They said they'd be back and they are."

"What? Who?" Several spoke at once.

"The banditos. I saw them from the cliff. Crossing the river. We must hurry."

Zachary felt as much as heard the panic in the room. "Hold on," he said. "How many were there?"

Almira took a deep breath. "Maybe ten. Not as many as before."

"Coming in midday as they are, they seem to assume the women are alone," McIntyre observed.

"And without weapons," Gordon added, "since they took the ones they had before."

The Rangers had already given the women the weapons and horses gained in their own encounter with such scoundrels. The four men were themselves well armed, each with a rifle, at least one pistol, and a knife tucked into a boot. Zachary ordered three of the women to take positions at upstairs windows; McIntyre and Gordon would remain on the ground floor; he and O'Brien would wait outside at the corners of the lodge. The children were to be gathered together in a back bedroom.

"I think they will find their reception a bit of a surprise, but let them come close first," he said.

The women were clearly frightened, but resilient and resourceful. They readily fell in with the plan. Then the entire house was quiet, waiting.

Presently a band of ten horsemen with two pack animals rode into the compound; they kept their horses at a walk. Zachary could see that they were men of experience, always cautious, but, at the moment, they were also confident, even cocky. Seeing one of them take a long swallow from a leather bag such as Spaniards often used for wine, Zachary wondered if they had all been drinking. They were dressed in a motley mixture of peasant wear and remnants of Spanish, French, and English uniforms. Several casually carried weapons across their arms and Zachary saw other rifles as well. They rode to within a few feet of the veranda.

The apparent leader rose up in his saddle and shouted in fractured

Spanish. "Buenos días, señoritas! We are back. Won't you come out and play with us?" He laughed and after a few seconds of silence from the lodge, he added in a cajoling tone, "Come on, pretty play-things. We know you are in there. We saw the smoke of your cooking fire. Don't make us come to get you."

Still no answer.

The man started to dismount and several of his companions were in the act of doing so as well when an answer came in the form of an explosion from an upstairs window. The bullet caught the man in the chest and spun him around; the movement scared his horse, which sidestepped with the rider's foot still in the stirrup. Now the horse truly panicked and its agitation spread to the others.

Pandemonium erupted among the visitors, who hastily returned fire or tried to do so even as they fought to control their mounts. Sur-prise was on the side of the lodge people, whose shots came from several vantage points. Soon enough, those of the would-be revelers who could do so turned tail and ran, leaving behind four dead and two dying companions.

It was late in the evening before they finished burying the dead and rounding up the stray animals, including one of the pack horses. The women exclaimed in satisfaction at discovering that that animal carried about ten kilos of flour and a container of tea. After the chil-dren had all been put to bed, the tired adults met in the drawing room. The tea tray materialized and they solemnly discussed the events of this hectic, sad day.

"You ladies did very well," McIntyre said. "Real soldiers, all of you."

"I am sorry I shot before I should have," said the woman who had fired that first shot. "I-I heard his voice—and it—it all came back to me—you know—what he—what he did to me—to us."

"Not to worry, Señora Vicente," Zachary said. "Try not to think about it—about him." Even as he said this, he knew such advice was futile, for few people can kill another without some emotional conse-quence.

Gordon added, "In any event, he got what he deserved. *That* one will never harm another woman."

"I don't care," Almira said just as though someone had challenged her. "I know the priest says revenge is wrong, but it felt good not to be a victim again."

Pilar raised her cup in a salute. "Gentlemen, we thank you."

A week later, José returned with his and Pilar's father and a contingent of ten Spanish soldiers in General Guzman's command. And two days after that Zachary, his three Rangers, and the baby Lucas, along with two pack horses and a nanny goat, left the compound with tearful good-byes ringing in their ears. The baby alternately rode in a basket attached to one of the pack horses or in the arms of his father or one of his honorary uncles. Instead of crossing the Pyrenees yet again, they headed for the port of San Sebastian, where they were confident of securing passage back to England. To Zachary's immense relief, they spent most of their nights along the way in villages with pensions or inns where servants were readily available to help with laundry and other needs one encountered in travel with an infant.

Within a month, the Rangers were all back in London, trying, with varying degrees of success, to cope with the return to civilian life.

After Easter, Sydney took her entourage back to London. She found the city ecstatic over the news of Napoleon's defeat and abdication. News of the victory at Toulouse was only slightly tempered by the fact that that battle occurred *after* the Corsican monster had given up the fight. Wellington was clearly the hero of the day and the Prince Regent was just as clearly determined to share in the duke's military glory. All London seemed set on a prolonged celebration, which would culminate in mid July with a state visit from Russia's Czar Alexander, Prussia's King Frederick, and the colorful Marshal Blücher.

As a still-grieving widow, Sydney felt she should refuse most of the invitations to balls and routs that arrived at Paxton House daily. However, she encouraged Aunt Harriet and Celia to accept any that might appeal to them, and she enjoyed listening to their accounts of their evenings. Sydney was content to take up her work with the Fairfax sisters in earnest now. Henry had never quite approved of her visits to Spitalfields, and she had respected his wishes. Now, though, she felt no such constraints.

Penelope and Priscilla Fairfax were middle-aged spinsters who had inherited a large fortune from their father, owner of a silk mill.

As daughters of a "cit," the two had little chance of making it into the higher echelons of society—nor had they ever aspired to do so. Their home in Spitalfields, an island of gentility in a sea of degradation and debauchery, offered a safe haven to some of the city's most neglected denizens. It was at times—and sometimes simultaneously—a home for unwed pregnant young women, an orphanage, and a refuge for abused women.

During her first stay in the city, Sydney had met the Fairfax sisters through a new friend, Lady Allyson Crossleigh, daughter of the Earl of Rutherford. One day the two young women had been out shopping with their maids in tow and a carriage driver and footman always near. As they strolled past the entrance to an alley, they heard a cry of pain and dull thumps and grunts. Both ladies instantly turned toward the sounds.

"Oh, dear," Lady Allyson's maid cried in a knowing tone.

"My lady, perhaps—" Maisie's cautionary note died away.

It was too late. Their mistresses had both rushed into the alley to behold a boy of seven or eight being set on by two boys of ten or twelve. The youngest one was curled into a fetal position as the older ones kicked at him.

"Stop that! Stop it this instant!" Lady Allyson made a grab for one of the older boys.

He slipped out of her grasp with a loud yelp. "Lawks! Jamie! Fergit 'im. Come on! We got 'is blunt."

The second attacker dashed past Sydney, who was already bending over the younger boy as he struggled to rise. Sydney helped him up and grabbed onto his shoulder when it was apparent that he, too, would try to flee.

"Are you hurt?" she asked.

"Not so's ya'd notice," he said and tried to wrench away. "Ye can let go o' me."

Sydney tightened her grip. "I think not."

Lady Allyson turned back in disgust. "The other two got away. I had the one and he just slipped out of my hand. Is this one hurt?"

"I believe he is only bruised." But when she ran a hand along his side, the boy gasped and flinched. "Perhaps not," she added.

"I'm that glad you got them two off'n me," the boy said, "but I'm all right now so ye can let me go." He seemed to be trying to act grown up, but Sydney detected little boy fear beneath the calm tone. She noted that his clothing was torn and dirty and that he was painfully thin. A street urchin, she decided.

Both women ignored him.

"You have no business being on the streets alone," Lady Allyson said. "We shall take you to your parents. Where are they?"

"Ain't got none," he muttered. "Now you just let me go." Again he tried futilely to wrench himself from Sydney's grasp.

She shook him by his shoulder. "What do you mean you have no parents?"

"I ain't got none," he repeated. "I get by on my own. Don't need any."

At this moment, Lady Allyson's footman dashed into the alley. "My lady, are you all right? Molly said—"

"I am quite all right, Nathan. Now if you will just take this lad in hand—"

"No!" the boy yelled and kicked and then cried out in pain as the footman picked him up.

"Careful," Sydney cautioned. "I think he may have a bruised or broken rib."

"All right, boy. Just calm down now," the footman said and held him more gently. It was clear the child was going nowhere.

The group made their way to Lady Allyson's unmarked carriage. The coachman and footman had been slowly following the ladies as they darted from shop to shop earlier.

"Fairfax House," Lady Allyson told the coachman. "Nathan, you ride inside with us to hold the boy." She and Allyson handed the coachman the packages they had retrieved as they exited the alley. Along with the two maids, they squeezed into the now crowded carriage.

"His lordship won't like your going to Spitalfields, my lady," the footman said.

Sydney thought this rather a bold comment from a footman.

"He need not know of it unless you feel compelled to tell him," Lady Allyson replied. She then explained to Sydney. "Papa has this bee in his bonnet that I need some sort of protection—from heaven knows what."

"What she needs is a keeper," the saucy footman muttered barely audibly, as he sat with the protesting child in his lap.

"This here's kidnappin'! Ye can bloody well hang fer that!"

"Here! You watch your language around ladies." The footman shook him, bringing forth an exaggerated yelp of pain. "Who'd want to kidnap the likes of you?"

The boy was clearly afraid, but he kept a sulky silence until they reached Fairfax House.

Permanent members of Fairfax House included Miss Penelope Fairfax, her sister Miss Priscilla, and three servants who, Sydney discovered later, were more like family members. Samuel Boskins, butler, footman, handyman, was an ex-soldier who had lost his right arm in a battle on the Peninsula; his wife was the cook-housekeeper; and there was a maid named Betty Lou. All had been rescue projects of the Fairfax sisters: the homeless Boskins couple from the streets and Betty Lou from a local brothel.

On this day, Sydney and Lady Allyson were ushered into the Fairfax drawing room and Mrs. Boskins presently appeared with some tea and biscuits. She reported that "the boy is settling down quite nice like—but he'll bear watchin'."

"Well, if we have learned nothing else in the last ten years and more," the angular, gray-haired, and usually austere Miss Penelope Fairfax said, "we have learned that if people—even young ones—do not want our help, it is wise not to press it upon them."

"But we do try harder with the young ones," Miss Priscilla said. Priscilla Fairfax was also gray-haired like her sister, more open in her demeanor, more ready to laugh.

In the course of this conversation and the one later in the carriage ride home, Sydney learned the scope of the sisters' work with the poor of Spitalfields. They not only provided "in house" care, but they also distributed donations to needy folk in the neighborhood.

"I do as much as I can," Lady Allyson said. "I pester people shamelessly."

"I shall be glad to join you," Sydney replied, delighted to have found a kindred spirit.

A few weeks later Sydney had been equally glad to learn that the boy—his name was Walter, but everyone in Fairfax House called him Wally—had, indeed, settled in nicely.

"I do not know how we ever got on without him," Miss Fairfax said. "He is very adept at running errands for us. And he is learning to read," she added proudly.

Now, on her return to London, Sydney was happy to lend the Fairfax sisters her support, moral *and* financial. It had, in fact, been Sydney's idea to expand the facility by purchasing the property next door. With proper renovations and additional staff, it would allow the Fairfax sisters to serve more people. Sydney was quite sure she could bury the expense among Paxton accounts.

She regularly turned down invitations to balls and musical soirees in her efforts to abide by society's unwritten but rock hard rules for grieving widows. She felt she owed Henry that degree of respect. However, she did make and receive morning calls. Among the regular callers at Paxton House now was Lieutenant Trevor Harrelson, late of His Majesty's forces in the Peninsula. He had made a call on Miss Carstairs his most urgent social obligation on his return to England. Sydney tried to listen only casually, even indifferently, whenever Lieutenant Harrelson mentioned his erstwhile commander, but she could not stop the little flip of her heart at any mention of the man—nor the shiver of apprehension at the control he might now hold over her entire life.

She learned some fascinating details of Zachary Quintin's exploits as a soldier and as an exploring officer, though she had to smile at the discretion the lieutenant employed in telling the tales in a London drawing room.

"But why did Captain—I mean Major—Quintin not return to England with you?" Celia asked the question Sydney was dying to ask herself.

She thought Lieutenant Harrelson seemed uncomfortable as he answered. "He—uh—he had to return to Spain for one last mission. Didn't need all of us. Tie up loose ends, so to speak."

"Oh," Celia said. "I do hope he will return in time for the grand celebrations of the state visits."

Sydney also refused to forego her interest in the theatre. It was one of the few interests she had shared with her husband. One night in late June she dressed carefully in a silvery gray silk gown trimmed in black to attend a performance of the famous Edmund Kean as Richard III. The theatre party, which had been planned for some time, included Sydney's friend Lady Allyson and her new husband, Lord Nathan Thornton, for the erstwhile saucy footman had turned out to be the younger son of a duke. Others were Aunt Harriet, Celia, and Lieutenant Harrelson. As the elegant Countess of Paxton entered her own box, she chanced to look across at persons just entering another box and found herself gazing directly into the dark eyes of Major Zachary Quintin.

CHAPTER 18

Sydney had braced herself for this moment. She was sure she had her emotions under control.

Lieutenant Harrelson had called two days ago. Seated in the family drawing room, he had delivered to Celia and Sydney the news that Major Quintin had not only returned to England, but he had not come alone.

"What do you mean he is not alone?" Celia instantly demanded.

"Brought his son with him," Lieutenant Harrelson said, then paused dramatically.

"His son?" Sydney and Celia spoke at once in surprised tones.

Harrelson nodded. "His son. The major married a Spanish lady in early 'thirteen."

"And you are just now telling us?" Celia accused.

Sydney was stunned. Zachary *married*? Somehow she had never imagined him with another woman in his arms. And they had had a child? Why not? she admonished herself. He had a right to a life of his own. Still, this news came as a profound shock.

Harrelson was answering Celia. "Couldn't tell you earlier. Had to be a secret. Army rules against it, you know. Also, they wanted to avoid the scandal broth likely when her father found out. High in the Spanish government, he is."

"So Major Quintin brought his wife to England?" Celia clapped her hands. "Oh, this is such a romantic story. Like Romeo and Juliet."

Still reeling inwardly, Sydney was glad to leave the conversation to the other two. Sunlight streamed through the windows and there was the occasional rumble of a carriage on the street below, but none of this registered with her.

"Hadn't thought of it like that," Harrelson said, "but you're right. Real tragedy here, too."

Celia frowned. "Tragedy?"

"The major's wife died. In childbirth."

"Oh, how sad," Celia said.

"When?" Sydney asked.

"Hmm. Seven or eight months ago, I think, but the major did not know until recently. He went back to Spain after Toulouse. Found out then."

It occurred to Sydney that Zachary had lost his wife within weeks of her losing Henry. She managed to make it through the rest of Harrelson's visit with an occasional murmur here and there, but her mind was in a whirl. Zachary was back. Zachary, who had so charmed a much younger Sydney. Zachary, whose kiss had been so mesmerizing. Zachary, who had been a party to Henry's duplicity. Zachary, who might now wield a frightening degree of power over the Countess of Paxton—and over her son.

When Celia and the lieutenant departed for a drive in the park, Sydney sought the privacy of her own bedchamber, where she spent a good deal of time pacing and considering dozens of "what ifs"— some wildly unreasonable, some within the realm of the possible, if not always the probable.

Finally, the ever practical Lady Paxton gave herself a mental shake. She would have to wait and see, then consider her options. But she deeply resented having to wait—being forced to react to someone else's position instead of acting on her own. With this rebellious thought, she reasserted control over her emotions.

Or thought she had.

Until her gaze locked with his in a crowded theatre. The fact that he was dressed in his army uniform, looking very much as he had when she had last seen him, on her wedding day, added to her confusion, though she knew all Wellington's officers were encouraged to appear in public in uniform during these days of celebration.

Now her careful control had deserted her. She felt a tightness in her chest and her knees suddenly seemed weak. She managed a slight nod in Zachary's direction and quickly averted her eyes as she took her seat in the front of the box, between Allyson and Aunt Harriet. She wished she had insisted on one of the rear chairs. She wished she had stayed home.

She tried unsuccessfully to keep her gaze from straying to that other box. So far it contained only two people, Zachary and a comely young woman. Less than a week in town and he already finds solace in female companionship? She immediately chastised herself for the pettiness of this thought. When she glanced again and saw an older couple enter that other box, she was more than a little vexed with herself, for she recognized Lady Leanora and her husband, Mr. Horatio Quintin, Zachary's parents. She had met them only briefly on a previous sojourn in the city.

Drury Lane had been one of the first of London's theatres to install the modern gaslights. Now as the house lights dimmed and the curtain rose, Sydney turned her attention resolutely to the stage. However, she actually absorbed very little of the inimitable Mr. Kean's performance. During the interval, she noticed that two other gentlemen had joined the party in the Quintins' box, one in civilian attire, the other in uniform.

Celia leaned closer to whisper to Sydney, "Did you see Major Quintin?"

Not trusting herself to speak, Sydney merely nodded.

Lady Allyson looked in the direction Celia indicated. "Lady Leanora is one of my mother's dearest friends. Come, Nathan, we must pay our respects," she urged her husband.

Celia, Lieutenant Harrelson, and Aunt Harriet all decided to "take a stroll" before the second half of the play. Sydney welcomed a moment alone. She noticed that there were now several people crowded into the Quintin box, but Zachary was no longer one of them.

A tap at the door to her own box heralded the arrival of a visitor. And there he was: the Zachary she had known in Bath, though his complexion was darker, the scar on his face faded now, and the lines around his eyes more distinct.

"Lady Paxton." He glanced around and seemed surprised to find her alone. "I hope I am not intruding."

"Major Quintin. No, of course not. Please. Have a seat." She was as nervous and unsure of herself as a green girl at her first grown-up affair.

He held her gaze for a long moment, then glanced away. He took the seat Lady Allyson had vacated. As he sat, he bent forward and she caught a faint familiar whiff of his shaving soap—which did nothing to help quell the riot in her innards. She tried to calm herself by inhaling deeply. They both started to speak at once.

"I think—"

"I have only—"

He smiled and gestured for her to continue.

"I heard only yesterday of your loss," she said. "Please allow me to express my condolences."

He nodded. "Thank you, my lady."

An awkward silence ensued. He broke it by saying, "I wonder if I might call on you next week to discuss the—uh—duties with which Cousin Henry charged me?"

"Yes, of course," she said, adopting the same businesslike tone he used.

"Will Tuesday next give you sufficient time to have the accounts and ledgers ready?"

"Yes. They are kept up to date. I think you will find all in order." She paused and again held his gaze for a moment. She hated this stiff formality between them. How did one bridge the changes wrought by time and events in lives lived in wholly separate worlds? She longed for the easy camaraderie of those days in Bath. But that had been a charade, hadn't it? "Would you like me to ask Mr. Stevenson to join us for this meeting?"

"No. That should not be necessary yet."

Just then Allyson and her husband returned, and Zachary stood.

"Zachary! I missed you," Allyson said with bubbly gaiety; she kissed him on the cheek. "I dragged Nathan to your parents' box specifically to make him known to you and your family. I want him to know all my childhood friends."

Zachary grinned at her. "It's nice to know that some people have remained the same in my absence. But Nathan and I are way ahead of you, Allie. We were at Sandhurst together. How are you, Nathan?" Zachary extended his hand, which the other man took warmly. "Congratulations on snagging one of England's most elusive beauties."

"Thank you. I must admit it took some doing." Nathan smiled indulgently at his wife.

"Zachary, you must come to dinner! I'll send round a card,"

Allyson said as the lights blinked to urge audience members to return to their seats.

Sydney wondered if Zachary's comment about some people remaining the same had been meant for her. After all, she knew him to be a master of double entendre; she still recalled vividly his toast at her wedding. She tried to shrug it off as the others returned and the play resumed.

The Countess of Paxton gleaned as little from the second half of the play as she had the first.

As he returned to the Quintin box, Zachary was mentally kicking himself: You handled that like an infatuated schoolboy. Sydney. What was it with her? That cool, formal politeness seemed out of character for the woman who had once argued so engagingly for the rights of women. She seemed apprehensive. Afraid. Of *him*? Tuesday could not come too soon.

Between now and then, however, there were other matters dealing with Henry's will that begged looking into. To this end, the next afternoon he climbed the steps of an elegant townhouse in the Mayfair district.

"Major Quintin to see Lady Ryesdale," he announced as he handed his card to the footman answering the door. He waited in a marble-floored foyer cluttered with a few too many pieces of marble statuary.

Presently, an older man, obviously a butler, came to say, "Her ladyship will see you, sir. This way, please." He was shown into a drawing room that might have been elegantly comfortable except that it, too, boasted a plethora of marble sculptures staring sightlessly at visitors. There were two women in the room.

"Lady Ryesdale?"

The younger woman stood and offered him her gloved hand. Slender with deep blue eyes and dark auburn hair, she was fashionably dressed in a lavender day dress. It crossed Zachary's mind that Henry had had an eye for pretty women. But this one had something of a haunted look about her.

"Major Quintin. I had heard of your return. May I present my mother-in-law, the Dowager Baroness Ryesdale?"

Zachary bowed toward the black-clad dowager, who merely inclined her head in a haughty nod. "I am honored, my lady," he said.

"You have a particular message for me, sir?" Lady Ryesdale asked as she gestured to a chair for him.

He remained standing. "Not a message exactly, but a matter I should like to discuss with you. Might I have a word with you in private?" he asked in a tone that would have been quite effective in a military setting.

"But of course," Lady Ryesdale said in what Zachary thought might be false brightness. "Mother Ryesdale? Will you excuse us?"

"Well, I never—" the woman huffed as she rose and lifted both her chins. "I shall be just in the next room."

The dowager left the door ajar, but Lady Ryesdale closed it firmly. Perhaps not so intimidated after all, Zachary thought. Lady Ryesdale again gestured for him to be seated and she took a chair near his.

"I assume you have some business to do with Henry?" she said quietly. "He assured me that I might trust your judgment."

Zachary liked that she made no pretense of dissembling about possible reasons for his visit. "Yes. As you undoubtedly know, I am guardian of both Henry's sons." Lady Ryesdale was not the only one who could speak frankly, but, like her, he also spoke in a subdued tone. "I should like to know if you are satisfied with the arrangements made for your son."

"I—I have not seen William in over five months."

"Five months? Five months? *Why?*"

"When Henry was alive, it was easier." There were unshed tears in her eyes. "He would have William brought to an inn in Richmond and we would drive down to visit him for a few hours."

"But now?"

"The dowager and George, the elder of her two younger sons, have forbidden me to see him. Punishment, you see."

"Punishment for having that baby?" Zachary asked.

"For that—and for the fact that their precious Ralph had to leave England. It was my fault, of course, that he was half drunk and challenged Henry to a duel." Her tone was bitter and her voice became a bit wobbly. "George and his mother have decided that if I have anything at all to do with William, I will be forbidden any association with James—the Ryesdale heir, you know—and, at only six years, he is hardly more than a baby himself. Imagine forcing a mother to choose between her children."

"They can do this?" Zachary asked in wonder.

"George was named guardian when Ryesdale had to be put in the asylum."

"I know it is *legal*," Zachary said. "I just wonder that people can bring themselves to *do* it."

She shrugged. "I am no longer surprised at what people can do in the name of Christian morality."

"I am so sorry, my lady," he said. "I think Henry feared such a turn. To your knowledge, is William well cared for?"

"His physical needs are satisfied—but he needs to be loved, too. He needs to know I love him. That his father loved him." Her tears spilled over.

Zachary stood and, still keeping his voice modulated so it would not to be heard beyond that closed door, he said, "Lady Ryesdale, I make no promises at this point, but I shall try to bring William to London so that you have at least an occasional opportunity to see him."

"Truly? You would do that?" Hope shone through her tears as she, too, rose. She fished a handkerchief out of a pocket, and wiped her cheeks.

He held up a hand. "I shall try."

He had barely stepped into the foyer when he heard that other door snap open and the dowager's querulous voice demanding, "What did he want?"

"Something pertaining to a girl I knew at school. Apparently his brother has formed an unsuitable attachment."

Zachary smiled at the Lady Louisa's quickly fabricated lie.

The next day Zachary journeyed alone to a village in Surrey, where he located the vicar into whose care Henry's William David has been consigned. The man served a rather poor parish and made ends meet by boarding and tutoring young boys while his wife looked after four infants in addition to her own brood of five young children ranging in age from a few months to eight years.

Zachary found the situation as Lady Ryesdale had described it. He had intentionally arrived unannounced, but he discovered the child William to be clean, well fed, and adequately cared for. Recalling his own limited experience in caring for one child after leaving the Ramirez compound, Zachary could only marvel at the couple's handling such a large household, even with their two servants to help.

He introduced himself to the vicar, a Mr. Milton, who cordially welcomed him and readily called for his wife to produce the fifteen-month-old toddler, William. She arrived with the child on her hip, but struggling to be let down. Zachary could not help smiling at the brown-haired, blue-eyed baby who certainly did remind one of his father.

"He's a very active little boy," Mrs. Milton said with a laugh. She set him down and he promptly made for the coal bucket near the fireplace. "Oh, no. You do not want that, young William." She grabbed him up and, sitting on a straight-backed wooden chair, pulled the child onto her lap.

"I must admit," the vicar said, "that we have wondered about the lad's connections. We knew of his father's passing, of course, and we continued to receive compensation for his care, but—" His voice trailed off.

Zachary explained that he had been in the Peninsula, but that he was now able to see to his responsibilities as the child's guardian. "I hope it will not prove an inconvenience to you if I should remove him to London."

"We shall miss him, I'm sure," the vicar said, "but there are always children like young William here who need a home and who have relatives willing to pay for their care."

Rich people able and willing to farm out their by-blows away from society's offended eyes, Zachary thought. It occurred to him that that could have been Lucas's fate had Zachary not returned to Spain when he had. This thought was downright frightening.

Two days later he still had not come up with a solution to the problem of young William. The truth was he had not yet settled on what to do about his own child. For the time being he was well cared for in the elder Quintins' household. Zachary's mother had seen immediately to the hiring of a nursery maid for her grandson—once she recovered from the shock of his existence.

On returning to England, despite being eager to see his family, Zachary had, along with Gordon, McIntyre, O'Brien, and Lucas, spent a day and a night in an out-of-the-way coaching inn on the outskirts of London before showing up at his parents' house. After booking rooms for his travel companions and a bed-sitting room for himself and Lucas, Zachary had asked McIntyre and Gordon to go into the city to locate and return with Harrelson and Richardson. These two were duly informed of the plan to protect the name of the baby Lucas, and Zachary was gratified, but not surprised, that they readily fell in with the secret marriage story.

"We are just glad we can now talk about it freely," Richardson said with a wink. "I suppose the peer will be none too pleased when he hears his fair-haired boy defied an official army edict, but at this point, what can he do?"

Zachary sat on a couch with Lucas on his lap. "If we keep as close as possible to the truth, there should be no slip-ups. And I am sure that one day Lucas will be as grateful to you as I am, won't you, my son?"

The baby smiled and rattled off a few unintelligible syllables.

The men all grinned at him foolishly, then Richardson added, "I must say, Quintin, you could not deny this one even if you were so inclined."

Harrelson pulled a watch from a pocket. "You know, Adam, if we left within the hour, we could make it back to town in time to make it to a couple of clubs and begin to circulate this story—or at least hint at it."

"Just don't do it too brown," Zachary warned.

The next morning Zachary, O'Brien, and Lucas appeared on the doorstep of the Quintin townhouse. The footman who answered the knock had been with the family for many years. He looked with surprise from Zachary to the baby in his arms and babbled something to the effect that the elder Quintins were still at breakfast.

"We shall announce ourselves, Thomas," Zachary said to the footman. "You see to O'Brien here. And see that we are not disturbed in the breakfast room."

"Yes, sir."

Holding Lucas close, Zachary strolled into the breakfast room to the familiar scene of his father behind a newspaper and his mother, her back to the door, sorting through the morning mail.

Sensing the door opening, she said, "Thomas, did I not hear the door knocker? Who in the world would call at this hour?"

"I don't know, my lady. Who?" Zachary asked.

His mother whipped around, her eyes widening. "Zachary!" she gasped and half rose from her chair, then caught sight of the baby in his arms. She paled and put a hand to her breast. "Oh. Oh, my goodness gracious."

His father, responding to his wife's outburst, looked over the edge of his newspaper and abruptly set it aside. "Oh, I say. This is a surprise."

"Rather," his wife said faintly, but she quickly rose and addressed her son. "Good heavens. Why did you not write us?"

Zachary closed the door to the breakfast room. He leaned awkwardly to kiss his mother's cheek and gestured for her to sit again as he took a chair at the table with Lucas on his lap. "This is Lucas, your youngest grandson."

"I can see that," his mother said. "He is the very image of you as a baby. But why—? Who—? Where is his mother?"

Zachary's father frowned. "I say, son, this is most unusual."

"Yes, Father, it is. But you know from your years in India that a war is likely to produce some very unusual—even bizarre—circumstances."

Lucas began to squirm, so Zachary reached for a piece of bread and broke a bit to hand to the baby. Zachary was aware of his mother's watching this action with surprised interest.

"Mother. Father. I shall give you the truth, but I must have your solemn word that it does not go beyond this room. Not Mary, not Julia, nor the boys. Only you."

His parents exchanged a look, then spoke in unison. "All right, son."

As succinctly as he could, he explained the circumstances of his relationship with Elena. When he finished, his parents sat in silence for a few minutes, his mother with tears in her eyes. The only sound in the room was baby Lucas, prattling.

"Did you love her?" his mother asked softly. Zachary knew the question came from his parents' own history: The Lady Leanora had given up much to marry her heart's choice.

"I think so," he answered honestly. "She was fun, exciting, and we got on well together. I certainly returned to Spain for her. Elena and I *would* have married. I would have brought my wife and son home to England."

"Well, that is good enough for me," Horatio Quintin said. "I shall tolerate no untoward talk about my grandson."

"There is sure to be talk," the practical Lady Leanora said, "but I have no doubt we can quell it. Now—let me hold this baby."

Zachary breathed a sigh of relief as he handed over his son and listened to his parents reveling over how beautiful, how alert, how active, and how smart he was. He had never truly doubted their acceptance, but he had, nevertheless, been apprehensive.

Prior to his meeting with Sydney, Zachary thought it prudent to learn what he could about the Countess of Paxton. With this in mind, he called on Lord Nathan Thornton and his bride, the lovely Lady Allyson. Nathan, younger son of the Duke of Halstead, had distinguished himself in the last year by helping to uncover a French spy. Zachary thought that eventually he would dearly love to hear all of *that* story, but for now there was the more pressing issue of his guardianship of all things Paxton.

Lord Nathan and Lady Allyson received him in a family sitting room in Rutherford House, home of her parents. The couple occupied a settee covered in rich blue and silver brocade. Zachary sat in a dark blue upholstered chair nearby.

"We are still looking for a place of our own," Lady Allyson explained. "Papa and Mama are in the country at the moment, so we are rattling around here by ourselves."

"By ourselves—with a staff of twenty or so," her husband said.

"I have come on a specific mission, my lady," Zachary began.

"Oh, for heaven's sake, Zachary. Don't you dare carry on with that 'my lady' and 'my lord' business with *us*! It is *Allyson* and *Nathan*." She looked to her husband for confirmation.

He merely shrugged. "It's easier to let her have her way."

Allyson ignored him and said, "Your mission, Zachary?"

"I should like to know about your friend Lady Paxton."

"Sydney? Why? Are you interested?"

Nathan shook his head. "My wife is a typical woman. She thinks every eligible male needs to be leg-shackled."

"No, it is not like that at all—" Zachary started.

Allyson interrupted. "Oh, I *am* sorry, Zachary. I quite forgot that story Adam Richardson—Viscount Kirkly—was telling at Almack's last night. It is true then? A secret marriage?"

Zachary nodded. He hated lying to these two, but already too many people knew the real story. "About your friend—" he prompted.

"What would you like to know? And why?"

"You know her late husband was my cousin?"

"Yes, of course I knew that. So—"

"So I am trustee of the entire Paxton estate—and guardian of the very young current earl."

"Oh, my goodness. I did not know that." Allyson was quiet for a moment and Zachary wondered how much she was editing what she might tell him. She shrugged and looked at Zachary directly. "Well. Sydney is a very bright, very capable woman."

"Not unlike her friend here," Nathan said, patting his wife's hand.

"Yes, I know that," Zachary replied. "I knew her briefly in Bath before she and Henry were married."

"Then you must know she is a very generous and caring person who will not hesitate to help others."

"Allyson," her husband admonished, "stop beating about the bush. Tell him about you and Sydney and the Fairfax sisters." Nathan turned to Zachary. "My wife and Lady Paxton are the principal patrons of the Fairfax sisters and their charity work."

"We help out now and then," Allyson said.

Her husband snorted. "Now *there* is an understatement if I ever heard one."

"What sort of charity work?" Zachary asked.

"Helping abandoned women and children, mostly," Allyson said.

"Rescuing street urchins," Nathan added, and somewhat to his wife's embarrassment proceeded to relate the story of the boy Walter.

Zachary could not help smiling. "That sounds like the Sydney I knew in Bath." If the others noticed his use of Sydney's given name, they politely overlooked it. He hurried on. "Do the Fairfax women take in these women and children on a permanent basis, then?"

"Sometimes," Allyson answered. "Most often they attempt to find homes for the children or positions for the women. Older boys are often apprenticed to tradesmen."

"You approve your wife's involvement in such matters?" Zachary asked Nathan. He knew immediately he had said the wrong thing, for Allyson sat straighter and had a challenging glint in her eyes.

Nathan chuckled. "As I said earlier, it is much easier to let her have her own way."

" 'Let her'?" Allyson glared at her husband.

"Anyway, they do good work," Nathan said.

Zachary took his leave soon after that. So Sydney, the rescuing angel of Bath, had turned into the crusading Countess of Paxton. He wondered what sort of social censure might come with that role. Something to ask his mother.

CHAPTER 19

Sydney sat at the huge oak desk in the Paxton House library, going over the account books yet again as she waited for the arrival of Major Quintin. She was nervous. She knew the major could find little fault with the accounts of the vast Paxton enterprises, for most showed modest or comfortable margins of profit, but how closely might he look at individual entries?

A knock at the library door heralded his arrival. But instead of ushering in Major Quintin, Roberts, the butler, bore a tray with a letter.

"This just came by special messenger, my lady."

"Thank you, Mr. Roberts."

Her immediate thought was that Major Quintin was postponing their meeting. Drat the man! She had been in a fret ever since that brief meeting in the theatre and he would make her wait even longer?

The message was not from Major Quintin, but from Viscount Hoffman. Since Henry's funeral, she had seen Lord Hoffman perhaps three times as they happened to be at some crowded social gathering at the same time. She felt her brow wrinkle in wonder and quickly read the missive.

> *My dear Lady Paxton,*
> *I have just learned some news that may be of particular interest to you, given Henry's antipathy to Percival*

*Laughton. Last year we knew Percival Laughton to be on
the continent as part of the entourage of the Princess of
Wales. To be precise, he was said to be in Italy. As you
know, the princess has returned to England (much to her
husband's dismay), and apparently Mr. Laughton has as
well.*

*To my knowledge, he has not yet shown himself in Lon-
don, and I think I would have heard if he had. I am under
the impression that he is rusticating at his family seat in
Derbyshire for the nonce, trying to recoup his finances a
bit. However, Percival Laughton is unlikely to remove himself from London for long, especially in these days of high
celebration of Bonaparte's defeat.*

*Henry was quite concerned—and not without cause—
that this rather unsavory relative might try to take advantage of you and your son. If I may be of any assistance to
you, please feel free to call upon me.*

Yours, etc.

F. Taunton, Visc. Hoffman

As she read the letter again, her initial fear hardened into a knot in
her chest. Her first instinct was to rush upstairs to the nursery to
check on Jonathan. But that was silly. She had been with him only
half an hour ago and all was well. Besides, just after Henry's death,
she had hired three additional footmen whose primary duties were as
bodyguards. One or more of these stalwart fellows was on hand
whenever Jonathan was taken out of the house—even for a simple
airing in the small park at the center of the square in which Paxton
House was located.

As she tried to tamp down her fear, Roberts appeared to announce
the arrival of Major Quintin. She hastily tucked the Hoffman letter in
her pocket and assumed her hostess mask.

She was momentarily startled at Major Quintin's appearance, for
instead of the military uniform in which she had always seen him before, he was attired in civilian dress: doeskin pantaloons, a dark green
tailored jacket, and Hussar boots. It struck her that this man would be
incredibly attractive no matter what he wore. They exchanged polite
greetings and she instructed Roberts to produce a tea tray.

"Right away, my lady."

"How would you like to proceed, Major?" She gestured at the desk. "I have the ledgers all right here—they include everything but the household accounts at the Hall. These go back only three years, but others are in storage at the Hall and will be made available to you as you wish." She knew she was speaking too fast, babbling, in fact, trying to cover her nervousness, trying to appear wholly at ease. But she could feel that letter in her pocket and she worried about what he might see in the books.

He held up a hand. "I will look at them in due time. Right now, I should like to be introduced to the current Earl of Paxton, if he is available."

"I think he is probably making life rather difficult for Nurse Watkins. Half an hour ago, he was wearing nearly as much of his lunch as he actually ate." She tugged on the bell pull and murmured instructions to the footman who responded.

Ten minutes later a nursery maid arrived with Jonathan in her arms. Sydney immediately took him into her own. The child babbled and Sydney said, "Actually, once in a while nurse and I can understand a word here and there. He does know how to say 'Mama.'"

At this, the little boy said, "Mama" and the three adults in the room all laughed.

Zachary shook the child's small hand and said in a formal tone, "I am pleased to meet you, my lord." He turned to Sydney. "A fine lad. He looks just like—like Henry, but he has your eyes."

She beamed and, with a kiss, handed her son over to the maid. Returning to the subject of the ledgers, she waved a hand toward the desk. "You will find here reports from the farms—proceeds from crops, sale of wool, and so on. I will be happy to leave you alone to peruse them at your leisure."

"That is very thoughtful of you, my lady, but if I am not intruding on your time unduly, I should like to go over them *with* you. This whole business is outside my usual realm of expertise, so I am sure to have questions."

"In that case, Major, we can work over here at the map table—more room to spread them out." She felt herself slowly relaxing, though she was very much aware of his mere presence in the room.

When their hands chanced to touch as they gathered up the books, she was startled by that same thrill his mere touch had given her in Bath so long ago. She quickly jerked away and she could see her action puzzled him. Soon they were seated side by side at the map table.

She sought to lessen the tension that she, at least, felt between them. "I must admit, Major, that when I first learned that Henry had named you guardian of all things Paxton, it came as a surprise."

"It was not a position I sought. However," he paused and held her gaze forcefully, "I accepted it. I did not expect—Henry did not expect—that I would ever have to assume it. Now that it is upon me, I intend to fulfill this duty as I would any other."

Was he warning her? She shifted her gaze and murmured, "Of course, Major. I quite understand."

He leaned back in his chair and seemed relaxed. His voice held a trace of the teasing challenge she remembered from Bath and there was a distinct twinkle in his eyes. "I wonder, Lady Paxton—would it be dreadfully offensive to your sense of social decorum if we went back to being *Sydney* and *Zachary* in private discourse?"

She smiled. "I should like that."

Roberts brought the tea tray in and set it at one end of the table. Sydney got up to pour a cup for each of them, then resumed her seat and began to explain the books.

"This red volume provides a quick summary of everything. These gray ones are numbered and labeled: farms, mills, mines, other properties—all of which are doing reasonably well despite the general state of the economy."

"And this tan book?"

"Frankly, that one causes me some concern."

"Why?"

"As you may or may not know, Henry was keenly interested in transportation—I suppose because getting goods from mills and mines to ports and markets is always a problem."

"And?" Zachary prompted.

"And he invested rather heavily in a canal system and in two companies—that is, two men, George Stephenson and Richard Trevithick—who are producing locomotives that run on rails."

"What is your concern?"

"In three years we have seen no return on these ventures. None."
Zachary rubbed his chin. "Hmm. I think my father has money in
the Stephenson concern. He may know something about it. However,
rail transport—other than within mines—is new. Sometimes it takes
years for such innovations to catch on."

She nodded absently. Every time she shifted position in the chair,
she felt that letter in her pocket. She remembered Henry's saying
Zachary would protect Jonathan. But could he? Would he? Zachary
had parental duties of his own now.

They continued to study the books for over an hour. That is,
Zachary studied and Sydney answered his occasional question. She
was deeply conscious of their physical closeness—the familiar warmth
and scent she associated with him. But there was something else, as
well. Almost a meeting of minds—a sense of shared purpose. But
even as they worked, her mind kept drifting to that letter from Viscount Hoffman.

After a while, Zachary said, "The numbers are beginning to dance
around like butterflies in my head. If you will agree, I should like to
take these and spend some time truly examining them."

Apprehension assailed her, but what could she do? Legally, he
could do whatever he wanted. Asking her permission was a polite fic-
tion. She shrugged. "Of course. You may do as you please with them."

He frowned slightly, but said, "Thank you." He stacked the books
neatly, then reached for his teacup.

"Let me refill that," she said, going into her hostess role again.

"Please." He sat back, his arm draped over the back of his chair.
"There is another matter I should like to discuss with you."

"Oh?"

"I do not mean to plague you with what might be a painful subject, but this has to do with Henry's other son. As you know, I am
guardian of that child, too."

"Yes. I do know that." She did not elaborate. She did not want to
admit that, since that last night before Henry died, she had studiously
avoided thinking of that other side of her husband's life. She knew he
had provided for the child and that was that.

"I recently visited both Lady Ryesdale and the child. His name is
William."

Sydney wanted to say, "I do not want to know his name. He is nothing to me." But she did not say this; she merely nodded and waited for him to go on.

Which he did. He told her as much as he knew of Lady Ryesdale's position and the arrangements for care of the child.

Sydney listened quietly, then said, "How very sad, but the child seems to be getting adequate care. Frankly, I am wondering what this has to do with me and *my* son."

"Perhaps nothing," he said. "But I know of your involvement with the Fairfax women and I was wondering if you thought they might be willing to take in this child on at least a semi-permanent basis? That way, Lady Ryesdale might at least *see* her child occasionally."

"'Semi-permanent'? Is that not an oxymoron?" She grasped at the inane to allow herself time to consider what he had said. He "knew of her involvement with the Fairfax women"? What did that mean? Was he investigating her? Why? How? Ah, Allyson. She should have foreseen this.

He smiled fleetingly. "I suppose it is contradictory. But what do you think?"

Sydney sat silent, unconsciously toying with a strand of hair at her ear. What *did* she think? It was surely most unusual to ask a wife—a widow in this case—to be involved in such a situation, and Zachary's bringing it up to her merely confirmed for her that Zachary had known of and condoned Henry's betrayal. On the other hand, Louisa and William were being treated with unnecessary cruelty, or at least crass indifference. Finally, she said, "I will ask Miss Fairfax and her sister. Perhaps they can handle this matter for you."

He gave her a questioning look, but said only, "Thank you."

As he rose to take his leave, she rose as well. Again, she felt Hoffman's letter against her leg.

"Uh—there is another matter," she said, and sat back down.

"Another matter?" he echoed, resuming his own seat and turning to look at her directly.

Now that she was actually facing the issue head on, she could not keep the tremor out of her voice. "Did—did Henry tell you about his—your—cousin Percival Laughton?"

"Yes, he did. But I knew of him long before, of course. His father tried to embroil my mother in an attack on her brother, Henry's fa-

ther. That was a huge error on his part. My mother may have been estranged from her family, but she loved them. Percy has been known
to applaud his father's efforts and bemoan their failure."

"Read this." She thrust the letter at him and watched as he read it,
then reread it.

"Hoffman is right to worry. Percy is capable of almost anything. I
trust you have taken precautions?"

She explained and was gratified at his nod of approval. He patted
her hand and said, "Try not to worry. My friends and I will look into
his activities. Tell your people to be extra alert, though, what with the
chaos of this royal visit and all."

"Thank you," she said. "Just discussing it aloud helps, I think. I
did not want to worry Aunt Harriet." She was keenly aware of his
nearness, his touch, and she remembered the ease with which they
had once discussed any number of topics.

His gaze searched her eyes, then shifted to her lips. Was he remembering that kiss in the park, too? Suddenly her mouth felt dry.
Involuntarily, her tongue darted out to moisten her lips.

He rose abruptly and gathered up the ledgers. "I must go. I shall
return these day after tomorrow."

Outside, Zachary found his coach had returned and waited for
him as he had instructed. He climbed in, leaned his head against a
squab, and cursed himself. How was it that she always made him feel
like a green schoolboy? He had wanted to kiss her as they sat there
together. He had wanted desperately to kiss her, even though she had
made such a fool of him three years ago.

He shook his head and deliberately turned his thoughts to the substance of their meeting. Perhaps Henry and Phillips had been right
after all to put such trust in a woman. Sydney certainly *seemed* to
have mastered the nuances of Paxton business affairs. He knew of
few women who would have the expertise—let alone the interest—to
jump into this male arena. He was sure his mother would have relied
on the steward and the lawyer, but Sydney, Lady Paxton, had apparently initiated the purchase of steam-driven weaving machines. And
what were those changes in workers' living conditions she had mentioned? Mill workers and miners were but foot soldiers in a different
kind of army.

He sensed that Lady Paxton, for all her "do-good" charity work, had been wholly indifferent to the plight of Lady Ryesdale and the child William. He did not think her angry or resentful—just, well, disinterested. For some reason, he found her reaction disappointing. Well, why not? Was she not reacting as a wife was supposed to react? That is, pretend her husband's mistress simply did not exist? Yet, according to Harrelson, Sydney had herself received Lady Ryesdale in Paxton House as Henry lay dying.

He shook his head over this—and over his own near slip: He had very nearly said Jonathan looked exactly like William. Which he did—except for the eyes. Both boys had inherited their mothers' eyes; William's were a clear blue, Jonathan's gray-green.

The next morning, as he did every morning, Zachary reported to the nursery suite to spend time with his son. He found Lucas in the common room of the suite he remembered from his own childhood. Tall barred windows let in an abundance of daylight, yet prevented a child's falling from an open window. Pictures of animals adorned the walls and a number of cupboards held a large collection of toys. Lucas was happily holding court from the "throne" of his grandmother's lap.

"He is such a sweet, happy child," Lady Leonora said. "His mother must have been a sweet, biddable girl."

Zachary emitted a bark of laughter at this. The image that popped into his mind was Elena returning from Arroyo Robles where she, Miguel, and other partisans had so gleefully mowed down a company of French soldiers. But this was not an image to share with his mother, so he merely said, "She had a mind of her own."

"That much is obvious in her willingness to defy the conventions of her society," his mother said. "I would imagine that was very hard for a young, protected woman of her class in today's Spain."

"Yes, I think it was," Zachary said, but he wondered if Elena had not actually been freed by the life fate had thrown at her. "Seems my lot in life to deal with strong women." He reached for the baby, who was flailing chubby arms toward him.

Lady Leonora gave up the child with a kiss, then settled back in her chair, a wooden rocking chair with a padded seat and arms. Zachary took a barrel-shaped chair nearby and held the bouncing, standing baby on his lap.

"You speak of Lady Paxton?" his mother asked.

"Yes—*and* the Lady Leonora, who also defied conventions, I think."

"I am sure it was much easier for me than for either of these young women. I had your father to support me. Lady Paxton has no one."

"She has her aunt and her cousin and God knows how many servants," he replied.

"Zachary, dear, do try not to be so obtuse. Mrs. Carstairs and her daughter do lend propriety to the household, but they also add to Lady Paxton's responsibilities. And, besides her own child, she must be concerned for the welfare of her dead husband's sisters, as well as her own brother and sister. It cannot be easy."

Zachary frowned. "You seem to know a great deal about the Countess of Paxton."

"Of course I do. Her husband was my nephew—or had you forgot that little detail? I have not foisted myself on her, but I see her about town now and then. I do hear things."

"And?"

"And I am quite sure I would like her if I knew her better."

Later in the day Zachary met the lawyer Phillips. He began by apologizing for not visiting the solicitor earlier.

"No apology necessary," Phillips said, gesturing to a leather couch in his office where the two sat on either end. "I knew you were back in town and I intended shortly to contact you."

"About anything in particular?"

"Yes. Percival Laughton."

"You don't say! I came here today wondering if he had made any overtures to you. I have just learned he is back in England."

"I've had no dealings with him directly," Phillips replied. "However, I did have a letter from a solicitor named Wharton inquiring about the terms of your guardianship of the young earl and suggesting that his client, one Percival Laughton, had a stronger claim to the estate than a soldier who was not only absent for such an extended period of time, but whose relationship came from a female rather than a male connection."

"Do I need to be worried?"

"Legally, I would not think so. Henry Laughton made his wishes quite clear. The documents are in order."

Zachary raised an eyebrow. "But? I hear some hesitation in what you are saying."

"Wharton is not the most ethical member of my profession. He may file a nuisance suit, but that is all it will be. However, I have had my people do some poking around. Percival Laughton *is* associated with people around the Princess of Wales, but he has other connections that one would definitely label 'nefarious.' And there's more."

"More?"

"He was deeply in debt when he left England. Mostly gambling debts accrued in some rather disreputable gaming hells. Those people are not inclined to be patient, but lately he has put them off with expectations of a windfall."

"Which for him can come in only two possible ways," Zachary said.

Phillips leaned forward on his end of the couch and pressed his hands to his knees. He nodded. "Right. Either he becomes the child's guardian or the child dies. I would bet that if he managed the former, the latter would be a certainty. And Laughton is rather desperate at this point. I have not wanted to alarm Lady Paxton unduly, but I think the man poses a very real threat to her son."

"She is aware and has taken precautions. I will do what I can to put a spoke in his wheels." Zachary stood. "Thank you—I think."

Phillips gave a rueful nod and offered his hand.

Zachary's next task this day was to consult his erstwhile Rangers and enlist their aid in foiling any plans Percival Laughton might be fomenting. He sent around notes to Gordon, McIntyre, Richardson, and Harrelson. They met in one of the lounge rooms at White's, perhaps the most exclusive of London's gentlemen's clubs. The five of them occupied a grouping of comfortable leather chairs in a corner. Zachary called for a bottle of brandy and glasses, which a waiter soon set on a low table before them.

Greetings and small talk over, drinks in hand, they toasted each other and absent friends, then Richardson said, "All right, Quintin, what is on your mind? I have a distinct feeling that you did not just feel a sudden urge to have a drink with us."

"Nor did I," Zachary said, setting his glass down.

"Something regarding Lucas?" asked McIntyre. "Don't tell me someone is spreading tales. I'll call the blighter out."

"No, it is not Lucas who may be in danger, but another child—the Earl of Paxton," Zachary said. "As you know, he is my ward. What you may or may not know is that Percival Laughton is next in line to the title."

"Percy Laughton?" Gordon said in disbelief. "I knew him in school. Such a weasel. Aren't the laws of primogeniture just wonderful?"

"So what do you want from us?" Richardson asked.

"Right now, not too much. Perhaps more later, though, and I wanted to alert you to that possibility. Just keep your eyes and ears open—I want to know the instant he returns to town, then I'll hire a Bow Street Runner to track his every move."

"Sounds like a plan to me," McIntyre said. "What do you think, Gordo? Want to hang around the gaming hells a while?"

"Why not?" Gordon replied. "Debauchery in a good cause. Can't leave London until after Prinny's big show at Carleton House anyway."

Richardson refilled their glasses. "While you two are down in the stews, Harrelson and I will hobnob with the upper echelons of that lot he was with on the continent. See how badly dipped he might be."

McIntyre affected an abused expression and said in a loud aside to Gordon, "Why do they always get the plush assignments?"

"Hey. You volunteered," Harrelson said.

"Regardless of who does what," Zachary said, "I'm grateful."

"Life being what it is, any of us may one day need the kind of help we can give you now," Richardson said.

The others all nodded.

Zachary looked around the group, his gaze settling on Harrelson. "I would not have Lady Paxton any more worried than she already is—so if we could keep this just among us?"

They all readily agreed and conversation drifted to more mundane matters, then the others left for their evening appointments and Zachary returned home for one of his least favorite tasks: examining account books.

His parents had gone out, so he could not use them as an excuse to procrastinate. He looked in on Lucas and spent a happy half hour playing with him before settling into the library and those infernal books.

He was not surprised to find that the Paxton earldom was one of the richest concerns in the United Kingdom—he had seen that much in the cursory glance he'd had earlier. Neither was he surprised at the diversity of its enterprises—previous earls had been capable stewards of their holdings. But he kept running across what he thought to be anomalies. None was in itself a huge issue, but taken together, they amounted to a tidy sum of several thousand pounds.

Tomorrow he would ask his father to confirm or refute his findings.

CHAPTER 20

After her meeting with Zachary, Sydney felt a sudden urge to spend time with Jonathan. She was confident that her son was adequately protected. Bessie Watkins, the maid charged primarily with his care, had been a Paxton employee for more than twenty years, and she was very fond of the child. Watkins was diligent in having a footman accompany her and Jonathan whenever she took him to the park. Her bedchamber was next door to Jonathan's and the maid bragged that she was a light sleeper. As in most London homes that had nurseries, this one was located on an upper floor and had bars on the window. Although these were primarily to prevent a child's fall, they would surely deter an intruder as well. Still, she wanted to reassure herself, so she went to the nursery and entertained him with a picture book. She loved hearing him laugh and try to imitate her imitations of cows mooing and dogs barking as he slapped enthusiastically at the pictures.

With Geoffrey visiting a school friend in the country for a few weeks, evening meals were all-female affairs. Usually Sydney gave this fact of her life little attention. Tonight, however, she noticed—and realized she missed just hearing a male point of view on various topics. Neither the younger girls nor Aunt Harriet and Celia were much interested in the political news of the day, though they eagerly followed plans for the grand celebrations of the allies' triumph over

Napoleon. Sydney had even less patience than usual with the adolescent chatter and giggles of Marybeth, Amy, and Anne. Aunt Harriet and Celia readily joined in the conversation centering on fashions and the adventures of Childe Harald in a new poem by Byron that seemed to have touched nearly every female heart in London.

After dinner she spent an hour in the music room playing the pianoforte as the three young girls practiced the steps a dancing master had taught them earlier. And even later, in her own sitting room, she tried to focus her mind on the words of Mrs. Radcliffe's latest novel. Finally, she admitted that her sense of dissatisfaction and ennui stemmed from that visit with Zachary in the afternoon. Images of Zachary, nuances of expression, variations of tone in his voice and laugh, kept intruding. She welcomed the interruption as Aunt Harriet and Celia, who were off to a ball, came to bid her good night.

"Don't you two look extraordinarily pretty tonight?" Sydney asked. "Celia, I knew that green silk was going to make up beautifully. Lieutenant Harrelson will not be able to take his eyes off you! Aunt Harriet, you should wear that shade of rose more often."

"You don't think it is too showy for an aging widow?"

"I keep telling her she really is not in her dotage yet." Celia adjusted the lace at her mother's neckline. "I think Admiral Crowley's friend Captain Thompson will be there tonight."

Celia and Sydney exchanged knowing looks at seeing the older woman blush.

"Sydney, I do wish you were coming with us," Aunt Harriet said. "There is no rule against your attending a ball, you know."

"Actually, I wish now I *were* going, but I sent my regrets, so—" She shrugged. "You two have a good time."

When they had gone, she gave up and let her mind concentrate on matters that had been struggling for attention all evening: Lord Hoffman's letter and Zachary's visit. Zachary had told her not to worry about Percival Laughton, but such advice was impossible to follow. Still, just knowing Zachary had taken an interest in that situation calmed her apprehension considerably.

From there her mind drifted to what he had said of Lady Ryesdale. Up to now, Sydney had studiously avoided that topic. She had felt deep sympathy for her husband's mistress when Henry was dying. She even felt she had achieved an unusual degree of equanimity about that relationship, but with Henry gone, she had allowed herself to put the whole issue at the bottom of a storage barrel of things that mattered. She need never deal with that sense of betrayal again.

And now Zachary had brought it bubbling to the surface.

She could not help relating to Lady Ryesdale's—Louisa's—predicament. Sydney tried to imagine herself denied access to Jonathan. The very thought of such was almost physically painful. *There, but for the grace of God, go I.* That old saw leapt unbidden to pull her to a full stop. Louisa was at the mercy of the man who was guardian of her heir-to-a-title son. Lady Ryesdale's situation was not unlike her own! William's plight was some strange and horrifying variation of the Bible story of Solomon deciding the fate of a child. Where to find a Solomon when you needed one?

She sighed. Tomorrow she would consult the Fairfax sisters. She could do at least that much for that other mother.

Zachary's examination of the Paxton ledgers was raising as many questions as it answered. He had quickly learned to distinguish between entries in Henry's or the steward's handwriting and those in Sydney's. To his dismay, the entries he found most disturbing were in Sydney's script. Without disclosing what it was that caused his concern, Zachary asked his father to look at certain entries as well as the overall picture. Using a magnifying glass and shifting from ledger to ledger, the elder Quintin scrutinized the items Zachary pointed out to him.

"Interesting," he said. "Some rather creative manipulations here. But to what end? Do you suspect thievery?"

"No. I did think of that early on, but it simply makes no sense. It would be like stealing from oneself. And it is not as though Paxton as a whole is losing money."

"But you think there could be greater profit?"

"Possibly. Or, the discrepancies are accounted for in something I am not seeing."

Horatio Quintin put his magnifying glass down on his desk blotter and leaned back in his chair. "Have you thought of just asking her?"

"Now there's a novel idea," Zachary said. "But I wanted to be sure I was not jumping to an outrageous conclusion."

"I think your instincts are right, son. I must say, though, overall, Paxton concerns have been handled very well in the last several months."

"I thought that, too," Zachary said, but he could not put from his mind that something peculiar was going on here.

In this frame of mind, he returned the books to Paxton House. He thought Sydney seemed nervous as she received him in the library again.

"I hope you found all in order." She took the books from him and turned to lay them on the desk.

"Actually, I did not," he said.

"W-what?" She stopped in mid-motion.

"I have some questions." He pointed at a long couch before which there was a long low table of inlaid oak. "If you would be so kind as to indulge me?"

"But of course."

Now she really did sound nervous, but she brought the books to the table and sat on the couch. He sat beside her, keenly aware of her nearness. He caught the scent of her perfume—the same scent she had worn in Bath. He took from an inside jacket pocket a piece of paper with his notes.

"Here, here, and here," he said, leaning over the table to show her particular entries, "there should have been more profit given the prices and volumes noted."

"But they do show earnings," she argued, "and the figures are balanced in the end."

"Sort of."

"What do you mean 'sort of'?" she challenged.

"I mean," he said in what he hoped was a patient tone, "there are some rather vague expenditures here. What does 'housing' mean? Certainly not Paxton Hall in Windham, nor this house. And 'schooling'? For whom? That of Henry's sisters and your own siblings? If so, why is tuition at Geoffrey's school and salary for a governess listed elsewhere? 'Supplies'? For what? And under properties, we have this strange listing, *etc*. What is it, really? It is an outrageous sum."

"Not really." She sounded defensive. "I-I can explain."

"I hope so." He leaned back and folded his arms across his chest. "Begin, please, with those 'housing' and 'schooling' entries in the ledgers labeled for mills and mines."

She seemed to brace her shoulders. Her voice was low, but firm. "They are worthwhile expenditures."

"For what?"

She spoke rapidly, as though she thought if the words came fast enough he wouldn't pay attention to them. "Improved housing for workers and—and schooling for their children."

"Am I hearing you correctly? You are taking funds that rightly belong to my ward and giving them to mill workers and miners? Are they not being paid adequate wages at the customary rate?"

She thrust her chin higher and spoke more firmly. Her eyes sparkled with a mixture of defiance and determination. "They are paid at the same rate as most others in their kinds of jobs. But that does not mean they are in any way adequate."

"According to whom?"

Her voice became even more vehement. "According to any caring, right-thinking member of the human race. Housing is provided as part of their wages, but it should be adequate shelter. We found people living in basement flats with dirt floors that turned into rivers of mud during a rain storm!"

Zachary absorbed this, then asked, "Schooling?"

"For the children."

"Children of mill workers and miners?"

"Yes."

"Why?"

"Why not?" she challenged. "It is to our advantage to have an educated work force."

"And where did that bird-witted idea come from?" he demanded. "Since when did one need an education to dig coal or throw a shuttle on a loom?"

She appeared to be trying to control her annoyance as she pressed her lips together. Then she said in a rather tight voice, "Put that way, one might train animals—monkeys, say—to perform those tasks."

"Look," he said, turning to face her more directly, "I respect the English working class as much as the next person. God knows they are the very core of our army—and the navy too—but they do not require literacy to perform their tasks. Soldiers and sailors are not quoting Shakespeare and Chaucer as they load rifles or fire cannon."

The set expression on her face hardened even further. "People are not merely attachments to the machines they operate. They have souls too."

"True, but their souls are not their employers' concern."

She reached impulsively to lay her hand on his forearm. "Oh, but they are, Zachary. Don't you see? We cannot—we must not—treat people like draft animals." Her eyes implored his understanding. Then she seemed to check her enthusiasm; she removed her hand and averted her gaze.

He was moved by her plea and surprised at the sheer power of his sudden physical response to her touch. Here was the girl he had admired so in Bath. Fighting the impulse to pull her into his arms and kiss her senseless, he coughed and said, "Uh—did Henry share this rather unusual view?"

"N-not at first," she admitted.

"But you managed to persuade him, eh?"

"I admit that I initiated our contact with Mr. Robert Owen, but then Henry and I met with him and Mr. Owen showed us what he was doing in his Lanark mill. Both Henry and I liked what we saw."

"Owen? Owen. I know I have heard that name. Ah, yes. The social reformer. Associated with Jeremy Bentham, is he not? 'The greatest good for the greatest number'?"

"Yes, he is."

Zachary shook his head. "Those radical reformers are bent on destroying the social fabric of this nation. The French example was not enough for them. But that is beside the point." He pointed at the ledgers. "What I see here is but an extension of your attempts to rescue street urchins. I truly wonder why Henry would ever have agreed to such."

She clasped her hands tightly in her lap and he could see that she was trying to control her anger. But why? The Sydney he had known in Bath would have rung a peal over his head.

Finally, she said, "Henry agreed for two reasons. First, it was simply the right thing to do." She paused and her next words were quieter. "Henry liked to play. He loved his sports. But he took care of Paxton people."

"All right. That is an admirable practice for a lord of the realm. The second reason?"

"Money."

"Money?" He raised an eyebrow.

"Profit, if you will." She opened one of the books. "As I said the other day, these books go back only three years. This early entry from the first of those does show a decided loss, though not a great one. Then we improved housing and after that we offered the schools. We also refused to allow children under ten to work in our mills or mines at all. Those ten to fourteen could work for us, but for only six hours a day and only if they attended classes six hours a week."

"No wonder you lost money. I wager you lost workers, too, when the younger children of a family were not allowed to work."

"We did," she admitted. "Several families, actually. But it was not difficult to replace those workers. And people work harder when they see real hope for a better future for their children. Our latest figures here more than justify what you so casually labeled a 'bird-witted idea.'" She pushed the book over to him.

He almost smiled at seeing at last a spark of that earlier Sydney. He took a few minutes to study the particular entries she pointed out. She sat rigid and tense as he did so. Then he gave her a rueful look. "All right. I stand corrected—for now, at least. And so long as this trend continues, I shall withhold my objections."

She relaxed and breathed a sigh of relief, but quickly tensed up again when he said, "Now—about that mysterious acquisition of property."

Her gaze was frank and open, but she emitted a nervous laugh. "Oh, dear. I do hope you will not be too vexed or fly into the boughs."

Feeling mesmerized by those gray-green eyes in which he saw a strange combination of apprehension and amusement, he could not help smiling. "Come now. I demand nothing less than a full confession."

She began to speak rapidly. "Surely you can see that the Paxton earldom can afford a bit of charity work."

"This sum goes beyond 'a bit of charity work.' Far beyond."

"I know. But it is for *such* a good cause and it is only this one time, you see, that it is quite so high and it will not be necessary again. I promise."

"Sydney, stop. You are babbling, my dear. Just tell me what it is."

"It's a house. In Spitalfields."

"Spitalfields! Good Lord. Why would you buy property in that area?"

She took a deep breath and explained. "Penelope and Priscilla Fairfax needed a larger facility to serve more children and this was right next door and available and—"

He held up a hand. "And it needed renovation and then they needed extra staff and then—"

She gaped at him. "You knew about it?"

"No. I am guessing."

"You—you won't insist we give it up or sell it, will you? I shall happily take a reduction in my personal allowance, but, please, do not say Fairfax House must cut back or sell its addition. They do so need the space."

He hesitated. On the one hand, he found her nervous worry amusing and endearing; on the other, he was annoyed and even hurt by it. "You haven't a very high opinion of me, have you?"

"I-I don't know what you mean." She averted her gaze.

He waited, silent, until she brought her gaze to meet his again. "Why else would you seek to play games with these accounts? Hiding expenditures about which you knew very well I, as your son's guardian and trustee of Paxton's interests, should have been consulted."

"You were not here," she protested.

"You made no attempt to keep me informed," he countered. "Even now that I *am* available, you have sought to somehow hoodwink me."

Again she averted her gaze. "I apologize. I—uh—it will not happen again."

"No, it won't," he said. She looked up, apprehension clear in her eyes again. He kept his voice level and firm. "I will not countermand any decisions you have made thus far, but in future, I expect you to abide by the spirit of Henry's directives. You may not like me—you may not trust me—but you must consult me."

"Yes, sir." She sounded resentful.

The tension was palpable. Gone was the friendly ease with which they had dealt the day before. He stood. He wanted to say something—anything—that would restore what they had once had, but then he reminded himself that that interlude in Bath had been a charade, a merry fling before her marriage.

"I shall take my leave, Lady Paxton. I trust we understand each other well enough now."

She started to rise. "Yes, I think we do. Oh, wait." She sank back down. "I must tell you—"

"What?"

"I—uh—spoke with the Misses Fairfax regarding Lady Ryesdale's son. William."

He resumed his seat. "Will they take him?"

"Well, yes, they *would*, but—"

"But what?" he interrupted. "Surely they are not squeamish about the circumstances of his birth. Not in that part of town."

"No, they are not."

"Then what is it?"

She held his gaze steadily now. "I think another arrangement can be made if Lady Ryesdale is amenable."

"And what might that be?" He was unable to hide his skepticism.

Now her words came out in a rush. "William should come here. He is Henry's son. Jonathan is his brother. They should grow up together. If Lady Ryesdale agrees, that is."

Zachary was flabbergasted. Two days ago she had seemed scarcely willing to acknowledge the other child's existence. "Are you out of your mind?" he blurted.

"Major Quintin!" Her eyes flashed anger. "That is the second time in a matter of only a few minutes that you have questioned my intelligence or my state of mind."

"I do apologize. But what you are suggesting is bizarre. Good grief! Have you given any thought at all to the talk there would be?"

She waved a hand dismissively. "No doubt it will cause a stir for a few days. However, society tolerated for years that *ménage à trois* in the Duke of Devonshire's household—his wife, his mistress, his legitimate and his illegitimate children all together at Chatsworth in happy bliss—or so we are led to believe. The *ton* will surely overlook my seeing to the care of one small boy."

His voice softened. "Have you considered all the likely consequences? What it might mean for your own family?"

"I am sure Aunt Harriet will agree with me. Celia will treat it as what it is—a nine days' wonder. Geoffrey won't care. The girls are still several years away from coming out—this will be old news by then. Jonathan will gain a playmate. I think one day he will applaud his mama's decision."

"It is an extremely generous proposal," he said, still trying to think it through.

"It needs only Lady Ryesdale's approval," Sydney said.

"You would receive her here?"

"Of course. Where else would she see her son?" She laughed. "I am not the Duchess of Devonshire. Louisa—Lady Ryesdale—will not be *living* here, merely visiting regularly. Surely that cold termagant who is her mother-in-law can have little objection to Louisa's paying morning calls on a fellow member of the *ton*. Can you at least present the idea to Lady Ryesdale?"

He nodded.

Sydney went on. "Should she object, William will be welcome at Fairfax House, but, honestly, Zachary, he would be better off here."

Her use of his given name told him that they might be in the beginning stages of restoring the ease they had once enjoyed in each other's company.

CHAPTER 21

Sydney paced in the formal drawing room as Aunt Harriet and Celia sat more or less calmly doing some needlework.

"Are you having second thoughts, my dear?" Aunt Harriet asked.

"Yes. I mean no. Not really. I am doing the right thing. I know that." Sydney glanced at the clock on the mantel. "I am just anxious about this first meeting and they are late."

Three days ago she had received a letter from Zachary saying that Lady Ryesdale had readily accepted Sydney's plan for William. In fact, he wrote, she had been exceedingly grateful and he enclosed a note from her that expressed just that sentiment. Now, Zachary was to have gone into Surrey to bring the child here. It had all happened much more quickly than Sydney had anticipated.

"They are not so very late. You know how undependable coach travel can be. Come. Sit. Pick up your book and read us another of Mr. Wordsworth's poems. Perhaps a shorter one this time." Aunt Harriet spoke as she might have to a ten-year-old and Sydney reacted dutifully and began leafing through the book.

Celia set aside her embroidery and said, "I should wonder if you were *not* having second thoughts. This is truly an extraordinary undertaking."

Sydney lifted her head. "You disapprove?"

"I did not mean to suggest that," Celia replied. "No. I quite admire you for doing this. I am not at all sure I could have behaved with such generosity in similar circumstances."

Sydney, feeling a little sad and envious of her cousin, said, "Oh, Celia, you need never think of such. *Yours* will be a love match. Your Trevor is besotted with you."

Celia blushed and said, "He has not asked me yet, you know."

"He will."

Sydney started to elaborate on this when Roberts entered to announce, "Lady Ryesdale, Major Quintin, Mr. and Mrs. Milton, and Master William."

Sydney stood to greet them. Zachary again wore civilian dress, but looked as disturbingly attractive as ever. He gave her an encouraging little smile that threatened to turn her knees to jelly. Lady Ryesdale, in a gold colored day dress, was the same beautiful woman who had knelt at Henry's bedside. The Miltons were in their thirties perhaps and were dressed conservatively, she in a gray dress with white lace at the collar and cuffs, he in a black coat and trousers. Mrs. Milton carried the child, who wore a blue coat with a matching wide-brimmed hat.

Zachary introduced the Miltons as the vicar and his wife who had cared for William since his birth. When all were seated in a grouping of two couches and several chairs, a momentary silence ensued, broken only by William's unintelligible chatter as he indicated he wanted down.

"No, Willy. Not yet," Mrs. Milton murmured to him, untying and removing his hat.

It was at this point that Sydney had a good look at the child—and nearly fainted. Except for those blue eyes, which he had clearly inherited from his mother, William looked exactly like Jonathan. Henry had passed on to both his sons his brown hair, the shape of his head, the arch of his brows, even the curvature of his lips. Sydney sat speechless. She glanced at Zachary; he gave her a slight nod of understanding. She thought he might have been waiting for her to make this discovery. She tried to think of something to say, but her mind was blank.

Lady Ryesdale, with tears in her eyes, leaned forward to look around Mrs. Milton and William, with whom she shared one of the couches. "I do not know how even to begin to thank you, Lady Paxton, for what you are doing. Please believe me when I tell you I do know what is at stake for you in all this."

"It is not so very much," Sydney said. "Perhaps I was remiss in not taking action sooner. Major Quintin deserves credit for bringing the matter to my attention." Looking at Zachary, she thought he looked slightly embarrassed.

"He was marvelous!" Lady Ryesdale said. "Just as Henry once said he would be. Why, he even thought to bring Mr. and Mrs. Milton along to ease the transition for William." She grasped the baby's outstretched hand.

Recalling that Zachary's letter had said he would go to Surrey, retrieve the child, and pick up Lady Ryesdale on the way to Paxton House, Sydney surmised that Lady Ryesdale had not yet held her son, and Sydney's heart ached for her. Sydney sucked in her breath as Lady Ryesdale held her arms out to William. She released her breath and noted a similar reaction from Mrs. Milton as the child hesitated but then allowed himself to be held by a virtual stranger. Again, Sydney noted tears in Lady Ryesdale's eyes.

Sydney said, "Aunt Harriet, if you will ring for some refreshments, I will show Lady Ryesdale and William to our nursery. Mrs. Milton, you are most welcome to accompany us."

"Thank you, Lady Paxton, but I think I will bid Willy good-bye here." She leaned close and kissed his cheek. "It is always so hard to say good-bye to them, isn't it, dear?" She addressed her husband in a tear-filled voice.

He reached from his chair near her and patted her shoulder. "That it is, my love. But our Willy's replacement is due in Surrey very soon, you know."

She nodded and wiped her eyes with a handkerchief.

Sydney led the way upstairs and Lady Ryesdale, hugging her son, followed closely. The baby looked alert and aware of his surroundings, but strangely issued no cry of protest at leaving the Miltons behind. She showed them the bedchamber first.

"There was another crib in the lumber room and this room is quite large enough to accommodate both comfortably."

"I like that William will not be alone at night," Lady Ryesdale said, patting her son on the back. "I think he is accustomed to having other children around."

Sydney waved a hand at a connecting door. "The nursery maid's room is right through there."

When they reached the playroom of the nursery suite, Sydney introduced Lady Ryesdale to Bessie Watkins. "Miss Watkins has agreed to see to the care of both boys," Sydney added.

Bessie Watkins had red hair with a few strands of gray, a profusion of freckles, and friendly brown eyes. She curtsied to Lady Ryesdale and said, "It's like I told Lady Paxton—two ain't much more work than one. Now three? That would be another story altogether. Just let me look at this fine young fellow." Up to now William's back had been to the nurse. On seeing him full on, she gasped. "Oh, good heavens! Oh, my goodness!"

"What? Is something wrong?" Lady Ryesdale asked.

Sydney smiled. "No. Watkins is just surprised. And here's why." She plucked her own son from a fenced-off area of the room that had a thick padding on the floor and was strewn with colorful toys. "Lady Ryesdale, Master William, allow me to present Jonathan, ninth Earl of Paxton."

Lady Ryesdale's gasp was an echo of the maid's. "Oh, my. They-they are so very alike. They might be twins!"

"Except for Jonathan's tattoo and the difference in eye color," Sydney noted as she sat on a couch and motioned for the other mother to join her. They sat half turned toward each other, with the little boys facing each other, flailing their arms, kicking their feet, and "talking" in their own respective languages. Nurse Watkins quietly slipped out of the room.

"Did you know?" Lady Ryesdale asked.

"Not until William entered the drawing room below several minutes ago. Major Quintin had seen both children, but he did not tell me they were mirror images of each other. Of course Henry knew, but he failed to inform me of that fact. To be perfectly honest, Henry rarely talked of you and William to me."

"That does not surprise me, Lady Paxton, as he rarely spoke of *you* to me."

They smiled ruefully at each other, then Lady Ryesdale said, "I fear we are likely to be the subject of *on dits* at every *ton* gathering in the next few weeks."

Sydney nodded. "At least until some duchess runs off with her coachman or Lady Caroline Lamb does something even more outrageous than before in her pursuit of Lord Byron."

Lady Ryesdale smiled. "Shall we pray for a scandal, then? What think you, my darling William?" She nuzzled her child and he giggled, setting off answering delight in Jonathan.

"In any event," Sydney said, "I think if we ignore the gossip and carry on as though our relationship is quite natural, the harpies will find other prey."

Lady Ryesdale nodded. "A good idea." She glanced at a large clock on the wall that would eventually serve yet again to teach Paxton children how to tell time. "Oh, dear. The time. I must get back. The dowager does not know where I am."

Nurse Watkins returned and Sydney and Lady Ryesdale put their sons into the play area, Lady Ryesdale doing so with a lingering caress of her son's hair. Both boys seemed to find the idea of a playmate intriguing.

"So far, so good," Sydney said. "However, I'm sure they will have their share of tears and quarrels."

"Undoubtedly."

As they left the nursery, Lady Ryesdale stopped in the hall to say, "Lady Paxton, I must tell you again how very grateful I am to you."

"Really, there is no need," Sydney said. "And since our sons are brothers and we will likely see a great deal of each other in the coming years, might we be *Sydney* and *Louisa*?"

"I should like that. I feel we might have been friends under different circumstances."

"We still can be." Sydney reached to squeeze Louisa's hand briefly.

When Zachary had returned Lady Ryesdale to that mausoleum that was the Baron Ryesdale's London home, and then seen the Miltons established in a coaching inn, he returned home quite pleased with himself and this day's work.

He went immediately to the nursery, where he was not surprised to find his mother on a couch entertaining Lucas. On seeing his father, Lucas emitted a squeal of delight and reached toward him. Zachary swept him into his arms and made silly noises against the baby's neck. This, of course, brought forth further squeals of delight.

Lucas loved it when his father helped him "fly like a bird"—that is, when Zachary, holding him in a horizontal position, would swing him around.

"Enough, Lucas," Zachary said with a laugh. As he sat next to his mother, he changed Lucas to the "horsey" game in which Lucas "galloped" on his father's outstretched leg as Zachary held him by the hands.

"How did it go?" his mother asked. Zachary had told his parents earlier of Sydney's plan to take in William.

"Very well, I think. Lady Ryesdale and Lady Paxton got on better than one might have expected and they reported that William settled in quickly."

"Well, they have to get along, don't they?" his mother said. "They are in this now for a long, long time—twenty years and more until those boys are grown."

"Hmm." Zachary shifted Lucas to his lap, where the baby quieted after a bit and actually fell asleep as Zachary and his mother continued to talk.

His mother went on, "I wonder if Lady Paxton really thought this through?"

"I thought you approved of her taking in this child."

"I do—though it is not my place to approve or disapprove. Nor anyone else's, but you know that will not stop the tabbies from having their say."

"Sydney realizes that."

"'Sydney'?" His mother raised an eyebrow.

He gave himself a mental shake for that slip. "I—uh—knew her in Bath before she married Henry."

"I see."

Zachary feared the ever-so-astute Lady Leonora saw far more than her son wanted her to. Her next words confirmed this.

"Did you know then that she was to marry Henry?"

He sighed. *In for a penny, in for a pound*, he thought. "Not until I saw her walk down the aisle. But she knew," he added bitterly. "It must have been a great joke to her."

"Oh, Zachary. I am so sorry. I knew you were terribly unhappy when you were here before your return to the Peninsula. I suspected some girl was the cause."

"It showed that much?"

"Only to your mother." She sat in thought for several moments, then said, "Tell me about that sojourn in Bath, if you will."

So he did. And in the process, he found himself finally letting go of some of his bitterness. When he was finished, his mother was again quiet for a while.

She shook her head. "I am trying to understand this. Henry told you he had arranged a marriage to a woman named 'Bella' who turned out to be your 'Sydney.' Do I have that right?"

He nodded glumly.

Just then the nursery maid came in. "It's time for Master Lucas's nap," she announced, then abruptly lowered her voice. "Oh, I see he is already having it. Would you like me to take him, sir?"

"Please." Zachary handed Lucas over and the maid left with him. Zachary leaned back on the couch.

"Are you still in love with her?" his mother now asked quietly.

"In love with her? I-I don't know. How could I have been in love with Sydney when I went back to Spain to marry Elena? My behavior was no better than Henry's, was it?" It occurred to him that here was the crux of his uncertainties about himself. For over three years he had held Henry in contempt even as he envied the man his wife, yet had his treatment of women been any better? Henry had married one woman while he had been in love with another. Had Zachary been about to do the same thing?

His mother interrupted his musing by grabbing his arm and saying vehemently, "Don't you dare make that comparison. Henry betrayed sacred vows. I have no doubt *my son* would have abided by his. Sydney was lost to you. Life does go on. You are human, Zachary. You met Elena when you were extremely vulnerable. I think she might have been too. You needed each other. From all that you've told us of Elena, she was a wonderful young woman. I think I would have welcomed her as a daughter just as I love the grandson she gave me."

"I am sure you would have—if I could have persuaded her to give up the fight for Spain, that is."

"Back to Lady Paxton." She spoke slowly. "I am inclined to think there is some sort of misunderstanding here. She does not strike me as the sort who would enter into a malicious joke that would bring another pain."

He reached to hug her. "Ah, Mother, some things never change. You are an incurable optimist."

"And what is wrong with that?" She rose. "Come. Your father should be home by now. He was helping plan the Lord Mayor's reception for the royal visitors." They were halfway down the stairs when she said, "Did you check the mail? There was a letter for you." The letter was from Adam Richardson—Viscount Kirkly now that they were back in England.

> *Zachary,*
> *Laughton has returned to London. He has taken rooms in a lodging house on the edges of an almost respectable section of the city. He was seen gaming at Watier's last night. I understand he was losing heavily.*
> *A.*

Richardson had supplied the address and a full description of Percival Laughton. Zachary immediately fired off a note with this information to the Bow Street Runners whose services he had hired previously. He was determined to leave no stone unturned in his efforts to protect Sydney's son. He did not stop to consider that he was acting on behalf of "Sydney's son" rather than his ward, the young earl.

Despite still being in half-mourning, Sydney decided to accept an invitation to an *al fresco* "breakfast" hosted by the Marquess and Marchioness of Rodham to celebrate the defeat of Napoleon and the safe homecoming of their son, Viscount Kirkly. The marchioness, once a reigning beauty in society, had, in her fifties, become a reigning hostess in *ton* circles. Invitations to Lady Rodham's entertainments were much sought after and this event at the Rodham estate in Richmond promised to be a huge affair.

Sydney dressed with special care, refusing to admit to herself that she anticipated seeing Zachary there. Her fashionable gown was a simple style in linen of a subdued jade green with ecru lace at a square neckline and elbow-length sleeves. Her hair was arranged in the popular Greek style with ribbons of ecru lace wound through it. She knew she would appear to good advantage.

And it was important that she do so, for this would be her first public appearance since taking William into Paxton House. Lady Ryesdale would also be among the guests. The two of them were sure to draw a good deal of attention. They had agreed they would present a united front to the gossips: friendly, cordial, dignified.

Sydney, Aunt Harriet, and Celia arrived at the party escorted by Lieutenant Lord Trevor Harrelson, looking resplendent in his army uniform, for uniforms were *de rigueur* for military men in these continuing days of national celebration. Besides a generous sprinkling of various military uniforms, Sydney noted other men and women in colorful array.

"Good heavens! Just look at all these people. I had no idea there would be so many," Celia said as they waited in line to greet their hosts. In a colorful cotton print of yellow and white with dashes of green, Celia looked very fetching on the arm of Lieutenant Harrelson.

"I think Adam said his mother had invited over five hundred," Harrelson said. "She does this every summer, but this year is special."

"She has certainly provided wonderful venues of entertainment for so many," Aunt Harriet commented.

And, indeed, the hostess has done so. There were four huge canvas pavilions situated about the grounds, each with tables and chairs and a buffet attended by several servants to see that no guest went hungry or thirsty. Other groupings of benches and chairs were scattered about in shady areas of the lawn. Two courses of paired sticks were laid out for guests who wished to play pall mall, an outdoor version of billiards played with colorful balls and mallets. And there were boats tied up at the river's edge. Sydney noted that several couples had already availed themselves of the boats, the ladies' bright parasols adding dots of color to the river scene. Off to the side of the party area, archery targets had been set up where young women might show off more than their archery skills.

Telling herself she and Louisa had chosen well for their first appearance at the same outing, and knowing that Jonathan was well protected at home, Sydney gave herself up to the not unpleasant task of having a good time. She was acquainted with the marquess and his wife, but had not met their son previously. Introduced to the Viscount Kirkly now, she thought he looked at her rather keenly as they engaged in the usual meaningless talk of a receiving line.

As soon as they were through the receiving line, Captain Thompson approached to claim Aunt Harriet for a stroll about the gardens. Sydney, Celia, and Lieutenant Harrelson also chose to stroll about, pausing frequently to chat with this or that friend or acquaintance.

Sydney kept looking about the crowd—discreetly, of course—hoping to see Zachary. Finally, she spotted him some twenty or thirty feet away. He was with two other soldiers, his parents, and another older couple and a young woman. Sydney recognized these three as one of the most garrulous members of Parliament, his gossipy wife, and his equally gossipy daughter. Just then Zachary's gaze caught hers and he smiled a greeting even as the young woman demanded his attention.

Sydney turned on hearing someone call her name. With little pleasure she recognized the speaker.

"Lady Paxton and Miss Carstairs. How lovely to see you here. I do so enjoy talking with old school friends." The Viscountess Ellsworth, the former Faith Holmsley, was accompanied by her husband, as well as Sir Thomas and Lady Fullerton, the former Elizabeth Kenmore. The two couples were with another gentleman whom Sydney did not recognize. She judged him to be in his late thirties; he was of medium height with thinning blond hair, very pale eyebrows and lashes, and ice-blue eyes. Unwilling to be rude to old classmates, even ones she liked as little as these, Sydney murmured greetings and would have moved on.

The viscountess pulled the blond man forward and said, "Lady Paxton, do allow me to present a dear friend. Actually, he is a connection of yours. Mr. Percival Laughton."

Celia gasped.

Lieutenant Harrelson said, "Oh, I say—"

Sydney was furious. She had no doubt at all that Lady Ellsworth knew exactly what she was doing, for there was a malicious gleam in her eyes and a sly smile on her lips. Sydney felt trapped. She could hardly create a scene by giving the man the cut direct.

He bowed. "Pleased, I am sure." He looked amused and self-satisfied at catching her off guard.

She was aware of several listeners nearby. Keeping her tone neutral and her voice low, she said, "How extraordinary that you should seek my acquaintance in this manner."

He laughed outright and said in a voice clearly intended for the bystanders, "Ah, but my dear Lady Paxton—my cousin, as it were—I have no doubt that if I called at Paxton House, you would send me away with a flea in my ear."

"Very probably," she said in the same controlled voice.

The amusement was gone from his eyes, leaving only ice. "Nevertheless, we have family business to discuss."

Before she could formulate a response, Sydney was suddenly aware of movement at her side. "Is this boorish fellow bothering you, Lady Paxton?" Zachary asked.

"Not anymore," she said, turning away. She placed a trembling hand on the arm Zachary offered.

"You needn't think I'll be put off so easily," Laughton said, still blustering.

Zachary, too, spoke in a low voice, but one laced with authority. "Any interest you have in Paxton affairs will be handled through me. Should you persist in annoying her ladyship, you will find the consequences most uncomfortable."

Laughton sneered. "Zany Zack to the rescue, eh? Oh, yes, your antics in Spain have not gone unnoticed. But your army bravado is meaningless here in England, cousin." He put a nasty twist on the last word, and Sydney thought he was playing to his Ellsworth-Fullerton audience.

"You wish," Harrelson said.

Zachary gave his friend a warning look and jerked his head indicating they should leave. He patted Sydney's hand on his arm. "Pay Laughton no mind, Sydney. His type are usually more bark than bite."

Behind her she heard Faith, Lady Ellsworth, say, "How very rude. We were taught better manners in school, weren't we, Liz?"

The sycophantic Elizabeth responded from her customary script. "Oh, my, yes."

These two Sydney could easily ignore. Despite Zachary's assurance, it was much harder to dismiss Percival Laughton's parting shot.

"This is by no means over, cousins."

CHAPTER 22

Mrs. Carstairs and Captain Thompson rejoined the group as Zachary steered Sydney to where his parents, Gordon, and McIntyre still stood. To his immense relief, the talkative parliamentarian and his encroaching wife and daughter had moved on.

Introductions and greeting accomplished as necessary, they all gravitated toward one of the pavilions where, sufficiently supplied with food and drink, they commandeered a large table seating twelve. As they sat down, Celia, responding to her mother's question, explained the incident to those who had either not seen it at all or had seen, but not heard what was happening.

Zachary was not sure who maneuvered the situation—he suspected his mother—but he was not at all displeased to find Sydney seated between him and his mother. Her physical closeness reignited the desire he had felt returning so forcefully that day in her library. Despite still unresolved issues between them, he wanted to reestablish the rapport of those days in Bath,

During a pause in general conversation, Gordon grinned at Zachary from across the table and asked, "So, Quintin, did you dispatch that devious devil back to his natural habitat?"

Zachary saw that Sydney was surprised at the ease and familiarity with which an ensign addressed a major. "Not quite," he answered, "though I think Harrelson was ready to take him on."

"I could have handled him had you not interfered," Harrelson said in a tone of mock hurt.

"With your usual grace and finesse, I'm sure," McIntyre said. "We remember that brawl in a Madrid tavern."

Harrelson looked embarrassed and Celia affected a shocked tone. "A brawl? Oh, never say you engaged in something so uncouth as a brawl."

Setting a plate of food and a glass of wine at an empty place, Adam Richardson joined the group. "A brawl? Not at my mother's party. She would be most vexed."

"Not here," McIntyre said. "That one Harrelson started in Madrid."

"Oh, that one."

"Couldn't let that Spanish captain get away with disparaging English horsemanship," Harrelson said.

"Well, he got his comeuppance the next day." Gordon proceeded to explain to the non-Rangers at the table. "A race. Harrelson's black easily outran the Spaniard's chestnut."

"My hero," Celia teased.

"No, Miss Carstairs. I fear you miss the point," Gordon said. "The *horse* won the race."

They all laughed and Harrelson said, "But with my superior expertise guiding him."

His friends snorted.

"Of course it was," Celia said soothingly and patted his hand.

Richardson's voice became serious. "I saw that little tableau a while ago. Didn't want to interfere and create a scene unnecessarily, but if you'd like me to have Laughton removed, it could be handled discreetly."

Zachary looked at Sydney to see her reaction to this idea. She did not immediately respond, but finally she said, "I think that would make matters worse. No matter how discreetly it was done, Mr. Laughton would have it all over town that Zachary and I had him thrown out."

Zachary was sure her use of his given name had been a nervous slip, but the idea that that was how she unconsciously thought of him gave him hope. Sydney was looking down, so did not see the momentary lift of several eyebrows around the table.

"As you please, my lady." Richardson nodded and exchanged a knowing look with Zachary.

Celia changed the subject. She directed her question to Harrelson, but in a normal tone that included everyone. "What did Mr. Laughton mean by that reference to 'Zany Zack'?"

"What?" Lady Leonora demanded. "Please explain, Miss Carstairs."

Celia repeated what Laughton had said.

"'Zany Zack,' indeed," his mother said. "What does it mean, son?"

Zachary, somewhat embarrassed, looked about to see his closest friends all grinning at him. "It is nothing. Just a soldier's joke."

All four women at the table looked intensely curious and even his father lifted one eyebrow. "There must be more to it than that," his mother said flatly. "Zachary? Trevor? Adam? You two ate enough of my ginger biscuits when you were boys. If you don't tell me the truth, I shall refuse to share the recipe with your future wives or cooks. Someone enlighten me!"

Richardson laughed and said, "That is enough of a threat for me, my lady. When the then Lieutenant Quintin first returned to the Peninsula, he was involved in—uh—several rather perilous incidents."

"We managed to read between the lines of the newspaper accounts," Horatio Quintin said, leaning back in his chair.

"Some jokester came up with 'Zany Zack,'" Gordon said.

Richardson went on. "Then when the peer—Lord Wellington—made him an exploring officer and he had his own team, we became 'Zany Zack's Rangers.' Started out as a joke, you see, but not anymore."

Celia's brow wrinkled. "Exploring? For what were you searching?"

The five Rangers laughed at the naiveté of this question and Harrelson explained. "We were mostly counting French soldiers. Also, finding routes through the mountains for our troops. Adam here is an excellent map-maker."

"It must have been very dangerous," Celia said.

No one seemed inclined to respond to this, but finally McIntyre did so with a shrug. "War is always dangerous."

"But you all survived and we rejoice at that," Celia said brightly, apparently willing to let this thread of conversation go.

"Um. Not all. The Rangers lost two good men at Toulouse," Gordon said. Zachary knew Gordon was still very bitter about that needless battle and its carnage.

"I am so sorry," Celia said, and others nodded or murmured their agreement with her sentiment.

Zachary was grateful when his mother changed the subject and lightened the mood by saying, "I must say, Adam, your mother has outdone herself this year."

As the day wore on, Sydney found she was doing precisely what she set out to do: have a good time. Partly because Celia and Trevor Harrelson were inseparable and Trevor was enjoying being with his army chums, and partly because Sydney herself felt so very much at ease with the Rangers' group, she spent most of the day in their company. After the meal in the pavilion, the group broke into smaller entities. Celia and Trevor seized the chance to be alone together, though in plain sight, by taking one of the boats on the river.

Sydney had been strolling about with Zachary and his parents when Horatio Quintin spotted an acquaintance. "Zachary, there's Lord Foxworth. You were asking about rail transport. He would be just the person to consult." He looked at his wife. "Do you mind, my dear?"

"No," Lady Leonora responded, "so long as I do not have to listen to another long dissertation on the intricate working of a steam engine and how such machines are going to make horses obsolete."

"There is a bench and some chairs over there." Her husband pointed to a spot nearby.

"Father, I think those might be better." Zachary pointed to a grouping twenty-five or thirty feet beyond. "More shade there."

So far as Sydney could see, the places were equally shady. She gave him a questioning glance, which he seemed to ignore as he summoned a footman bearing a tray of glasses of lemonade. Then she noticed that these seats were near one of the pall mall games—the one in which Lieutenant McIntyre, Ensign Gordon, a man in civilian attire, and three young women were playing.

"We'll be right back, my dear," the elder Quinton said to his wife.

Sydney saw Zachary stop for a brief word with McIntyre, who nodded and glanced her way, then looked off in another direction. As she followed his gaze, she saw Percival Laughton staring at her. He turned away, looking resentful. She switched her attention when her companion spoke.

"I am so glad for this moment alone with you, Lady Paxton. I hope I am not intruding to bring up what might be a delicate subject, but I did want you to know that I quite admire what you have done for Lady Ryesdale's youngest son."

"Za—uh—Major Quintin told you?"

"He told his father and me soon after you proposed it to him, but by now, of course, I have heard it from other sources as well. You must know it is quite the *on dit* of the moment."

Sydney grimaced. "I did suppose that there would be talk. Thank goodness my son and his brother are so young that gossip is irrelevant to them."

Lady Leonora gave her an admiring glance. "You are a remarkable young woman—but then I was sure you would be."

Sydney did not know how to respond to this, so she sipped her lemonade to cover her confusion.

"Tell me about your name," Lady Leonora said abruptly.

"M-my name? What about it?"

"Henry told Zachary he was marrying a woman named 'Bella' who turned out to be someone named 'Sydney.'"

"My given name is *Sydney Isabella*. I was 'Bella' as a child. The family, the neighbors—including Henry—knew me as 'Bella.' Some still refer to me that way—when they are not intimidated by the titled Lady Paxton."

"So when did it change?"

"My mother's name was *Sydney*. I loved her very much. She died when I was twelve. I missed her terribly and I suppose—childlike—I felt closer to her in using the name she shared with me."

"How sad to lose your mother as you were coming into that most difficult period of growing up."

"Losing a parent is difficult at any age," Sydney said, thinking of her father.

They sat in thoughtful silence for several minutes, enjoying the pleasant day and sipping their drinks, but Sydney did not find the silence discomfiting. She spied Aunt Harriet and her sea captain some distance away and smiled.

Lady Leonora followed her gaze and smiled, too. "Do you think Mrs. Carstairs and the captain will make a match of it?"

"If he has his way, they will. However, I doubt Aunt Harriet will contemplate any major change in her life until Celia is settled."

"That does not appear to be too far off," Lady Leonora said. "Trevor seems quite smitten."

"His family may object, though. A duke's son and a sea captain's daughter?"

"Family objections are not always insurmountable problems," the older woman said dryly.

Remembering what she knew of Lady Leonora's marriage, Sydney smiled and shrugged. After all, her own marriage to Henry had not been a union of social equals.

Again they sat in companionable silence for a few moments.

It was interrupted by the appearance of Adam Richardson, Viscount Kirkly, with his mother, the Marchioness of Rodham, on one arm and Lady Ryesdale on the other. "May we join you?" he asked.

Sydney thought half of London's social elite had their attention focused on this section of the marquess's elaborate garden. Seeing the hand of Zachary Quintin in this meeting, Sydney gave Captain Richardson a knowing look and mouthed a "thank you" to him. He grinned.

When the newcomers were seated, Lady Leonora addressed the marchioness. "You have surely outdone yourself this year, Margaret. Whatever will you do for an encore?"

The marchioness preened. "I feel sure we will come up with something. My granddaughter is making her debut in two years."

"Already? But I remember her as a baby," Lady Leonora said.

"They grow up so fast," the marchioness said.

"That they do. But it is such a delight to watch them grab at whatever life has to offer them. I swear Zachary's Lucas will be walking within the week," Lady Leonora said. "He just learned to say *Papa*— at least we think that is what he is saying."

"And, Lady Paxton, you now have *two* little ones in your nursery." The marchioness thus introduced the topic that was on the minds of so many of her guests. Sydney noticed that several of these had moved casually to be within hearing distance.

Richardson stood. "If you ladies are going to talk babies, I think I will find someone to discuss horse racing or sailing."

The women laughed at him and waved him on, then Sydney responded, speaking primarily to Louisa, but clearly enough for the on-lookers.

"Yes. Our boys seem to be adjusting to each other quite nicely. My Jonathan is learning to share and his brother William is happier now. He cried a good deal that first night, but less each day since. You must visit again soon, Louisa."

"Thank you, La—uh—Sydney. I shall."

Sydney winked at her and Louisa smiled back. *There*, Sydney thought, *the first hurdle taken.* She knew her own frankness and the easy accord between her and Louisa would be the talk of every London drawing room the next day.

That night Sydney lay in bed reviewing the day and replaying certain images. Most of these, to one degree or another, involved Zachary. She knew very well he had prevented a recurrence of that encounter with Percival Laughton by ensuring that wherever she was, there would be at least one of the Rangers nearby. It had all been very discreet and very thorough. He had himself been at her side much of the day and she rejoiced in the easy rapport between them—and in the twinges of desire she felt whenever he looked directly into her eyes or their hands happened to touch.

She rolled over and stared blankly about her. Light from a nearly full moon slipped through gaps in the drapes to turn pieces of furniture into ghostly shapes.

As sleep continued to elude her, she recalled Lady Leonora's question about her name. Was it possible Zachary really had not known whom Henry was marrying? That seemed unlikely, yet it would explain a good deal—like that insulting toast at the wedding breakfast. Zachary must have thought she knew he would be at the wedding, and he must have known then of Louisa, but to what extent? Certainly now Zachary and Louisa exhibited none of the characteristics of a long-standing friendship. In fact, just today, Louisa had said to Sydney and Lady Leonora, "Major Quintin's visit came as such a surprise. Imagine having a stranger effect so much change in one's life."

She pounded her pillow into yet another position. Had her distrust and resentment been misplaced? If so, it may have served one positive purpose: it had prevented a silly schoolgirl's dwelling on what might have been as she tried to build a life around her marriage. A marriage built on a lie. Still, it had not been so very different from dozens of others.

She wondered what Zachary's marriage had been like. What kind of woman had his wife been? Lieutenant Harrelson had said she was a Spanish gentlewoman—and a partisan fighter. The two images did not fit somehow. What was it that had made him love her? Or had he loved her? She knew from her own experience that factors other than love often brought—and kept—people together.

In another London townhouse Zachary too was finding sleep elusive, though his had been a very long day. It started shortly after breakfast with a meeting with the Bow Street Runners who were keeping Percival Laughton under surveillance. He had met them in their office, a small drab windowless room that contained two scarred desks and an assortment of chairs as well as a small table with a teapot and several dirty cups. A large detailed map of London hung on the wall.

"You have something to report to me?" Zachary asked, taking a chair.

"We do." John Ruskin, the older of the two, leaned back in the chair behind his desk, his hands hooked into the pockets of his vest. "As you know, your fellow Laughton has rooms in a lodging house. He's real close to the woman who runs it. Real close, if you get my meaning."

Zachary waved his hand impatiently. "I have no interest in whom the man takes to his bed."

"His lady friend has a brother named Daniel Olson. It appears that Laughton is engaged in some sort of business with this Olson fellow. Olson has a sometime partner known only as Scrubb."

"Have you any idea of the nature of Laughton's affiliation with them?"

"Not yet," Ruskin admitted, "but the association bears watching."

Ruskin's younger partner, a man named Lowell, swung his long legs and feet off his desk and stood. "These are some rough types." He circled an area on the map with his hand. "Operate here mostly — in Seven Dials." Lowell had just named one of London's most notorious districts. Respectable men avoided the area even in daylight.

"Usually press gangs, prostitutes, and so on, but they've been known to expand their activities to burglary in the more elegant parts of town."

"And murder," Ruskin said from his desk. "You want someone to disappear, they will see to it—for a price. Kidnapping would be within their services."

Zachary nodded. "You are quite right: the association bears watching."

Later, when he saw Laughton accost Sydney, Zachary wanted to wipe away the man's smirk with a resounding facer, but, mindful of the time and place, he restrained himself. He did, however, enlist the aid of his Rangers in making sure it did not happen again. He also shared with them the information he had had from the Runners.

"I think we should just take him out of the picture," Gordon said. "Treat him like the scum he is. Threatening a baby, yet."

"This is London, Gordie. Have to wait 'til he does something," McIntyre said.

Gordon was not persuaded. "Bah! An ounce of prevention seems in order."

"For now, we just watch," Zachary warned.

"I hear his creditors are becoming impatient," McIntyre said. "They won't want him running off to the continent again."

The day after the Rodham garden party, Paxton House was besieged with morning callers. Sydney had anticipated this onslaught, so dressed carefully in a day dress of mauve muslin trimmed with a wide black sash at the fashionable high waist. A large bow in the back had streamers hanging nearly to the hem. A black and white cameo hung from a silver chain around her neck.

She mentally dismissed many of the callers as eager gossips whose primary interest was in harvesting some seed of sensation they could then plant in the next drawing room. Sydney, Aunt Harriet, and Celia adroitly turned the conversations whenever someone asked a question or dropped an innuendo about how and why William had become attached to the Paxton household. He just had, and that was that.

One particularly aggressive dowager voiced a desire "to see those dear little children. Might she just peek into the nursery?"

Sydney skewered her with a look of utter wonder. "I am sorry, ma'am, but we do not display children like denizens of a freak show." The affronted woman, obviously used to getting her own way, huffed and departed.

"That was neatly done," said Zachary, who had arrived a few minutes earlier with his mother and Lieutenant Harrelson.

"I've probably made an enemy for life," she replied.

"Well, if it is true that one is judged by the friends he chooses, it must also be true of the enemies one makes. I think your reputation will survive."

"Hmm. I think there may be a compliment in there somewhere, so I thank you."

He grinned and gave her a mocking bow, then turned to join Nathan and Allyson Thornton as Sydney was called upon to greet arriving guests. Finally, the crowd of visitors thinned appreciably, leaving special friends who had been invited to stay longer: the Quintin party, the Thorntons, and Louisa, a late arrival who had slipped away to the nursery almost immediately.

Celia and Trevor had had their heads together for several minutes. Now Trevor said, "I assume everyone knows Vauxhall Gardens is presenting an extravaganza of the Battle of Vitoria." Vauxhall Gardens was a popular amusement park offering balloon ascents, tightrope walkers, and concerts as well as other entertainments. The gardens themselves were quite spectacular with long walks and byways that were especially attractive to lovers. High sticklers frequently disapproved.

"Yes. So?" Zachary asked.

"So let us get up a party to attend—say on Saturday," Trevor said.

Celia said, "Oh, Sydney, do say you will approve. You know you have wanted something special as a diversion for the girls and Geoffrey and his friend. It would be such fun."

Geoffrey had returned to town, bringing his friend with him, precisely for the royal visit and such celebrations.

"What do you think, Aunt Harriet? Lady Leonora?"

"Certainly—if we have sufficient escort. I am sure Captain Thompson would happily join us," Aunt Harriet said. "Geoffrey and his friend are old enough to serve in that role as well."

Lady Leonora looked at her son, who nodded. "I haven't been to

Vauxhall in years," she said. "In my day, young people enjoyed excursions there immensely."

"It's settled, then," Sydney said. "Allyson, Nathan—you will join us, won't you?"

When her husband also nodded his assent, Allyson said, "Of course. As Celia says, it will be great fun."

CHAPTER 23

The Paxton-Quintin party for the excursion to Vauxhall was an eclectic group of varying ages. Aunt Harriet, Captain Thompson, and the elder Quintins represented one end of the age spectrum. Next came Sydney, her cousin, and their friends, including Lieutenant McIntyre. Sydney's young family members, along with the street urchin Walter made up the youngest part of the group. After gaining the approval of Miss Fairfax and her sister, Sydney had invited Walter to join them as a reward for his helpfulness to the sisters and for his diligence at learning his letters.

"Wally will be so pleased," Penelope Fairfax had said. "He works very hard, you know."

"I am glad to hear it," Sydney replied. "It is always nice when we win now and then."

Penelope nodded. "I feel certain we have won over our Wally, but that wretched woman, Alice Barnet, still tries to lure him back to her lair—or steal him!"

"So far, he has been clever—and fast—in eluding her," Priscilla said.

Ringside seating at three tables had been arranged at Vauxhall Gardens. Once again, Sydney happily found herself seated beside Zachary, conscious of his every small movement, the warmth of his body, an occasional hint of that spicy combination of scents that was just Zachary.

The program consisted of a preliminary concert during which everyone enjoyed a supper of such foods and drinks as the Gardens provided: cold chicken and thinly sliced ham, lemonade, ratafia, and wine. Then came the extravaganza featuring a reenactment of the Battle of Vitoria, the turning point of the war in the Peninsula. Using a megaphone, an announcer with a sonorous voice explained each scene. The orchestra musicians with loud horns and drums added to the explosive sounds of cannon and other weapons, shouting men, and neighing horses in the arena. The audience jeered figures wearing large caricature masks of Joseph Bonaparte and his entourage and cheered those depicting Wellington and his army. The smell of smoke hanging over the arena added to the battle atmosphere. There were exaggerated "deaths" and a generous amount of red paint to simulate blood. Sydney decided that the general public was getting its money's worth in sensationalism and gore.

Seeing the pleasure the youngest members of the party took in the spectacle, Zachary, Harrelson, and McIntyre—who had all lived through the Battle of Vitoria—made few comments on the show's authenticity during the performance, though Sydney did observe them exchanging skeptical looks now and then or rolling their eyes. A musical interlude followed the battle show. The three young girls, Marybeth, Amy, and Anne, begged to be allowed to walk along some of the paths.

"Only if Geoffrey and Mr. Atkins will escort you," Sydney said, casting her brother a questioning glance. At almost fifteen, Geoffrey was already as tall as many men and his friend, Reginald Atkins, was of a similar size and build.

"Please, Geoffrey," Marybeth said.

"Sure. Why not?" Geoffrey said with a show of nonchalance, though Sydney suspected the two boys were as eager to move about as were the girls.

Seeing disappointment on Walter's face, Sydney added, "And you must allow Walter to accompany you."

"All right," the girls chorused.

Walter's eyes lit with delight and he scrambled from his seat.

"Mind that you stay on the main paths that are well lit," Sydney cautioned.

"We will."

When the young folks had left, Horatio Quinton said, "So, tell me, you who lived through it, did this performance come even close to the reality of Vitoria?"

McIntyre responded. "The basic premise of the show conveys an overview and the underlying truth is accurate enough."

"Hindsight provides perspective," Zachary said. "We certainly did not know *then* that Vitoria was the turning point."

Lord Nathan Thornton had also served in the Peninsula, but had been called home a year before the Battle of Vitoria to serve a purpose similar to that of the Rangers, but in England. He now chimed in with, "I doubt anyone in a given battle or other mission ever sees much beyond his own tiny piece of the giant jigsaw puzzle of a cataclysmic event."

"True," Captain Thompson said. "Have to let writers and historians sort it out later."

"And they usually get it only half right," McIntyre said.

"Perhaps half a loaf is better than none," Lady Leonora said.

Anything she or anyone else might have added to this sage comment was cut off by the sudden appearance of the twins, Anne and Amy. The girls were running, holding their skirts hiked indecorously above their ankles, and screaming, "Sydney! Come quickly! Help!"

Sydney jumped up, as did Zachary and the other men at the table. "What is it? What happened?" she asked.

The girls were out of breath.

"A woman," Anne said.

"And a man," Amy added.

"They grabbed—"

"Wally and Marybeth."

The twins were used to finishing each other's sentences.

"They were behind the rest of us," Anne went on.

"Room for only two on the path," Amy explained.

"Marybeth screamed."

"So did Wally."

"Geoffrey and Reggie chased—"

"Told us to get you—"

Instantly, Zachary took charge. "Come. Show us where. Harrelson, McIntyre, Thornton—see to the entrances. They must have a carriage."

"Here, son. You may need this." Horatio Quintin handed Zachary a small pistol from an inside pocket of his jacket.

Zachary looked surprised, but took it and said to the twins, "Let's go."

"I'm coming, too," Sydney said.

"I'll notify the Vauxhall people," Captain Thompson said. "They must have guards all around this place."

It was only a matter of a very few minutes, but it seemed much longer. Sydney felt she was seeing the scene from afar even as she lived each fearful second. She and Anne quickly followed Zachary and Amy.

Terror gripped her. Marybeth. Sweet Marybeth. She could not imagine life without her baby sister. And Walter was turning into such a nice lad. She heard Zachary's questions as they hurried to the spot.

"A man and a woman. Did you see anyone else?"

"No, just those two," Amy said.

"Did they say anything?"

Amy glanced back at Anne who said, "The man didn't say much. Yelled when Marybeth bit his hand."

Amy added, "The woman grabbled Wally's arm and twisted it. She said something like 'you won't get away from me again, you miserable brat.' He kept pulling to get away, but she held tight."

Alice Barnet, Sydney thought, her terror increasing tenfold, for the Barnet woman ran one of London's most notorious "flash" houses. Originally intended to provide for and protect abandoned children, these facilities were training grounds for pickpockets and prostitutes. The people who ran them—mostly women—pocketed any money the children brought in. Images of Marybeth forced into prostitution and of Walter sent back to that sordid life threatened to undo Sydney. She struggled to tamp down her nausea.

"Here. This is the place," the girls said.

The gravel on the path had been seriously disturbed.

"Walter and Marybeth did not go quietly," Zachary observed. "With luck, they will slow their captors."

"They went that way." Amy pointed.

A few minutes later, the path parted, branching off in three directions, but Geoffrey's friend Reggie Atkins was there to show them the way. The boy was very excited and spoke in short bursts as he pointed to the right. "Geoff is still following them. We almost caught up to them. He told me to wait here to show you the way."

"We are near the west entrance," Zachary said.

"You girls stay close with Mr. Atkins," Sydney ordered, hastening to keep up with Zachary.

Moments later, they reached the entrance where gas lamps on either side of the gate illuminated a chaotic scene.

Two adults were trying to cram two wriggling, screaming youngsters into a carriage whose driver was yelling, "Hurry up!" as he tried to hold his team steady. A third youngster, Geoffrey, clawed at the man, trying to rescue his sister. The man, taller and much heavier than the boy, managed to thrust him aside. Geoffrey stumbled and fell, but quickly scrambled to his feet and began the assault anew.

The woman already looked frazzled as Walter kicked and screamed, "Let go o' me. I ain't goin' with you."

"Oh, yes you are, brat. Now shut your mouth an' get in there." One by one, she pried his fingers loose from the edge of the carriage door as she still held onto his other arm and tried to avoid his thrashing feet.

Meanwhile, the man kept trying to fend off Geoffrey and control the equally uncooperative Marybeth.

"Yeow!" he yelled. "She bit me again!"

"Don't let her get away," the woman said. "That Fish woman will pay good money for her. She's just the right age."

This remark hit Sydney like a slash of sleet, cold and brutal, for she knew who "that Fish woman" was: the madam of a brothel that catered to clients who preferred very young girls.

Zachary rushed forward. "Stop! Stop right there! You are going nowhere with these children." He jerked at the arm with which the woman held Wally, thus spinning her off balance and allowing the boy to escape.

The man was so startled at the interruption that his grip on Marybeth loosened and she quickly fled to Sydney's side, crying in relief. Wally, too, immediately rushed to Sydney. She now cradled a child under either arm.

The coachman, apparently seeing no profit for himself in this scene, whipped up his team and pulled away, leaving Alice Barnet and her male companion standing on the side of the street. Zachary released his grip on the woman's arm, but drew the pistol his father had given him and motioned for the two to stand together. The woman was not yet ready to give up, though.

She shouted at Sydney. "That boy is mine. You can't have him."

"Are you his mother?" Sydney asked.

"No, but—"

"Then he is not yours."

"Yes, he is. His mother sold him to me. He is my property."

Sydney looked down at Wally's upturned face. His stricken look told her this was true. She hugged him even closer.

By now the Vauxhall guards had arrived and were ready to take charge. And right on their heels, Trevor Harrelson appeared and said, "Confound it! I missed everything."

Zachary put away his weapon. "It must have escaped your notice, madam, that England abolished slavery several years ago."

"Don't matter. I paid good money for his services," she said with a note of triumph.

"But not the clothing he wears," Zachary said. "Should you choose to pursue this matter, I will personally have you charged with trying to steal his garments—a crime for which I am sure you know you could be hanged or transported."

"That's true, Alice. Best give it up," her assistant said.

"Hmpf." She turned away in a show of contempt, but Sydney detected a trace of fear at the mention of hanging or transportation.

By now, Amy, Anne, and the Atkins boy had caught up with them and stood watching the altercation.

Calming and comforting Marybeth and Wally, Sydney said, "You are all right now. You are safe. I want you to go back with Geoffrey and Reggie and the twins." She glanced at Trevor and said, "Lieutenant Harrelson, would you mind going with them?"

"Be glad to, my lady."

As Geoffrey, his friend, and the girls nodded their assent to this idea, Sydney added, "Stay close and stay on the main path. The fireworks will start soon. Aunt Harriet will be worried. You must tell her and the others what has happened. We will be along soon."

The Vauxhall guards took down the names of the Barnet woman and her companion and forbade their ever returning to the gardens, but did not release them yet.

Sydney was furious at the thought that they were getting off so easily for what they had attempted to do. *Attempted.* In that word lay the problem. Were she to pursue the matter, the newspapers—never mind ordinary gossips—would consider it a godsend, what with the names of some of the people even remotely involved. And probably in the end for something only attempted, but not achieved, the result would be the same.

Reading the frustration on Sydney's face, Zachary said, "You think they deserve far more severe punishment, don't you?"

"Yes. It's outrageous. That woman and her ilk send children out to beg and steal knowing full well they can be hanged for stealing as much as a—a handkerchief. Hanged! One little boy having only six years cried on the gallows for his 'mommy.' And—and what she planned for Marybeth—" Sydney burst into tears.

Zachary could not help himself. He simply stepped closer, took her in his arms, and held her tightly as she sobbed. He knew she was suffering shock and relief over what might have been. "Don't cry, Sydney. Please don't cry. Your sister is safe. Wally is, too," he murmured, stroking her back. "You can't save all London's street urchins."

"But—but there shouldn't—shouldn't be any—to save," she said through sobs that were subsiding.

At this point McIntyre and Thornton arrived. McIntyre raised an eyebrow at seeing Zachary embracing Sydney, but made no comment.

Thornton turned to Zachary. "You want us to make sure these two just quietly disappear, Major? Easy enough to do in the dock area."

Sydney stepped away from his embrace and Zachary felt a sense of loss, but reacted to Thornton's suggestion by scowling at the two miscreants. Their fear clearly showed that they knew the idea was feasible and these soldiers were undoubtedly capable of performing such a deed. After all, London was a city with no police force, a city in which unspeakable acts were carried out in darkness every night. Zachary deliberately let them stew in their fear as little enough payback for what they had put those children through.

He held their gaze, trying to convey a full measure of his contempt. He fervently hoped they thought he really would carry through on such an act. Finally, he said. "Yes, it is a good idea. Excellent, in fact." He paused. "But, frankly, we haven't the time tonight. We have their names. We know where they live and operate." His voice hardened as he turned directly to the would-be kidnappers. "If either of you ever—in any way—annoys Lady Paxton or any of her associates, we *will* come after you. In fact, you might find it healthier to move your activities elsewhere. Perhaps take up some honest work?"

Even through their relief, the two glared at Zachary and Sydney, but they nodded and then quickly scurried away like the vermin they were.

When they had gone, Thornton said, "I doubt they will repeat this particular offense. But those two represent just a hint of the greater problem. How long—how long before Parliament discovers a back-bone to give us a police force?"

Recognizing this as a rhetorical question, the others did not respond.

"Allyson will be worried," Thornton added and began to walk rapidly back to the arena. McIntyre quickly joined him, leaving Zachary and Sydney, her hand tucked in his elbow, bringing up the rear. Sydney was very quiet. Zachary was certain she was caught up in the aftermath of the near disaster she had just experienced. He had seen such reactions many times in the last few years. He wanted to wipe away her pain, to bring back the joy and contentment of the early part of the evening.

Back on the main path with its string of gas lamps hanging from trees, Zachary steered her into one of the conveniently situated, dimly lit alcoves. She made no protest as he slipped an arm around her and lifted her chin.

"Are you all right?" he asked.

"I am now."

In her eyes he saw relief and gratitude and an indefinable something else. Longing, maybe. He couldn't help himself; he lowered his mouth to hers. With no hesitation, she responded passionately, her arms around his neck, her need as urgent as his. He hugged her even closer, his hands caressing her back and she leaned in to him. He buried his face in the curve of her neck.

"I have dreamed of this for so long," he murmured.

"I have too. Nearly three years."

He pulled back to look into her eyes. "Really? Since that day in the park in Bath?"

"Yes. Since then."

He kissed her again, a long, searching exploration of her mouth and was delighted as she responded in kind. Fully aware of his own intense desire, he thought she felt the same, yet he could not bring himself to take advantage of her vulnerability. She had, after all, just suffered a very traumatic experience.

A loud boom brought them back to their senses even as the sky above them radiated brilliant light.

"The fireworks," she said. "We must get back."

"If you insist."

"I insist." She gave him a kiss that started as a friendly, joking peck, but quickly evolved into something deeper, far more intense. When they separated ever so slightly, she said weakly, "I insist."

He grinned. "All right. But this is unfinished business, my lady."

She nodded, her eyes reflecting her ready agreement.

They returned to the tables where others were already oohing and aahing over the fireworks spectacle. Zachary's mother gave him a small nod. Allyson directed a knowing smile at them. McIntyre lifted a thumb slightly, but no one commented on their tardiness.

For Sydney, Zachary's kiss brought back not just the joy of the evening, but also the joy of those earlier days in Bath. She chastised herself as a silly schoolgirl, but faced the next day with eager anticipation. When she received a small bouquet of violets the next morning, she thought her heart might burst with happiness. Yes. Definitely a schoolgirl reaction, she noted, not at all that of a young matron.

Regardless of her renewed feelings for Zachary, she was mindful of the narrow escape she and hers had had with the Barnet woman and that awful man. In the afternoon, accompanied by one of the "bodyguard" footmen and a maid, besides her coachman and another footman, Sydney visited the Fairfax sisters. As usual in her visits to that house, her coach was laden with foodstuffs, linens, and used clothing that Fairfax House would use itself or distribute to others.

The Misses Fairfax greeted her warmly, and over a tea tray Penelope said, "Wally told us of his narrow escape. And your sister! I do hope she will not have nightmares over this."

"Marybeth is quite strong," Sydney replied, accepting a proffered cup. "She seemed her usual bubbly self at breakfast. How is Wally today?"

"He is fine. Really. You must not worry. He is a very resourceful lad," Priscilla said. "He is out with Boskins at the moment, delivering a cooker for a family over on Everdon Street."

"He was very excited about the show," Penelope said. "He simply could not stop talking about the spectacle of the battle and the fireworks. He is quite the envy of every child in the neighborhood."

"Some adults too," Priscilla said.

"I'm glad." Sydney remembered that stricken look on his face when the Barnet woman said his mother had sold him. "I think his earlier life was full of misery."

"However," Penelope said, "Wally's enthusiasm and anticipation before the event may be why Alice Barnet happened to be at the gardens at all. He must have mentioned it to another child and where he would be got back to her."

Priscilla nodded and said, "When I did the marketing this morning, I heard talk on the street about her attempt to snatch him. Barnet's place is in a neighborhood some distance from ours, but such news travels fast."

"Especially when it involves Alice Barnet," Penelope said. "That woman never has been one to suffer in silence."

"And now she thinks herself mightily abused," Priscilla said.

Sydney leaned forward to set her cup on the tray. "Should I worry excessively?"

Priscilla responded. "Um—not excessively. I think she received a real fright last night. Still, she associates with some truly despicable types that hardly deserve to be called human beings."

"So, just be cautious, my dear," Penelope added.

When she arrived home, Sydney was disappointed to find she had missed a visit from Zachary.

"He seemed ever so sorry to have missed you," Celia said in a casual tone but with a sparkling glint in her eyes.

"Celia, don't tease," her mother admonished. "Major Quintin wanted to inform us that he is going out of town for—I think he said—three days."

"Oh." Sydney tried to keep the disappointment from her voice. Three days? Three whole days?

"He is to accompany his sister, Lady Islington, and her two children from Warwickshire to London," Celia said, all teasing gone. "Seems Lord Islington has business on the continent, but will return in time to escort his wife to the Prince Regent's grand soiree at Carleton House."

"I see," Sydney said absently. She was still trying to absorb the idea of three days. But she had to laugh at herself. What was three days compared to three years? She was impatient that the relationship between her and Zachary be carried to the next level, whatever that might prove to be. If his kisses at Vauxhall were any indication, he was equally eager for that to happen.

The three days passed more quickly than she had anticipated. On the first day, she went shopping. Shopping was never her favorite activity, but it might be nice to have a new gown for the prince's extravagant affair. Rumor had it that he had invited nearly a thousand of his intimate friends to help him and the visiting royals honor the Duke of Wellington and other Peninsular heroes. On the second and third days, Lady Paxton was seen making a number of morning calls—certainly engaged in far more socializing with her peers than had been the case in the last several months.

For six months after Henry's death, she had adhered faithfully to society's dictates for a grieving widow. In this case, the widow of a husband who had not loved his wife, who had been unfaithful throughout the marriage. While it was also true that she had not loved him as a wife perhaps should, it was equally true that she had been totally faithful to her vows. In fact, she had forced herself not to dwell on what her life might have been with someone who stirred her senses as Zachary Quintin did.

And now, for an additional three months, she had been in half-mourning, curtailing her activities and dressing very soberly. Enough was enough. She would not behave outlandishly –Lady Paxton was no Caroline Lamb—but she would look better and enjoy herself more than she had these past few months.

And if a certain army major's eyes lit with appreciation and he sought her company, it would be worth a bit of censure for bending the rules.

On the third day, it was with eager anticipation that she looked forward to a dinner party being hosted by her friend Lady Allyson.

CHAPTER 24

Sydney, who never fussed much about her attire for a given party or event, changed her mind repeatedly in preparing for Allyson's dinner party. Finally, she settled on a gown of iridescent teal silk with a silver overskirt, a low-cut neckline, and off-the-shoulder cap sleeves. With it, she wore silver colored kid gloves and her aquamarine necklace made of stones of graduated size, the large center stone teardrop-shaped and resting at the top of her cleavage. Dangling earrings were smaller aquamarine teardrops. Her hair was again arranged in the Greek style with curls framing her face.

She gazed at herself in the looking glass and said to her maid, "Maisie, you have worked a miracle this time."

"You look very fine, my lady."

Before descending the stairs to the drawing room to meet Aunt Harriet and Celia, Sydney went up to the nursery. Jonathan has been out of sorts all day, his cheeks warm, but not truly feverish.

She found Nurse Watkins in the playroom sitting on the floor with William, who was giggling on hands and knees, trying to catch up with a wind-up toy monkey skittering across the rug. The maid immediately stood as Sydney entered.

"What a lovely gown, my lady."

"Thank you, Watkins. The dressmaker did a nice job, did she not?"

The toy lost its momentum and William began to howl. The maid lifted him into her arms and he quieted, but reached toward the toy, which Sydney had picked up to rewind. She leaned over to kiss him on the cheek, but his interest was focused on the toy in her hand. She smiled ruefully. "So much for trying to gain masculine attention." She handed the toy to William and said to the maid, "I came to check on Jonathan."

"He's sleeping—at last," Watkins said as she returned William and the toy to the floor. "It's just as I thought, my lady. He is getting a new tooth. One of the back ones. It broke through just this afternoon. I moved his crib into my room so if he cries in the night, he won't wake this one."

"Good idea. And thank you, Watkins." She waved "bye-bye" to William, who waved back somewhat distractedly, the toy monkey still absorbing his attention.

In the drawing room her aunt and cousin were waiting for her, Aunt Harriet in a violet silk gown and Celia in a pastel pink cotton with deeper pink rosebuds embroidered along the hem and scattered about the skirt. It was Wednesday. The mother and daughter were off to Almack's, London's most exclusive social club, for its weekly assembly.

When Sydney complimented her dress, Celia affected a small moue. "I do wish the patronesses were less strict about dress. It just seems silly to insist that all young unmarried women appear as fresh-faced debutantes."

"Now you mind her p's and q's," Aunt Harriet said to her daughter in a light tone. "When you are an old married lady, you may flout convention. Certainly if those dragons of decorum could refuse the Duke of Wellington admission because he was wearing trousers instead of knee breeches, they would think nothing of refusing you a voucher to attend."

The coach dropped Sydney at Rutherford House first where the Thorntons were still in residence, then went on to Almack's. As Sydney entered the drawing room, her hostess rushed to her side.

"Don't you look lovely," Allyson said. "That color is perfect with your eyes. I am so glad you are not in gray or something equally drab."

"I confess that I am tired of those colors, too," Sydney said, "but I suppose the high sticklers will find fault."

Allyson hooked her arm into Sydney's. "Well, let them do so. We who matter won't. Besides, all England is celebrating, so the rules are relaxed."

Sydney laughed and felt fully at ease now. "If you say so." She surveyed the room—discreetly, she thought—looking for Zachary.

"He's not here yet," Allyson said softly.

"Who?"

Allyson gave her arm a shake and said in the same soft voice, "Don't you dare play Miss Innocence with *me*. Zachary will be here—the Quintins are just a bit late."

"Oh."

Since it was their home, Allyson's parents were officially hosting the party their daughter had planned, but Allyson was performing many of the hostess duties, in part because so many of the guests were her and her husband's particular friends.

"I think you know most of our guests. Mama and Papa came back to town for the celebrations."

Sydney chatted amiably with the Earl of Rutherford and his countess. She had always liked them and even envied them, for she thought theirs was the sort of marriage she had once envisioned for herself.

She and Allyson moved on, for Allyson seemed intent on seeing that her friend was known to and accepted by everyone. Two younger couples stood together and Sydney thought she heard Allyson mutter something like "birds of a feather" just before making her known to the foursome.

"Lady Paxton, allow me to introduce Nathan's brother, the Marquess of Eastland, and his fiancée, Lady Dorothea Newsome." They were a striking couple. The marquess was tall, blond, and some seven or eight years older than his brother. He was dressed impeccably in dark evening wear and a quizzing glass dangled from a silver chain about his neck. He used the quizzing glass to inspect this mere mortal being presented to him. Sydney wanted to giggle, but managed to keep a straight face as she curtsied to them. The fiancée, nearly as tall as Eastland, had thick, very black hair that was pulled back in an elaborate braid that showed off a widow's peak on her high forehead. Her complexion was fashionably pale and her gown was gray silk trimmed with black lace.

Sydney said, "May I offer felicitations on your forthcoming marriage?"

"We have had to postpone our nuptials," the woman said. "I am still in mourning for my stepmother." She gave Sydney's gown a pointed look.

Sydney was sure the look was intended to intimidate, but again she controlled an urge to giggle.

Allyson turned to the other couple, whom she introduced as Baron and Lady Edmund Lawton. "My sister Clara and her husband. Their name is the same as yours, Sydney, but spelled differently."

"How interesting," Sydney said politely. "Perhaps at some ancient time the names were the same."

"Oh, I should not think so," his lordship said.

"Perhaps we should have it researched to be sure," his wife said.

"I doubt that would be necessary, my dear," her husband said.

"There is something to be said for ignorance regarding some matters," Sydney observed. While Sydney had not previously met Allyson's sister or the sister's husband, she knew from little bits of information Allyson had let drop from time to time that they were rather "high in the instep." This encounter confirmed that impression.

Allyson urged her on and said quietly, "Don't you think Lady Dorothea will make a perfect duchess one day?"

"I think *she* thinks she will," Sydney replied.

Sydney was glad to see Adam Richardson and Cameron McIntyre among Allyson's guests. She had enjoyed time spent with them at the Rodham party. Then the butler announced the arrival of Quintin family members. She was thrilled when Zachary, having done the polite greetings routine, sought her out to make her known to his sister, Lady Islington. Zachary's sister was two years older than he and looked very like her brother, with the same dark good looks that Sydney admired in him. She was more outgoing than he, quick to try to ensure that those around her were at ease and amused. They talked of Lady Islington's journey and the trials of traveling with young children.

"Thank goodness Zachary was able to accompany us," his sister said. "He was very helpful in entertaining my two. That seems to be a recently acquired skill." She gave him an arch look. "I certainly do not recall it in the pre-Lucas days."

"I have learned a lot from my son," Zachary said.

A few minutes later Allyson was pairing up her guests and ushering them from the first floor drawing room to the dining room on the ground floor. Sydney saw that her friend again bent the "rules" somewhat, but she managed to satisfy the sensibilities of those who held their own consequence in high regard, and she had seen that others simply had pleasant dinner companions. Sydney found her partner very pleasant indeed: Zachary.

"You can thank me later," Allyson whispered.

The dinner itself was lavish and tasty—Rutherford had an excellent cook—and the conversation lively, centering on recent and current celebrations of Bonaparte's defeat. Sydney was enjoying herself thoroughly and joined the discussions readily despite being distracted by the sheer magnetism of her particular dinner partner. When the ladies withdrew to leave the men to their port and politics and sport, she felt keenly the loss of his closeness.

Allyson, seated next to Sydney in the drawing room, leaned close to say, "They won't be long. I gave Papa and Nathan strict orders: only one round of drinks."

Sydney blushed at being so obvious. "Thank you—I think." She changed the subject to tell Allyson about the progress on the extension to Fairfax House, for Allyson, too, had been instrumental in seeing that project to fruition. She had just finished when the men returned and, for Sydney, the party resumed its earlier liveliness. Again Zachary sought Sydney's company. She noted a raised eyebrow or two at this, but chose to ignore the reactions of others.

Lady Rutherford had just called for the tea tray when the butler entered to speak quietly to Lord Rutherford. The earl immediately but calmly strolled over to where Sydney stood talking with Zachary, Richardson, and Lady Islington.

Lord Rutherford touched Sydney's elbow to draw her slightly aside. "Lady Paxton, there is a Paxton footman in the waiting room of the entrance below. He says it is urgent that he speak with you."

She gasped, unable to control her shocked surprise. No Paxton servant would have called here now except in the most dire emergency. "Jonathan!" she cried and hurried from the room, Zachary right behind her. A man in Paxton livery paced the floor in a room scarcely larger than a dressing room, with stark whitewashed walls, a padded bench and two padded chairs.

It was Cosby, one of the three footmen who had been added to her staff after Henry's death.

"I came as quick as I could, my lady. It's Master William. Someone snatched him."

"Snatched—? William? But how—?"

"Just tell us what happened," Zachary said, his hand gripping Sydney's elbow.

Before he answered, the footman looked at Sydney, who nodded. "I went up to relieve Grady at the regular time to do so, and I found him lying on the floor in the hall, unconscious. Miss Watkins was in the nursery common room, gagged and tied to a chair. She'd been reading in there, you see, so as not to disturb the little earl with her reading light in her own room."

"But the boys?" Sydney's initial panic was only slightly assuaged by the man's calm demeanor.

"The little earl is fine. Still asleep when I left. But they took Master William."

"Oh, my Lord!" Sydney felt herself swaying and was grateful for the steadying arm Zachary slipped about her waist.

"They. How many?" Zachary asked.

"Two, so far as we know. They could've had someone outside watching. But Miss Watkins saw only two."

"How did they get in?"

"From the alley. Broke in through the kitchen side door. Cook had the night off an' the kitchen maids was all playin' loo in the servants' hall. They come up the back stair an' conked Grady afore he even knew they was there." He paused. "I'm real sorry, my lady. I checked that side door myself earlier. Locked, it was."

"How long ago did this happen?" Zachary asked.

"We're thinkin' maybe two hours ago."

Sydney was impressed with Zachary's calm probing for information, but she also felt nearly hysterical at this devastating news. Was Jonathan *really* all right? And poor William. Where was he? Would they hurt him? Louisa. Louisa had to be told. How did you tell a mother you had allowed her son to be kidnapped?

"I assume you came in a coach?" Zachary was asking the footman.

"Yes, sir. The coachman come back after takin' the ladies out."

"All right. Here's what we do," Zachary said. "You take Lady Paxton home. Then have the coachman take you to Almack's to ask Mrs.

Carstairs and her daughter to return home immediately. I suspect that Lieutenant Harrelson will be there. Bring him, too."

"Yes, sir."

Zachary opened the door. A Rutherford footman hovered in the entrance. "Bring Lady Paxton's cloak, please."

Draping the cloak over her shoulders, Zachary gazed into her eyes and said, "I'll make your excuses above stairs. Try to stay calm. Richardson is here. So is McIntyre. We'll get him back. I promise."

He wanted to kiss her, but not with those servants looking on. As soon as she was out the door, he dashed upstairs to tell Allyson and Thornton and his parents what had happened. They, in turn, would convey the information to anyone who had a need to know. He pulled Richardson and McIntyre aside and elicited their help. Thornton took the three of them into the sitting room of the suite he shared with his wife in order to discuss a plan of action in relative privacy.

"Percy Laughton must be behind this," Zachary conjectured, "though we cannot ignore the possibility of that Barnet woman. However, she would be far more likely to snatch a poor person's child off the street than one whose parents had the means to offer pursuit. On the other hand, revenge can be a powerful motive."

"Why would Laughton want *William*?" Richardson asked. "One would think if he were to snatch one of them, it would be the earl."

"Right," McIntyre said. "But what if they just grabbed the first child they saw in the Paxton nursery? What if it's neither Laughton nor Barnet—but some random kidnapping for ransom?"

"That's possible," Thornton said.

"Yes, it is," Zachary agreed. "And if that is the case, it will make our catching up to them much more difficult, for we will have to wait for a ransom demand. If Laughton is behind this, I doubt very much that he did this deed himself. Not his style. He'd be off somewhere establishing an alibi for himself."

"So, where do we start?" McIntyre asked.

"With Laughton. He's the most likely suspect and," Zachary added grimly, "the most likely to harm the child he sees as a threat to his ambitions."

"You will need a carriage," Thornton said. "And you cannot go about the city in those army coats." He immediately dispatched a footman to have a carriage readied and brought around. Then he disappeared into what must have been his and Allyson's bedchamber for several minutes. He returned with a brown and a black jacket and a brown cotton shirt. After a bit of trading around for fit, Richardson and McIntyre donned the jackets and Zachary the shirt as Thornton disappeared again.

He reappeared to say, "Here. We may need these too." He handed over three pistols and shoved one into his own waistband.

"You keep an arsenal in your bedchamber?" Zachary asked. "And what do you mean 'we'?"

Thornton seemed slightly embarrassed, like a child caught stealing a biscuit. "My wife enjoys shooting, too. And surely you did not think of leaving me behind. You'll need a driver."

Within another ten minutes, Zachary had sent off a note to Bow Street, Thornton had informed his wife of what he was doing, and the four of them settled into a Rutherford landau to be on their way.

When they arrived at Laughton's lodging house, Zachary was not surprised to find Laughton gone. Nor to find his landlady less than eager to help them find him. They sat in the carriage trying to determine what their next move should be. It was very dark. Gas lighting had not yet reached this section of the city, so the only sources of light were a half moon high above murky clouds and an occasional splash of light from an undraped window.

Ruskin and Lowell arrived in a hackney cab as they debated and informed them that earlier in the evening Laughton had been seen entering a gaming hell in the Seven Dials.

"Entering, but not leaving?" Zachary asked.

"He could have left by a back door," Ruskin conceded, "but his usual behavior is to stay put in one of those places for several hours. We may have made a mistake, but since we were already in that part of town and Laughton seemed set for a while, Lowell and I decided to find out what we could about his new best friends, Olson and Scrubb. Of course, had we known of that missing child, we would have stuck closer to Laughton."

"That task required both of you?" Zachary asked.

When the Runner hesitated, Adam Richardson answered. "In Seven Dials, a man asking questions had best have someone to watch his back."

"True," Zachary agreed. "So, Ruskin, what did you find out about Olson and Scrubb?"

"They move around a lot. Right now Scrubb lives with a whore who works the Charing Cross area and Olson has a room in the back of a fishmonger's shop in the Dials." He named the exact locations.

"We'll start with where those two live," Zachary said. "They are just the types Laughton might use for such work as this. Ruskin, you and Lowell go back to that gaming hell. If Laughton is still there, one of you keep watch on him and the other report to us at one of these places. If he is gone, try to find out where and when."

"Yes, sir."

The Charing Cross location proved fruitless. No one had seen either Scrubb or his woman since noon that day. Zachary cursed the trip as a waste of time and worried anew about poor little William. Anger and frustration kept showing him images of Lucas scared and helpless. Once the carriage—an open landau with two shuttered lanterns—reached the Seven Dials area, they drove slowly past the fishmonger's shop, pretending to be drunk and to have wandered here unwittingly.

"Where'd you say this light skirt lives?" McIntyre asked in a loud "drunken" voice.

"Uh—here, sh-somewhere." Richardson stood up and feigned looking around for the right building. It was far darker in this section of the city. "Veronica," he called loudly and plaintively and fell rather than sat back down.

They heard shutters fly open and bang against a wall on the second floor of the building next to the one that had the fishmonger's shop. A man leaned out and shouted, "Shut up! They's some as needs our sleep!"

"Sleep when you're dead," Richardson shouted back, then said, "Well, we know for sure one of these flats is occupied."

The fishmonger's shop was on a corner. As they passed over the cross street, they could barely make out a delivery alley behind the shop. The main street itself seemed empty, though two doors down was a pub of sorts. Its open door emitted a rectangle of subdued light and a cacophony of sounds: people talking in loud, drunken voices, arguing, singing, and the plinking tones of three or four stringed musical instruments.

Zachary called a halt. "Adam, Cam, let's check out the rear of the shop. Nathan, drive on. Give us plenty of time to scout out the situation. Can't leave horses like these on a street in this part of town at any time."

"Take one of the lanterns," Thornton said.

The shop faced onto a main thoroughfare; it was shuttered and dark. The ground floor of the building was raised two feet above actual ground level and there was undoubtedly a cellar beneath. On the side street were two steps leading up to a door that probably led to a hall and stairs for access to other rooms. Zachary tried the door. It was not locked. The alley smelled of rotting fish. Light from an open window above revealed a jumble of debris and garbage. "Watch your step," Zachary cautioned, as his boots slipped on something soft and spongy. There was also a door here in the alley and Zachary thought it must lead directly to the shop. It was locked.

The sound of a small child crying hysterically assailed their ears as they stood beneath the window, listening.

"Scrubb, can't you do something to stop that caterwauling?" a male voice growled.

"I give 'im a piece o' bread. He threw it on the floor." It was another male voice.

"Well, give it back to him. Or pick him up. Or something. You got a kid. You should know how to deal with him."

Scrubb grunted and said, "Ain't seen my boy in ten years 'n' more." But he apparently did pick the child up, for the tone of his cries changed momentarily, then resumed their pitch.

The window, set off to the side of the alley door, was too high for any of them to see into the room from the ground. "We need to get a look inside," Zachary whispered.

"Could just rush them," McIntyre responded. "Have surprise on our side."

"We don't even know that's the right baby, do we?" Richardson asked. "Besides, he might get hurt. Especially if they are armed."

They stood in silent frustration. Zachary ran a hand through his hair. Finally, Richardson spoke again.

"Quintin, you are the only one who knows William. If we braced ourselves against the wall, you could stand on our knees and perhaps see in."

Zachary mentally measured the distance. "That might work."

With their help and bracing himself against the wall, too, he managed to look into the room. It had a bed, a table, three wooden chairs, and an unlit coal fireplace. There was also a nightstand that probably held a chamber pot and a dresser with a wash basin and a ewer. All this Zachary saw in a mere glimpse, for his attention riveted on the human figures in the room.

William. And two men. William, alive and so far looking none the worse for his ordeal, though Zachary's heart wrenched at seeing his tears of fear and despair. Once more, a vision of Lucas in such a circumstance flashed across his mind. William was dressed in only a nappy and a nightshirt. His feet were bare. The two men looked to be in their mid to late twenties. The one holding William was an exceptionally big man with already thinning dark hair; the other had a full head of sandy hair. Dressed as dock workers, they were unkempt and dirty. They sat at a table on which could be seen the remains of a sparse meal. The dark-haired one had William on his knee and seemed to be trying to distract him. So that was Scrubb; the other must be Olson. Zachary saw no sign of a weapon other than a bread knife on the table.

He motioned for Richardson and McIntyre to let him down. They moved slightly away from the window, and he had just finished describing the layout of the room when they heard the crunch of boots approaching. They quickly covered the lantern and flattened themselves against the wall under the window. Then they heard the visitor throw open the door to the room above.

"Ah, my little treasure. My ticket to the good life. Come to Cousin Percy." The speaker apparently snatched William from Scrubb's arms, for the child let go with a loud screech of fear and rage.

Zachary mouthed "Laughton." Richardson and McIntyre nodded.

"Now look what you done. He was startin' to quiet down," Scrubb said.

"He'll quiet soon enough once he hits the river. Just make sure you do it where the river currents will wash the body ashore while it is still recognizable. They have to be able to identify him—not just another unwanted baby tossed away like so much flotsam and jetsam."

William was still squalling.

"Here. Take him," Laughton said in disgust. Then he gave a snort of surprise. "What the—?"

Now Laughton was furious. "You idiots! You blithering damned idiots!"

"Wha—?"

"Who you callin'—?"

"You got the wrong damned brat," Laughton roared. "This isn't Paxton."

"He was the only baby we saw in the Paxton nursery." This was Olson's voice.

"How do you know it ain't him?" Scrubb asked. "Babies all look alike."

"Look at his feet. Paxton heirs always have a tattoo on the inside of their right ankles. A pair of crossed swords."

"Well, you didn't tell us to look for no bloody tattoo." Olson sounded both belligerent and defensive.

"An' we didn't see but one baby," Scrubb said.

McIntyre touched Zachary's shoulder and whispered, "Shouldn't we put a stop to this?"

"If we go charging in there like a mad bull, that little boy will get hurt," Richardson said, also in a whisper.

"Let's give it another minute or two," Zachary said. "If they come out, they will come one at a time through that side door. It will be easier to take them."

Within the room Laughton was still fuming. "What a mess. This is no good to me at all. You'll have to go back and get the right brat."

"I ain't goin' back there," Olson declared.

"Me neither," Scrubb said. "Never do the same house twice. Bad luck, don't you know?"

"Then you don't get paid," Laughton threatened.

"We'll get paid if you know what's good for you." Olson's threat sounded more ominous than the other's had.

"Look—I'll pay you twice as much if you go back for the other boy." This time it was a desperate plea, not a threat.

A long silence followed, broken only by William's pitiable cries.

"Too risky. They might have figured it out by now. Too risky by half."

"I'll find someone else then." Laughton's voice sounded as though he had turned away. "Right now, I have a hackney cab waiting." The listeners heard the door open.

"What should we do with this kid?" Scrubb asked.

Laughton apparently turned back. "I don't care. The river? Leave him on some church doorstep. Do what you will." The door snapped shut.

Scrubb was heard to mutter, "Don't seem right to drown 'im just because he don't got that tattoo. No profit in that."

Zachary and Adam crouched on either side of the steps to the side street outer door, their weapons drawn. As Laughton's boots touched the ground, Zachary said softly, "Good evening, Laughton. Only I suppose it is more accurately morning now, isn't it?"

"Wha—? You!" Laughton started to reach for a weapon.

Zachary pressed his own pistol against Laughton's ribs. "Don't even think about it. I would truly enjoy pulling this trigger. Quietly, now."

Richardson relieved Laughton of his weapon and they nudged him into the alley where McIntyre still listened beneath the window. Tearing Laughton's own neck cloth into long strips, they tied his hands behind his back and a gag over his mouth, then forced him to sit in the muck on the ground.

"They're trying to decide what to do," McIntyre whispered. "Right now they are opting to give the boy to Olson's sister to leave as a foundling."

"I think that will prove unnecessary." Zachary motioned Richardson to guard the prisoner. "If he moves, kill him," Zachary said, venting his own cold fury. "Come with me, Cam," he said to McIntyre.

They went to the side street door, opened it, and boldly walked down the hall to where they saw light under a door. As they pushed into the room, Olson, his back to the door, said, "Forgot something, did you?" Something in Scrubb's expression caught his attention. He twisted to face two drawn pistols.

"As a matter of fact, we did," Zachary said. "Hand over that child."

"Not so fast, your lordship, sir," Scrubb said sarcastically. He was a big man—even bigger than he had seemed initially. He still held William on his lap. "See this here little neck?" He caressed the child's neck with a huge hand. "I could break it just like that." He snapped the fingers of his other hand. "Be like breaking the neck of a kitten."

Zachary cursed himself for not seeing this possibility. He lowered his weapon, as did McIntyre.

"Get their barkers, Dan." Scrubb stood, still holding William, whose sobs were more subdued for the moment. Zachary and McIntyre turned over their guns.

Scrubb said, "Now, you two stand aside as me 'n' Dan here take our leave."

Daniel Olson seemed unused to having a weapon in hand at all, and especially inept with one in each hand. Such firepower in the hands of the ignorant was extremely hazardous, Zachary reminded himself as the two men backed toward the still open door, Scrubb first, still holding William.

As they passed Zachary, William cried out and reached toward this person he apparently recognized with positive feelings. That suddenly stiff little body in his arms seemed to startle Scrubb, whose attention was momentarily diverted and he was unaware of the man in the doorway behind him who dealt him a resounding blow to the head. Scrubb uttered a small grunt and, already unconscious, slowly sank to his knees—still with the baby in his arms—then down completely.

McIntyre dove at Olson's legs. Olson dropped one of the guns, but fired the other. Zachary felt a burning sensation when the bullet grazed the flesh of his forearm as he reached to untangle William from the prostrate form of Scrubb. McIntyre, having knocked the inept Olson to the floor, managed to retrieve both weapons.

Ruskin, with Lowell right behind him, stepped into the room and said casually, "Well, you almost managed without our help. Bow Street's reputation remains intact, though."

He and Lowell—more prepared in this regard than Zachary and his Rangers—put manacles on these two prisoners. Richardson prodded a begrimed and smelly Laughton into the room. The Bow Street men removed his gag, but saw that he was bound more securely than before. Scrubb had regained consciousness, but still seemed woozy.

Zachary hugged William close, saying over and over, "It's all right, little man. You're safe. I've got you. Nobody's going to hurt you anymore." He continued to hold him with one arm as McIntyre used a knife to open his other sleeve and wrap his wound tightly with strips from a handkerchief.

Ruskin said, "We'll see to these three. There are two hackney cabs out there on the street—ours and his." He jerked a thumb at Laughton. "Your carriage is out there, too. We'll let you know when they come up on the docket at Old Bailey. Kidnapping. That's a hanging offense, you know."

Zachary saw Laughton blanch at this, but the other two were more stoic. "Thanks," he said, lifting his wounded arm in a salute of sorts.

As they clambered into the landau, Thornton said, "You fellows had all the fun. Next time I want to play too."

"With luck, there won't be any next time," Zachary said. He held William on his lap, glad to see the exhausted baby fall asleep with the swaying of the carriage.

"By the way, Quintin," Richardson said, "you owe McIntyre and me new breeches for our uniforms."

CHAPTER 25

Sydney arrived home to find the entire household in an uproar. Her first concern was to reassure herself that Jonathan was all right—he slept soundly—even as she worried about William. Where *was* he? Why? Why had someone taken William? Roberts had already seen to barring the door the intruders had used. Bessie Watkins was more frightened than injured by her ordeal, but Sydney sent her to bed and ordered another maid to move Jonathan's crib back into the boys' room and to stay with him for what remained of the night.

There seemed two possible explanations for this disaster. First, it was a bizarre, horrible mix-up. Those scoundrels who had taken William had been after Jonathan. In that case, Percival Laughton was somehow involved and she recalled very well how Henry had felt about his cousin. In the second possible explanation, William was the target and the only ones who might remotely consider taking such measures against baby William were Lady Ryesdale's in-laws. Her intuition told her the first explanation was by far the more probable. She prayed fervently that Zachary could find William and bring him home safe.

Even though he had been at Paxton House such a short time, and even though she knew and welcomed the fact that William had a mother who loved him, Sydney had grown to love this child as her own. She marveled at his growth, felt sorrow at his pains just as she did with Jonathan. The boys were very alike in appearance, but already no one who knew them had any difficulty telling them apart. Perhaps because he had so far been an only child, Jonathan was quieter, more self-contained, while William was more gregarious, eager to share.

"I never expected to love William so much," she said tearfully to Aunt Harriet and Celia, who had come in moments ago along with Trevor Harrelson.

The four of them sat in the smaller family drawing room with the door ajar, simultaneously sharing their anxiety and trying to avoid it as they waited.

"Have you informed Lady Ryesdale yet?" Aunt Harriet asked.

"I sent a note saying we had an emergency and ask that she come here as soon as possible. But, frankly, at this hour, I have no idea when, or even if, she will get it. That is such a strange household."

No one had a response to this.

They tried to reason out the who and why of such a terrible deed. Sydney shared her initial thoughts on the matter.

"If Laughton *is* behind this, that baby's life may be in real danger," Harrelson said. "However," he added on hearing all three women gasp, "I happen to know that Zachary has had him watched ever since he returned to London. The major will have things in hand."

"I just keep thinking of that poor, scared little boy in the hands of some ruffian," Celia said.

"He is such a sweet child," Aunt Harriet observed. "It is just so unfair that innocent children are often made to suffer so."

Sydney appreciated their sharing her worry, but she only half listened, attuned as she was to any sound of someone arriving below. Finally she heard the pounding of the door knocker, but the voice that followed was not the one she wanted to hear. It was Louisa's voice, not Zachary's.

Louisa, in a rather drab green cotton dress and no jewelry, entered the drawing room, saying, "I came as soon as I could. What is it? Has something happened to William? Is he ill? I must see him."

Sydney patted the cushion of the couch next to her. "Come and sit down, Louisa." She took Louisa's hand in her own. "William is not here."

"Not here? What do you mean 'not here'?" Her voice rose in panic.

Not knowing how else she might put it, Sydney simply blurted out, "He has been kidnapped."

"Kidnapped? My William? Why, for heaven's sake? Who?"

"Major Quintin and his friends are looking for him now," Aunt Harriet said, obviously trying to inject calm into the discussion.

"In a city of a million people and more? Oh. Oh. Oh." Louisa took deep breaths trying to control her sobs. "T-tell me what happened."

As matter-of-factly as she could, Sydney did so, but she could not stop the tears streaming down her face.

"But *why*?" Louisa persisted. "I-I thought he would be so safe here."

Sydney choked back a sob as she said, "I think it may have been an accident—that they may have mistaken William for Jonathan. Henry's cousin, Percival Laughton—"

Louisa's eyes held sheer terror as she said, "Oh, my God! Henry always distrusted him. Thought him capable of almost anything."

Harrelson now said, "It may be possible, Lady Ryesdale, that it was not a mistake, that William really was the target."

"William? Oh, I shouldn't think so. There is no title associated with William—nor a great fortune."

"It is no secret in the clubs that Baron Rysedale's family disapproved of your—uh—relationship with Paxton," Harrelson said.

"That is true," Louisa admitted. "But they direct their venom at *me*. They do not recognize that William even exists."

"What if he suddenly did not exist?" Aunt Harriet asked gently.

Louisa took time to think before she responded. "I cannot see either the dowager or her son George sullying their noble hands in such a thing as housebreaking or kidnapping. Ralph would have done so, but they wouldn't. And of course Ralph has been out of the country ever since—since—"

"That duel," Harrelson said, and she nodded.

There seemed nothing else of substance to say on the matter, so Sydney said, "Well—now we wait." She rose. "I'll have Roberts bring us some coffee."

A predawn glimmer of light shone through gaps in the drapes when at last they heard a clamor in the entrance below, then the muffled sound of boots on carpeted stairs. Suddenly Zachary stood framed in the doorway, holding a sleepy looking William on one arm.

"Oh, thank God," Sydney said.

Louisa rushed over to gather her son in her own arms and shower him with kisses. Sydney could not resist just touching him and stood with one arm embracing Louisa's shoulders and the other hand caressing William's back.

As Zachary moved farther into the room, Richardson and McIntyre followed him. Aunt Harriet stepped into the hallway briefly, then resumed her seat as Sydney invited the newcomers to sit as well. "Please. You must tell us what happened."

Richardson gestured at his stained breeches and scuffed boots. "We are hardly fit to be in an elegant drawing room."

"Fiddlesticks!" she said. "We are so happy to see you and to have William back safe that we would welcome you covered top to toes in mud—or—or worse."

Roberts and a footman entered with trays: more coffee and a pitcher of ale and a pitcher of cider along with glasses and cups. Roberts said quietly to Sydney, "Cook is preparing an early breakfast, my lady." Sydney caught Aunt Harriet's eye and mouthed a "thank you."

When everyone had a drink of choice in hand, she said, "Now—do tell us."

"It was Laughton, just as we thought," Zachary began. He recounted the rescue mission with an occasional correction or elaboration from the other two—as well as incoherent but happy interjections from William.

The next day Sydney had additional locks put on outside doors, and she spent hours in the nursery with both boys. Every day that week Louisa somehow managed a visit to Paxton House for an hour or so. Sydney was glad that not once had Louisa blamed her for William's ordeal. For Sydney, the rest of the month of July was anticlimactic—historic celebrations of the end of the war notwithstanding.

The Prince Regent's much talked-of gala at Carleton House went off as planned, but in the event turned out to be something of a disappointment. Not that her expectations had been so very high to start with. She was quite sure she had received an invitation only because her late husband had lent nominal support to the Tories. These days the prince—who had once allied himself with his father's Whig enemies—now that he was regent, actively courted the Tories.

While Sydney applauded the prince's celebration of genuine heroes, she deplored his use of such celebrations to shore up his own political interests—especially as so often he seemed to be trying to belittle his estranged wife in the process. The grand affair at Carleton House had started in early afternoon on a very hot day. Military men in full dress uniforms were forced to stand in parade formation for long periods of time. Many of them suffered heat stroke—all because one self-important buffoon wanted to show off, Sydney thought, but she wisely forbore voicing this opinion aloud.

In order to accommodate the hundreds and hundreds of guests, giant tents had been erected on the lawn. The whole affair was incredibly crowded. And what a waste of money, she thought. All those lobster patties, rich pastries, and champagne for people who had probably never known what it was to be hungry, while even within the city—let alone the country at large—were thousands who were this very instant experiencing hunger pangs. Moreover many of them were members of the newly demobilized army the regent was so intent on honoring.

Sydney had arrived at this affair on the arm of one of those being honored, Major Zachary Quintin. She knew the Rangers had come under duress; but a sovereign's invitations amounted to a royal command that could not be refused. The guest of honor was, of course, the Duke of Wellington, who appeared in a resplendent army uniform with medals and colorful sashes awarded by both domestic and foreign entities. Nevertheless, the duke's attire seemed starkly simple next to that worn by the English Prince George, the Prussian King Frederick, and the Russian Czar Alexander.

As they waited in a long line to present themselves to the dignitaries, the Rangers talked quietly among themselves.

"I hear Prinny had that uniform made especially for this extravaganza," Lieutenant Harrelson said.

Ensign Gordon snorted. "A puffed-up uniform to fit his puffed-up claims of having actually led troops into battle."

"Careful, Gordie," McIntyre warned. "You'll have us thrown out of here before we meet the royals. Then what will you tell your grandchildren one day?"

"That I served honorably with men of honor," Gordon replied.

"Hear. Hear," Captain Richardson said.

When they at last reached the dignitaries, instead of merely acknowledging Major Quintin and the Rangers with a nod and a handshake as he had others, Wellington, in a booming parade ground voice, said, "Ah, Quintin, I see you brought most of your Rangers home. Saved me writing those letters, for which I heartily thank you. Great job, all of you."

Sydney felt Zachary's arm tighten under her hand as he said in a controlled, neutral tone, "Thank you, your grace."

There was murmuring among other guests at the great man's singling out these few and for the rest of the evening, the Rangers were singly and collectively much admired. Sydney was proud of her friends, especially Zachary, but she was anxious for this evening to end and she knew they were too.

As she and Zachary waited for their carriage, Sydney was glad to see two very welcome faces: those of Allyson and Nathan.

"Can you imagine what the Fairfax sisters could do with what this grand show must have cost?" Allyson asked rhetorically.

"Allyson, enough, my dear," her husband admonished only half-jokingly.

"But, darling—"

"No. Enough. Much as you'd like to do so, you cannot save the whole world and you cannot deny others their right to be extravagant and ostentatious if they so choose."

"I agree with you," Sydney said to Allyson in a stage whisper. "An *army* of hungry poor people might be fed on this night's leftovers."

Nathan threw up his hands. "I surrender. I cannot fight two of you. 'Tis a pity we have no women in Parliament."

Their carriage finally arrived and Sydney sank into the seat with a sigh of relief as Zachary gave the driver instructions then climbed in beside her. She was keenly aware that not since the Vauxhall Gardens excursion had they been so alone together, for McIntyre, who had accompanied them here, was leaving later with Gordon. A carriage lantern offered only muted light, but never had Zachary looked more attractive to her.

He slipped an arm around her to draw her closer. "Now, about that unfinished business between us," he murmured and kissed her. She had anticipated this, had wanted this for days. He was not comforting a distraught friend this time. He was seeking, needing, and claiming a lover's response. One she eagerly gave him. Her lips parted and the kiss deepened. When his hand moved to cradle her breast, she gasped at the flood of desire that swept through her.

She pulled away, albeit reluctantly. "Zachary, we—"

"Too much too soon?" he asked, his voice husky.

"Not exactly."

"Good." He settled his lips on hers again, thus reigniting that incredible desire.

She felt almost deliciously helpless, but found herself able to withdraw again. "Zachary," she said, suppressing a soft laugh, "I am not making love with you in a rolling carriage."

In a pretense of thinking this over, he said, "Hmm. Am I to assume you object to the location, not the idea of our making love?"

She felt herself blushing, but she answered boldly. "Yes. You may assume that."

He grinned. His kiss this time was more subdued, but full of promise. "I can wait."

In the next few days, Zachary saw Sydney only intermittently and fleetingly. He sent her a fresh bouquet of violets with a one-word, unsigned message, "Waiting." His sister and her family were still in town. Also, his younger brothers had come for the celebration and insisted he join them for rounds of fisticuffs at Gentleman Jackson's Boxing Salon and to inspect horses at Tattersall's market. His mother so enjoyed having all her children around her that Zachary hadn't the heart to disappoint her by skipping out on family dinners. His younger sister Delia, who had made her debut just this year, demanded that he escort her to Almack's.

Sydney was also at Almack's, along with her aunt and her cousin—and the ever-present Trevor Harrelson. Zachary thought Sydney might be bowing to the strictures of the patronesses, for she wore the silver gray gown she had worn to the theatre when he had first arrived in town. He was able to persuade her to one dance, but not the waltz that he so dearly wanted. Later, he overheard someone comment on the phenomenon of seeing Lady Paxton on the dance floor and counted himself privileged.

Another time, he talked with her briefly as he escorted his mother on a morning call at Rodham House.

In addition to family duties, two other matters occupied him in those days following the Carleton House reception. The first was selling his commission. He had mostly enjoyed his stint with the army. It had given him a sense of achievement, but it was time to move on. He needed to devote himself not only to the business he would one day inherit from his father, but also to the affairs of the young Earl of Paxton. Richardson and McIntyre were also selling out. Harrelson hadn't made up his mind yet, but Gordon was staying in.

And he met with the lawyer, Phillips.

"I am concerned that Percival Laughton may somehow manage to cheat the hangman and continue to present a threat to my ward."

"I think the chances of that are so remote as to be impossible," Phillips assured him. "If he cheats the hangman, it will be because one of his former cohorts wants to send a message to other debtors and has Laughton killed in prison. Happens all the time. Newgate is a cesspool."

"At the risk of seeming to dance on another's grave, I suppose there is something to be thankful for in that," Zachary said.

Phillips nodded his understanding, then said, "As mastermind of that bit of unmitigated evil, Laughton is done for. Now, the other two might get off with being transported, but it would be for at least twenty years—and I don't see either of them being able to afford passage back to England at the end of that time. No, I think your young ward is safe."

"I am sure his mother will be glad to hear that."

Then—finally—Zachary was able to be alone with Sydney from time to time. He invited her for a drive in the park. Soon the drive turned into a regular occurrence. They met at a variety of social functions—a dinner party, a ball, a musicale—sometimes by chance, sometimes by arrangement. They were often seen with their heads together in heated or laughing discussion. They attended theatre productions, but always with family members or friends. He was delighted that they had regained the simple companionship of their sojourn in Bath and he restrained himself from pushing her lest he break the spell. They rediscovered mutual interests, though—just as in Bath—they did not always agree. He did not press her, but he did send her another bouquet with the note, "Still waiting."

One morning in late August, Zachary came down to breakfast to find only his mother there before him. She waited until he had filled his plate, poured his coffee, and sat down next to her before she said, "All right, Zachary, are you or are you not going to marry that girl?"

"Who?" he asked, stalling.

"Whom," she corrected, "and don't play games. Lady Paxton. The two of you spend an inordinate amount of time together."

"Her year of mourning is not up," he said, still stalling.

She rolled her eyes. "It almost is. Besides, given the nature of her marriage and the circumstances surrounding her husband's death, I doubt anyone would look askance were she to push the clock ahead a bit. Well, not anyone who matters."

"I'll take your views under advisement." He leaned close to kiss her on the cheek.

That afternoon when he called at Paxton House, he found Sydney in the library, struggling with some ledgers the steward had sent on from Windham. "Do look at these figures," she said. He did so and they quickly sorted out what had seemed to be a problem. "I need a break," she said, flexing her shoulders. "Come. Walk in the garden with me."

They strolled aimlessly for a while, then sat on a stone bench that was secluded from the house by surrounding trees and bushes—a tiny oasis of nature in the heart of the city.

"Lady Paxton!" He pretended shock. "You lured me out here for a tryst."

"Actually, I didn't," she said, "but it is a good idea, is it not?" She lifted her face invitingly.

"A very good idea," he whispered, beginning a gentle assault on her mouth.

They sat quietly for several minutes, just holding each other and relishing the closeness. Then she spoke hesitantly.

"Zachary, you've told me much about Lucas and what a delight he is in your life. Tell me about his mother. Tell me about your wife."

He felt himself go very still. Here was a moment of reckoning. He pulled away slightly and twisted so he could see her reaction to what he said. "Elena was not my wife. She might have been. She would have been, but she wasn't."

She held his gaze steadily. "But Trevor told us—"

"The Rangers agreed to help me protect Lucas. They all know the truth. My parents know. And now you."

She was quiet for a time and he noticed the birds twittering in the trees around them. Then she said, "Tell me about Elena."

"Where to start. She was a bit of a paradox." He grinned. "Perhaps most women are. She was sweet and generous and loving. Fiercely loyal. Beautiful. The French called her *La Belle Diable*. The beautiful devil. She did not hesitate to kill in cold blood when she thought doing so would serve the cause of Spain."

"She sounds very strong."

"She was that." He still held Sydney loosely in his arms and nuzzled her neck. "'Tis my lot in life to love strong women. My mother is a strong woman. So are you."

She slanted her head to allow him better access to her neck. "Did you love her?"

"Yes, I think I did. But I have to admit that a saucy English girl with gray-green eyes often got in the way—even though she was utterly lost to me."

In response to this, she turned to kiss him fiercely.

Sydney was pleased that Zachary had chosen to confide in her. And he had almost admitted to loving her! She understood fully his wish to protect Lucas from the pain a sanctimonious society could cause an innocent child. If only such a ruse could have saved William from some of what the future might have in store for him. Still, many a prominent family in England had members who had, as it were, been born on "the wrong side of the blanket." Some of those offspring had become valued members of society and made positive contributions to the nation.

Ah, but those were hardy souls who could hold their own against all comers, she told herself. Well, William would have to become one of those. She fervently hoped that love and family support would be enough. Meanwhile, she mustn't borrow trouble from an unknown and unpredictable future.

Three days later, Zachary arrived in civilian attire—a brown jacket and doeskin breeches—to take Sydney on an excursion away from the city. She wore a sprigged muslin frock in soft blue-green and carried a matching parasol. Zachary lifted his eyebrows in appreciation when he saw her and she felt deliciously scandalous in going off with him alone even for just an afternoon outing. But, after all, she was not some green schoolgirl who needed to be watched and protected constantly.

He had arrived in a curricle drawn by a team of matched grays. On the seat in the back where a boy servant—a tiger—might normally sit, a large basket was strapped into place.

"A picnic? We are going for a picnic?"

"Ah, see what you've done already," he cried in mock despair. "Gone and ruined my surprise, she has."

"I love picnics," she said.

They drove in relative silence as he maneuvered them through London's hectic midday traffic with everything from elegant coaches to farmers' carts vying for road space and trying to dodge careless pedestrians darting hither and thither. Once they were out of the city, with newly mown fields on either side of them, she breathed deeply of the fresh country air.

"Nice," she said.

They left the main thoroughfare and turned onto a country lane that consisted of two ribbons of sand with a runner of grass between them. They passed a large, well-kept stone farm house with a thatched roof and attendant outbuildings.

"Are we trespassing?" Sydney asked.

"No. My father owns all this land." He made a sweeping gesture and then chuckled. "He thinks its value will triple, at least, when the city expands out here."

"Does he not mean *if* it expands?"

"No, he is adamant—when."

"It is a lovely location," she said. "I hope it remains fresh and pristine."

"I used to spend entire summers out here. Mother would move the family to the farm and Father would ride back and forth every day. It was a long ride, but he said it was worth it."

He now guided the team across an open field to a copse of birch and elm trees next to a small river. He jumped down to tie the team in a shaded grassy area, then reached to help her down. His hands lingered at her waist and he drew her close to kiss her lightly—at first. That it deepened to something more intense was not his doing alone.

They drew apart and she asked, "Did you bring me out here to seduce me?"

"Well—yes—that is—partly—if you are willing. If not, we will just have a nice meal and drive back to town." His gaze seemed to say, *The choice is yours.*

"I—uh—see. You are tired of waiting."

"Oh, I can still wait—if I have to."

She looked away and said in almost a whisper, "You won't have to."

He uttered a whoop of triumph and whirled her around as they kissed again. He carried the basket to a patch of grass under a giant elm hanging over a pool in the river. He took a blanket from the top of the basket, spread it on the ground, and moved the basket to the edge of the blanket.

"I don't suppose I could persuade you to remove your clothes and jump into that pool with me," he said.

She gave him an arch look. "You suppose exactly right."

"Well, at least take off your shoes and stockings and we'll wade along the edge."

He was already removing his boots and socks. Her unruly mind reveled in the implied intimacy.

He gave her a questioning look as she still stood at the edge of the blanket. "Do you need help?"

"No."

She sat abruptly, kicked off her slippers, and reached beneath her skirt to loosen a garter. She felt suddenly shy, but this was Zachary and wherever this was going, she welcomed it. The task accomplished, she wriggled her newly freed toes and laughed in delight. He reached for her hand to help her to her feet and continued to hold it as they walked the few steps to the water's edge. The grass felt cool and sensual against her bare feet. She released his hand to use both hers to keep the hem of her dress out of the water.

"This is wonderful!" she said. "I've not done this since I was a little girl."

"Perhaps next time you will agree to our baring more than our feet and we will jump in the pool."

The idea of such a "next time" caused her heart to jump.

"I can't swim," she said.

"I'll teach you."

They splashed around at the edge of the water for a while, then retreated to sit on the blanket. Zachary rummaged around in the basket and came up with two crystal glasses and a bottle of champagne.

As he struggled briefly with the cork, she said lightly, "You take this seduction business very seriously, don't you?"

He did not answer as he filled the glasses then set the bottle aside. He lifted his glass in a salute. "Today, I do." They kissed and sipped and kissed again. He took her glass and set it aside along with his. He took her hand and said, "You may recall that I said I brought you out here *partly* to make love with you."

"Yes . . ." She responded hesitantly.

"This is the other part: Will you marry me?"

"Wha—?" She thought her heart would leap out of her chest.

"I want to do more than make love. I want to love you, live with you, grow old with you—forever." He went on, hurriedly, as though he were afraid of her response. "I love you, Sydney, and I think you love me too."

"Oh, yes, I do. I do love you." She threw her arms around his neck, spilling both glasses of champagne, and said, "Yes. Yes, I will marry you."

Lunch and more champagne were temporarily forgotten as they sealed this troth in the most exquisite way possible. The former Miss Sydney Waverly finally knew exactly what some married women whispered about and she felt all the ecstasy that any girl dreamed of experiencing with a lover.